Charles Betrand Lewis

Sawed-Off Sketches, Humorous and Pathetic

Charles Betrand Lewis

Sawed-Off Sketches, Humorous and Pathetic

ISBN/EAN: 9783337086275

Printed in Europe, USA, Canada, Australia, Japan

Cover: Foto ©Andreas Hilbeck / pixelio.de

More available books at **www.hansebooks.com**

SAWED-OFF SKETCHES;

HUMOROUS AND PATHETIC.

COMPRISING

*ARMY STORIES, CAMP INCIDENTS,
DOMESTIC SKETCHES, AMERICAN
FABLES, NEW ARITHMETIC;
ETC., ETC., ETC.*

BY

C. B. LEWIS ("M. QUAD"),

OF

The Detroit Free Press.

NEW YORK:
COPYRIGHT, 1884, BY
G. W. Carleton & Co., Publishers.
LONDON: S. LOW & CO.
MDCCCLXXXIV.

Stereotyped by
SAMUEL STODDER,
42 DEY STREET, N. Y.

CONTENTS.

————◆◆————

HUMOROUS SKETCHES.

AMERICAN FABLES.

DOMESTIC SKETCHES.

SAWED-OFF SKETCHES.

HUMOROUS SKETCHES.

"JUST LIKE A BOY."

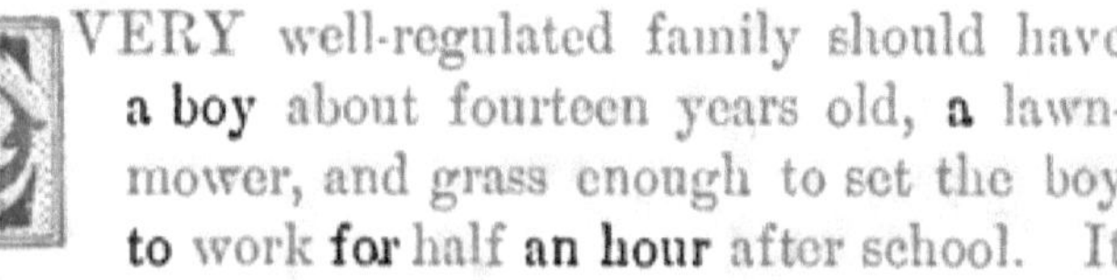

VERY well-regulated family should have a boy about fourteen years old, a lawn-mower, and grass enough to set the boy to work for half an hour after school. It is an interesting study to see a boy shoving a lawn-mower around. Off comes coat, vest, and hat as he goes out, and he vividly realizes that President Hayes got his first start by cutting half an acre of grass before breakfast—and it was cut mighty poorly at that. No boy can strike a bee-line with a mower. He starts out to do it, but he sees a boy on stilts up the street, and he stops to rest. He has just started off again when he sees a boy with a ball down the street, and it is also time to oil the mower. He has just braced himself for a new effort when a stray dog comes trotting along, and it is that boy's duty to watch that dog out of sight. He turns and shoves the mower along for about ten feet, and then he must have a drink of water. If the old gent is at home a boy can drink a gallon of water and get back to his work in about twenty minutes, but all depends on circumstances. If he gets back he stands and wonders whether it is a right or left-handed mower, and why it wasn't rigged to run itself.

If a rap on the window admonishes the boy that procrastination is the thief of time, he buckles right down to business and rushes the mower over four brick-bats, a hoop, and several coal clinkers, and then comes an examination of the knives. Let a boy get in the shade with a good brace for his back, and he can examine a lawn-mower from basement to garret in about half an hour. At the end of the second cut across the sward it is a boy's duty to scan the heavens and see if any kites are up.

A good boy can do this in about fifteen minutes, and he can put in ten more looking across the street at a whitewashed fence and a cat. By this time he feels hungry, and when he has hunted the house over for cake it is high time to go around the corner and see if that Smith boy has got that bird-trap finished.

HE LAID THAR.

IT was down below Bowling Green, Ky., on the line of the Louisville & Nashville Road. It was court day in the town, bringing in a large crowd, and the "celebrated Indian doctor," was there with his wagon and his cures. He harangued the crowd for forty minutes before he made the least impression, and then an old man began to edge up in a sneaking kind of way.

"Do you suffer with dyspepsia?" asked the doctor.

"Yaas."

"Then my compound of forty-four different kinds of root will cure you."

A woman advanced and took the old man by the the arm and whispered:

"Lemuel, you hain't got dyspepsia no more'n our cat, and you shan't buy nuthin'!"

"Madam, is that your husband?" asked root and herbs.

"Yes sir."

"I notice that his liver is out of order. Let him take one bottle of my Elixir and he will be restored. Let him neglect himself three months longer and he fills a dishonored grave."

The old man was going down for a dollar, but she stopped him with:

"No, you shan't! Smartweed tea and vinegar

will rinse the liver as clean as a whistle, and we've got both in the house!"

"And I—ah—and I—ah—notice that he is predisposed to dropsy," continued the doctor, as he waived his bottle around. "This Elixir cures dropsy in forty-eight hours. Neglect the disease and a funeral procession is seen winding its horrid way over these romantic mountains."

The old man went down again, but the wife gave him a push and called out:

"Dropsy! why, you old idiot, you never had energy enough to get it, and if you ever do I'll cure you with sage tea and kerosene oil."

"And I—ah—and I—ah, discover that his blood needs replenishing," continued the doctor. "My Elixir contains twelve kinds of iron, and is warranted to furnish new blood at the rate of a gallon a day. Some of the best blood in America is the work of my Elixir. President Garfield was about to order twenty-four bottles the day he was shot. Go into the White House and you'll find it on the side-board. Jay Gould uses it, Vanderbilt will have no other!"

"Jerusha, I'll have it!" said the old man. "I want about eight gallons of new blood the worst way."

"You don't!"

"I do!"

"You shan't have it!"

"I will!"

Then she shut her teeth hard, drew a full breath, and seizing the old man by the back of the neck and the coat tails she **ran him through the crowd** and **steered** him under a wagon with the remark:

"Now, you lay thar! If **this** family has got any disease I can't tackle and cure inside of two hours I'll leave and let you run the ranche! Now I'll see to old Elixir!"

But the doctor was a man of policy. When he saw her coming and noticed the color of her eyes, he locked up his medicine-chest and calmly began:

" Fellow-citizens, I **desire to** call your attention to these suspenders at twenty-five cents per pair, **and** by the way here is a cake of **scented** toilet soap **for** the lady who prevented her husband from admitting his constitutional ailments **in the** presence of a life-insurance agent. Who takes the first pair?"

FIXING THE DOOR.

THERE was a crack under the kitchen door—a crevice large enough for one to put a hand under—and early in November Mrs. Cripso began saying.

"Now, Cripso, don't let this day pass without nailing down a cleat to stop that crevice. It will let **in** more cold this winter than two tons of coal can drive **out.**"

And Cripso began replying:

" Certainly, my dear—certainly, That crevice **shall be stopped** this very day."

On fifteen different occasions in November she reminded him of the fact that he had forgotten the crevice. In December the number of occasions was twenty. During the month of January she spoke of it twenty-two times. In February she began referring to the matter at each meal, and the other day she nailed him down with the remark:

"Cripso, I am going down town, and I'll stop on my way and ask a carpenter to come up and fix that door."

"I'll fix it."

"No, you won't! You just let it alone. I'll have a carpenter here before night, and that door will be fixed."

"I say I'll fix it myself—right away—now," and in five minutes he had saw and hammer and cleat, and was at the job.

Mrs. Cripso went off chuckling over her victory, and upon her return her husband said:

"Well, the old crevice is shut up."

"You fixed it, eh?"

"Fixed it better than any carpenter you could have sent up, and in ten minutes, too. Come and see."

She took one look at his work and then sat down and whispered:

"Cripso, you just missed it by a hair's breadth."

"What?"

"Being born a fool! You have nailed the cleat to the floor inside the door!"

So he had. He had shut the crevice and door

too, and when he came to realize it he walked slowly out into the back yard and tried to saw his head off on the clothes line.

------◆◆◆------

HE WON'T PAY.

I GOT that notice this forenoon," he remarked as he handed the printed slip into one of the ward windows at the Water Office yesterday.

"Y-e-s, I see," replied the clerk as he handed it back.

"I am notified," resumed the citizen, "that the water is to be shut off from my house unless I pay rates at once."

"Yes, sir."

"Is this despotic Russia or free America?"

"I guess so," sighed the clerk as he looked over a lot of figures.

"Then you'll shut my water off, will you?"

"I presume we will."

"I don't believe it? We've been frozen up for ten days, and if anybody can find any water to shut off they may try it on."

"Frozen, eh?"

"Frozen tight as a crowbar, and whose fault is it? You contract to give me so much water daily or weekly or monthly for so much money. Where's my water to-day?"

" Then **it's** frozen ? "

" Frozen ?   Didn't **I say** every **water-pipe in** my house **was frozen as solid as** the Rock **of** Gibraltar? And whose fault is it ? "

" I see," murmured the clerk.

" **What do you see ?**   Do you see me going around the **neighborhood borrowing water, or do** you see **those frozen** pipes. The landlord **says he** didn't **freeze 'em up !** "

" **No ?** "

" And I didn't."

" That's so."

" But the weather did.   Am I any more responsible **for** the weather than you are?   Why **don't you** run your water over a heater in the winter and **take** the chill off ? "

" **I think we will.** "

" **And now I won't pay until** I get water ?   No, **sir ! I will see you hung first !**   You can go up and **dig and pick and turn** your old **rods** around, but you can't **scare me into** paying ! "

" I know it," was the brisk answer.

" **You** may advise **me to** light a candle and crawl under the house and knock **the top of my head** off against the joists, but I won't do it !   **You** may advise hot bricks, but I'd like to see myself holding hot bricks against the cold pipes to please anybody ? **Warm** rags will sometimes do the business, but am I going **to** hunt **all over** Detroit for rags and burn half a ton **of coal to warm 'em ?** "

" No," softly said the clerk.

" And **don't** you forget that you are **a servant of** the public, either ! "

" Never ! "

" And as **I** said before, shut off **and be** hanged to **you** ! "

" Yes."

" And I will move ! "

" You will."

" And you may sue **for the** amount and I will fight you **to** the highest **court in** the universe ! This monopoly can't bluff me for a cent ? "

" That's so," was the calm reply, and the citizen walked out as stiffly as if his legs had been drilled for water-pipe and there had been a freeze-up.

THE LITTLE **WIDOW** BRIGGS.

A SPAN of ponies attached to an emigrant wagon, containing a woman and three children and various household goods, halted on Grand River avenue yesterday to have a blacksmith set a shoe for one of **the** horses. As the woman seemed to be alone, or at least had no man in sight, the smith asked :

" Old man sick ?"

" No, sir ; I buried him up the country a year **ago.**"

" Then you are **a** widow ?"

" I reckon I am, and **my** name **is** Briggs."

"Which way are you jogging?"

"Going southwest—may be into Indiana."

"Got sick of Michigan?" continued the smith as he pared away at the hoof.

"Well, the State is good enough," she slowly answered. "Some mighty fine land, good schools and tolerable weather, but I had to get out of where I was. I lost a pound a week right along for the last three weeks."

"Ague?"

"Humph! I'd like to see the ague upset us! No, sir! My husband wasn't cold before I had an offer of marriage! It wasn't a month before I had three of 'em. Why, it wasn't six months before their tracks were as thick around my house as cat-trails on the snow!"

"Had your pick, eh?"

"Pick! I could have married anybody from my hired man up to a chap who owned a section of land and four saw-mills. They came singly and in droves. They came by day and by night."

"And you—you—?"

"Say, you!" she exclaimed as she drew herself up, "do I look like an idiot?"

"No, ma'am."

"Well, when I fling my three children at the head of a second husband and give up the $800 in cash in my pocket you can call me an idiot. No, sir! I repelled 'em."

"And they got?"

"They had to. Susan, hand me that second husband repeller. It's in the back end of the wagon."

The girl hunted around and fished up a hickory club four feet long, and the woman held it out for inspection and said:

"There's hairs of six different colors sticking in the splinters, and these blood-stains are the pure quill. You can judge whether they sat there and made love, or tore down the front fence in their hurry to reach the woods."

"By George!" whispered the smith after a long inspection. "Well, I guess you don't want to marry."

"K'rect, sir. If you have any old widowers in this town, or if you know any one between here and Indiana who wants a headache that will last all winter without any letting up, just put 'em up to begin to ask me if my heart don't yearn for love and my soul rattle around for some one to call me darling!"

WHERE HE HAD US.

There were seven or eight of us in the smoking-car, and by and by the conversation turned upon hotels. Six of the crowd were going to stop off at the same village in Georgia, and one of them re-marked:

" Well, gentlemen, you can make up **your minds** to go through purgatory to-night."

" Why ? "

" Well, there is only one hotel in the town, **and** that is run by **the meanest** man south of the Ohio River."

" Do you know **him ?** " asked a chap who was suspected of **being a lightning-rod agent from** Chicago.

" I rather **reckon.**"

" And what's he mean about ? "

" Everything. **He** has bugs in his beds, **uses** beans in his coffee, his rooms are dirty, **and he's a** robber in his charges."

" And there's no other hotel ? "

" No. **If** there was he wouldn't get custom **enough to keep a cat** alive. He's the meanest man **in the State of** Georgia, and if I ever catch him outside **of his town I'll** put a head on him ! "

" I move **that we resist any** swindle on his part," said **a** drummer from Chicago.

" If I find **bugs I'll fire the bed out** of the window," said a patent-churn man **from Ohio.**

And thus it went **on** for half **an hour,** everybody anticipating and predicting, but the conversation finally closed by the originator remarking :

" Well, we'll have **to** put up with it, I suppose, but you can make up your minds to see the meanest, low-down, hang-dog tavern-keeper in America."

It was after dark when we reached the village, and **after** delaying awhile with the baggage five of us rode up together in the 'bus. The sixth man had disappeared, and we didn't see him until we reached the hotel. Then he was discovered behind the desk, a pen over his ear, his coat off—in fact, he was the identical landlord himself! One after another walked up, took a look at him and fell back, and we had adjourned to the veranda and were talking of sleeping out on the grass that night when he came out and said :

"Gentlemen, will you **walk** in and **register?**"

One followed the other, and though we all remained **until the** next **evening,** not a word was said nor a hint dropped about the conversation on the cars. It was only as the **train** was ready to **go** that he shook hands all **around and kindly** remarked :

"The meanest, **low-down,** hang-dog tavern-keeper in America **hopes to** see one and all again. Have a cigar, gentlemen?"

We sent him a gallon of wine and a box of cigars from Augusta, **but** he was still our **creditor.**

MISSISSIPPI 'SKEETERS.

THE railroad station at Mississipi City is located among the pines, and the way the mosquitoes were biting there even in April, was enough to keep a mule **moving.** After awhile we got to talking about the insects, and I asked **a native** of the country :

2

“ Are they thicker than this in the summer ?”

“ Thicker ! Why, in July there’s a million to one !”

“ And larger ?”

“ Larger ! Why, sir, one of the regular ’skeeters of this section could carry twenty of these on his back and still fly high !”

I thought I’d down him at once, and so continued :

“ Now, sir, answered me truthfully. Do you believe that six of your biggest mosquitoes could kill a mule if he was tied up out here ?”

He looked at me in amazement for a minute and then went to the door and beckoned in the man sitting on a box and watching the horses. When the man came in the native said :

“ William, you remember that air roan mule o’ yours ?”

“ I reckon.”

“ In perfect health, wasn’t he ?”

“ He was.”

“ Could run like a deer and kick like a sawlog ?”

“ He could.”

“ And he was all alone in a ten-acre lot, William ?”

“ He was.”

“ And two of them mud swamp ’skeeters got arter him one morning and run him down and killed him and devoured both hams and sucked every drop of blood in his body? William, speak up !”

“ Stranger, if they didn’t then I hope to be chawed to rags!” said William, and he said it exactly like a man who wouldn't have allowed there were two 'skeeters if he hadn't been earnestly convinced of the fact. He walked out doors, and a deep silence fell upon us two, broken only after a long interval by the native saying :

"I've allus kinder suspected that them two 'skeeters had assistance from a hoss-fly, but I can't prove it. I kinder think the hoss-fly held him down till the murder was committed!"

THE NEW "ANNIHILATOR."

BRIGHT and early yesterday morning, before one-tenth of the citizens of this county had shaken off the effects of the glorious Fourth, Prof. James K. P. Burlingame made his appearance on several streets in Detroit almost at the same moment. You would have known him to be a professor, even if you had seen him tangled up with the wheels of a butcher-cart. That tall plug hat, carrying the stains of years—that linen duster girted at the waist—his long hair hanging down to keep his shoulders warm was a dead give-away on his title.

The Professor came here to dispose of individual rights to use his "Fly Annihilator," and he didn't let thoughts of the next Presidential election set him down on a bench. His piccolo voice inquired of a woman at the front door of a house on Congress street east :

"Madame, have you ten seconds to spare this morning ?"

"No, sir !" was her prompt reply.

"Very well, then, you will miss seeing my Fly Annihilator," he remarked, as he walked off. "Thousands have missed it to their everlasting sorrow—thousands have accepted it and been made happy for life."

"It's some kind o' pizen," she called after him down the street.

"Warranted free from all drugs or chemicals dangerous to the human system, and recommended to people troubled with sleeplessness," he called out back, as he briskly retraced his steps.

"I've got screens in every window, and yet the flies get in," she continued, as he opened his satchel on the steps.

"Of course they do—of course. A fly is like a human being. Bar him out and he is seized with a desire to get in at any price. Tell him he can't and he will or break his neck. Fling away your screens and depend entirely on my fly annihilator, warranted to kill on sight, and can be worked by a child four years old. This is the application."

He took from the satchel an eight ounce bottle filled with a dark liquid and provided with a small brush, and holding it up continued :

"One 25-cent bottle does for twenty doors, and I give you directions how to make all you want. No poison here—nothing in this bottle to trot little children up to the cemetery."

"Why, you don't put it on the flies, do you?" she asked.

"Not altogether, madam. Any child can use it, as I said before. Just watch me a moment."

He swung the front door open, and with the brush applied the mixture to the back edge, giving it a thin coat from top to bottom.

"Now, then," he said, as he swung the door back, "flies like sweet. This mixture is sweet. The fly alights on the door, and you swing it shut and he is jammed against the casing and crushed in an instant. Every door is capable of killing 1,000 flies per day. If you have twelve doors your aggregate of dead flies will be exactly 12,000. When you have crushed about 2,000 on a door take an old knife and scrape them off and begin over again."

"Do you suppose —— !" began the indignant woman, but he interrupted her with:

"Don't suppose anything about it, except that it will mash flies and never miss. All you have to do is to open every door, apply the mixture, and then shut them in succession. If you have twelve doors and twelve children, you can leave it all to the children. And only twenty-five cents per bottle."

"Do you think I want all my doors daubed up with flies and molasses?" she shouted, as she made a cuff at the bottle.

"Just as you prefer, madam," he quietly replied. "Some do and some don't. Some won't have it at any price, and others even set up extra door in the back yard in order to use lots of it. I'll warrant this liquid to draw 'em, if you'll only open and shut the doors."

"I won't buy it—I won't have it!" she shouted as she jammed the broom against the door.

" Very well, madam—very well. If you prefer a fly on your nose to one on the door I can raise no objections. Remember, however, that this is my farewell tour previous to appearing before the crowned heads of Europe, and you will not have another chance to secure the annihilator. All you have to do is to take your sewing on your lap and open and shut the door at regular intervals."

" If my husband was here he'd—he'd——"

" He'd buy the right for this county and make $20,000 in two months, but as he is not here we'll bid you good day and pass on. Sorry, madam, but some folks prefer to kill their flies with a pitchfork, and the man with pitchforks will call here in fifteen minutes."

----•----

NOT A SHYLOCK.

A DAY or two ago a man who was at the Central Depot to take a train suddenly cried out that some one had stolen his valise, and he began such a hulla-baloo that everybody had to be interested.

" I sot that 'ere satchel right down thar' and stepped to the door," he explained to Officer Button, " and when I returned it was gone."

" Well, you should have been careful. We are not responsible for such losses."

" You ain't eh? Whar's the President?"

" Out of the city, sir."

" Whar's the Gineral Manager?"

" He's sick abed."

" Whar's the Superintendent?"

" Won't be here till 4 o'clock."

" Wall, now, somebody's got to make good that loss or about a dozen men will go to the hospital for six months apiece!"

" What was the value?"

" Fifty dollars and not a cent less!"

" What were the contents?"

"I had twelve shirts, a new suit of clothes, an overcoat, and lots of other things."

" Was it a carpet-sack?"

" She was."

" One handle gone and the lock broken?"

" Yes, one handle was gone, and I had her tied with a string."

" Is this it?" asked the officer, as he took the baggage off a bench not six feet away.

" Great snakes! that's her!" chuckled the owner.

In handing it to him the string broke, the bag flew open and out rolled two old shirts, a pair of socks and five or six paper collars—all there was in it.

"Then these are the duds you wanted $50 for?" queried the officer.

"No, sir!" was the indignant reply. "I should have taken the money for loss of time and damage to my feelings. I'm no Shylock, sir!"

SITTING DOWN ON A DOG.

A WOMAN and a terrier-dog reached the Union Depot yesterday half an hour before the time of the Grand Trunk train for Buffalo, and while the woman sat down in the waiting-room as the best thing she could do, the dog made the tour of the room several times and then curled up on a seat not far away to get a wink of sleep before being turned over to the tender care of the baggage-man. All things were so-so when a young man with a good deal of cane and watch-chain and necktie sauntered in and took a cool survey of the various females. The one nearest the dog not only had a young and pleasant face, but she was all alone. After satisfying himself of this the young man advanced, made a graceful bow and inquired:

"Beg pardon, but do you go East?"

She nodded.

"Ah! I thought so. If you have any baggage I shall be most happy—ah—shall be most happy to—"

He had all the time been preparing to sit down

beside her on the dog, and the sentence was not yet
finished when he sank gracefully back. Some dogs
have been sat down on so often that they don't mind
it, but this terrier had always been a pampered pet,
and had been given proper time to shake off sleep
and get his legs under him. When suddenly buried
under 140 pounds of masher his ideas must have
been terribly confused, but not for long. A clock
couldn't have ticked over six times when the young
man began to rise up and whoop, and he was scarcely
up when he made a course for the door which upset
every band-box and satchel for a width of ten feet.
As he went out of the door a black object let go of
him and trotted back, and it was only when the dog
began rubbing against the baseboard to restore himself to his former round shape that any one was able
to discover why the frenzied young man had left in
such a hurry.

"SA-LUTING THE BRIDE."

There was a marriage at the upper end of the
Detroit, Lansing & Northern Road the other day.
A great big chap, almost able to throw a car-load of
lumber off the track, fell in love with a widow who
was cooking for the hands in a sawmill, and after a
week's acquaintance they were married. The boys
around the mill lent William three calico shirts, a

dress-coat and a pair of white pants, and chipped in a purse of about $20, and the couple started for Detroit on a bridal tour within an hour after being married.

"This 'ere lady," explained William as the conductor came along for tickets, "are my bride. Just spliced fifty-six minits ago. Cost $2, but durn the cost! She's a lily of the valley, Mary is, and I'm the right-bower in a new pack of keerds. Conductor, sa-lute the bride!"

The conductor hesitated. The widow had freckles, and winkles and a turn-up nose, and kissing the bride was no gratification.

"Conductor, sa-lute the bride or look out for tornadoes!" continued William as he rose up and shed his coat.

The conductor sa-luted. It was the best thing he could do just then.

"I never did try to put on style before," muttered William, "but I'm bound to see this thing through if I have to fight all Michigan. These 'ere passengers has got to come up to the chalk, they has."

The car was full. William walked down the aisle, waved his hand to command attention, and said:

"I've just been married, over thar' sots the bride. Anybody who wants to sa-lute the bride kin now do so. Anybody who don't want to, will hev cause to believe that a tree fell on him!"

One by one the men walked up and kissed the widow, until only one was left. He was asleep.

William reached over and lifted him into sitting position at one movement and commanded :

"Ar' ye goin' to dust over thar' an' kiss the bride ?"

"Blast your bride, and you, too !" growled the passenger.

William drew him over the back of the seat, laid him down in the aisle, tied his legs in a knot and was making a bundle of him just of a size to go through the window, when the man caved and went over and saluted.

"Now, then," said William, as he put on his coat, " this bridle tower will be resumed as usual, and if Mary and me squeeze hands or git to laying heads on each other's shoulders I shall demand to know who laffed about it, and I'll make him e-magine that I'm a hull boom full of the biggest kind of saw-logs, an' more comin' down on the rise. Now, Mary, hitch along an' let me git my arm around ye !"

———•◆•———

HE CUT LOOSE.

At half-past 8 o'clock Monday morning an aged couple who had driven thirteen miles to see the circus, hitched their team near the Western Haymarket. When old Dobbin had been secured they moved across to the big tent and the woman said :

"Now Perry, don't get excited. A circus is a

circus the world over. We'll go slow, see everything on the outside, and then jog back hum."

" Mebbe we'll go in," replied the old man.

" Mebbe we won't! You solemnly promised me over and over agin before we left hum that you wouldn't go in, and I shall hold you to it. We'd look purty in a circus, wouldn't we ? "

" I didn't promise nuthin' about side shows," observed Perry as they edged along with the crowd. "Here's them wild men of Bunkio or Barney-oh, or some such place in Europe. I've allus heard and read of 'em, and I've allus said I'd see 'em if I ever got a chance."

" Perry Baker, are you demented ? " she asked. " You let me catch you sneakin' into a side-show and I'll never live with you another day."

The dulcet tones of the keeper of a lemonade stand now fell upon their ears, and the old man was licking his chops and bearing off in that direction when his wife checked him with,

" What you after now? 'Tain't five minnits since you swallered a pint of cold tea, and you ain't a bit thirsty ! Perry, don't you undertake to sneak out of your solemn promise ! "

The couple got along down to where the living skeleton and the fat woman and great contortionist held out, and the man at the door called out :

" Right this way, old man ! This is your only chance to see a living man weighing only twenty-two pounds ! "

" I'm a comin' ! " shouted Perry in reply.

" Not a rod—not a foot ! " said his wife, as she seized his arm.

" I'm a-goin' to see that skeleton if it takes a leg ! It's the fust **chance** I ever had, and **it** may be the last ! "

But he didn't go in. She walked him aside, dodged two peanut-stands, crawled under three wagons, just missed a **snake** exhibition, and held him up on the outskirts **of the crowd** and calmly remarked :

" You promised and promised, and now you want to break it. Perry Baker, we're goin' back hum, and when we git out past the toll-gate you'n I will have a settlement."

" What's the harm **in a** circus, Mary ? " he argued.

" It's the principle of the thing. It's settin' a bad example and wastin' money. Come along ! "

" Say, let's go clear around the tent."

" **Not** a rod."

" Let's have one glass of lemonade ? "

" Not a swaller, Perry. You come hence ! "

He crossed to the wagon with her, and she climbed in. While she was lifting herself up he bolted, and when she turned around he was gone—mixed up with the circus crowd. She stood up and called him by name as loud as she could yell until a policeman ordered her to stop, and then she got down and said to a boy about 16 years old :

" Bub, I want **you** to come with me. My old **man** has cut loose, and he'll never stop seeing wild men and living skeletons and fat women and red lemonade as long as he's got a cent left."

" How much'll ye give ?"

" I'll give ye a quarter, if we find him. I want to steal up on him before he knows it. I want to find him in front of the only boa-constrictor on the North American continent, and I want to open a performance which will discount this circus all holler."

She was last heard of at the door of the circus. Having failed to find him elsewhere she was about to pass in when the ticket-taker objected.

" But I'm looking for Perry."

" Can't help it, ma'am."

" I won't be in only long enough to lead him out."

" Can't go in without a ticket, ma'am—don't get in the way ! "

" Won't you find out if Perry is in there ? " she persisted.

" Can't leave the door, ma'am—better get a club and wait for him ! Fall back—fall back—tickets on this side ! "

BEING KIND TO A STRANGER.

AMONG the passengers in a parlor car on the Lake Shore Road, was a handsome woman, whose husband shared the seat with her and who would have been picked out as a quiet, sedate, absent-minded man. The seat opposite was occupied by a flashily-dressed young man, with a lady-killing twist to his mustache, and he was considerably surprised when the husband handed him a daily paper, with the remark :

"Have a glance at the news ? Plenty of excitement around the country, I observe."

The young man was busy with the paper for half an hour, and then the husband offered him a popular magazine. This entertained him for an hour, and he had scarcely closed the book when the good man reached over with :

"Have a cigar. These are prime Havanas, and I know you will enjoy one."

The young man accepted with thanks, and naturally made his way to the smoking-car, where he put in nearly another hour, but without the other's company. When he returned he was greeted with :

"Perhaps you'd like to look at the latest novel ? Very interesting, I assure you."

He read until weary, and upon being offered another cigar replied that he was to leave the train at the next station, and added :

"I want to thank you again for your many courtesies."

" Oh, don't mention it."

" You never saw me before ?"

" Never."

" Don't know my name ?"

" No."

" Then tell me why you were so very courteous to an entire stranger."

" Young man, I will explain. In times past when a loafer sat and stared at my wife as a steady job I got up at the end of an hour and broke his neck. This made me much trouble and expense, and I changed my programme. I now carry books and cigars to bribe them. Had you been going a hundred miles further I should have offered you a drink of brandy, a new puzzle, two more dailies, and another cigar, and my wife would have secured quite a rest."

" Sir ! I——"

" Oh, it's all right—all right ! It was cheaper than throwing you out of the window, and I hope you'll get up to the hotel safely. Good day, sir— good day—glad to have met you !"

And that young man with the lady-killing mus- tache and crockery-colored eyes and hair parted on an even keel picked up his grip and walked out with- out being certain whether he had been mashed in a collision or pulverized under a land-roller.

HE WANTED TO POSE.

A RESIDENT of Park street **had a** photographer **come** up the other day for the **purpose** of taking a view of **his** residence, and the **man of** the camera had just got in position when along came an old coon with a buck-saw **on his** arm, and wanted to know what was **up.**

"Going to **photograph** the house," **was the** reply.

"**Then** I guess **I'll** pose," remarked the **old man.** "**I'll take a** position at the left of the gate, **and** represent the **statue** of Industry."

The members of the family **came out and arranged** themselves, and the man called **out:**

"Here, old man **you** want to get **out of** that!"

"**Can't** I represent Industry?"

"**No, sir.**"

"**Can't I** stand **over** there and represent Laziness?"

"No, **sir!** We don't want **you** in **the** group at all."

"Lemme represent the Sleeping Beauty."

"You go away."

He drew off to one side, the passing teams halted **to give** the artists a chance, and directly the plate was **made.** Everybody rushed forward when **it was ready for** inspection, and the **old** man was one of **the first. As** the plate was held up he giggled and **tickled,** and finally burst into a loud laugh. He had dodged around the corner of the house and his full figure was revealed behind the family.

" What do you represent in that attitude ?" sternly inquired the photograper.

" Well, I reckon that's a pretty good pose for Contentment."

" Very well. I will now represent Dissatisfaction."

And the artist took the festive old chap by the the ear and walked him out of the crowd and put in a couple of kicks which changed the pose of Contentment to that of Sorrow.

THE MAN ON THE VERANDA.

Up on Park street the other evening the boys fixed up a straw man in an old suit and placed him on a veranda in the melancholy twilight. He hadn't been in position above ten minutes when rlong came a specimen who had been blasted out of the lower stratum of life, and he leaned his elbows on the fence and called out:

" Good evening, mister. Is this the place where they wanted the back yard cleaned out ?"

The straw made no reply.

" I think this is the place," continued the other. " I was a speaking to the lady, and she said as how I was to call this evening for ten cents, being as she pitied my misfortunes."

The straw man was silent.

"Which was **very kind of her indeed,** because I am powerfully broken down. **I may be** wrong, but I dunno. I'll be on hand early in the morning. I **allus likes to** keep my word, **you know!**"

If the straw man knew he **didn't let on.**

"Yes, **she** said **she felt for me, and** she said I must **be sure to** call for **the ten** cents. **Being** as you are her husband **I** presume **you** might **hand** me the money yourself."

Still no response.

"In which **case** my gratitude would **be eternal, you know. Cast** thy bread upon **the waters and it shall return fifty per cent., or some such thing. You couldn't make it a quarter, could** you? **That** would make **it a cast worth** casting, you know. The profit on that, after **many days,** would be half a dollar, you see."

It is doubtful if the man saw.

"Being as I'm in a little hurry, and being as **I** haven't had anything to eat in several days, perhaps it would be well to close this transaction **at once. If** you wanted **to make** it half a dollar instead **of a** quarter, why I——"

Jut then **a** potato tickled the wayworn traveler's **ear,** and another raised his hat several inches. He bounded to the center of the street like a cat, wheeled **around,** and peering through the darkness, he called **out:**

" Mister, three minutes ago I looked upon you as a great statesman, but a man which will heave rock instead of arguing the question hain't fit to run a yaller dog convention ! Good night, sir. If you have that 'ere back yard cleaned it'll be after you have apologized for this uncalled-for attempted assassination !"

THE GAME THAT "JEEMS" PLAYED.

There was an awful time in a farm-house near Pontiac last night. We haven't received any particulars, but solemnly believe that a certain husband whose front name is " Jeems " was made to wish he'd never been born into this deceitful world.

There arrived on the Western express yesterday morning a nervous, wiry, black-eyed woman of 40, who kept closing and opening her fingers all the time, as if she was clawing noses or pulling hair. She had a straight business look in her eyes as she got off the train, and one of the hackmen at the depot-door ventured the opinion that she had come into the city to foreclose a mortgage or make up a " shortage " on wheat.

" Sir ! " began the woman as she walked up to the depot policeman, " I want answers to a few questions."

" Yes, mum—just so," was the humble reply as he followed her into the waiting-room.

"Now, then," she continued as she took a seat, "I live near Pontiac. My Jeems was in here the Fourth of July, and didn't get home till midnight. He came in here on my money, and I want to know how he spent it. Here is his bill of expenses as he made it out. He has put down $2 for riding up town in a hack."

"That's twelve shillings too much," replied the officer.

"Just as I thought—just exactly!" she whispered as she put down the figures. "Here he has got down one dollar for seeing the balloon go up."

"Not a balloon went upon that day, madam."

"Just as I thought—just exactly! He looked as innocent as a lamb when he wrote that down, but he didn't know me! Here is eighty cents for riding across to Canada and back."

"That should be ten."

"Just exactly what I thought last night when he kissed me and said it was an awful price, but lots of comfort," she observed as she put down "70" opposite his figures. He has it, down here that his supper and dinner cost him $1.50 per meal at the Central Market. It strikes me that three dollars would buy two pretty festive meals."

"You can knock off about two dollars and a half from that," said the officer after he had figured a bit.

"Just exactly as I thought. He smiled as softly as an angel when he wrote that down, but he was smiling at the wrong woman! While I was home milking the cows and having an awful headache he was eating his high-toned meals like a second John Jacob Astor! And now he has put down fifty cents for seeing the bears."

"The what?"

"He says it cost him fifty cents to go into a menagerie and see the bears," she explained.

"If there was a menagerie in town on that day then I didn't hear of it," solemnly remarked the officer.

"Just as I thought—just as I thought! Went in to see the bears, did he? Well, he'll see several menageries when I reach home! Here is one more item. He says he paid $2 to see the rope-walk."

"It was free," replied the officer.

"Yes I thought so—thought so when he sat there and looked so loving and fatherly and said it made his hair stand up. There'll be a ' walk ' when I get back home, and somebody's hair will stand straight up! That's all, and I'm much obliged."

"You won't kill him all at once, will you?" pleaded the officer.

She looked over his head at the wall, breathed hard, clenched her hands and answered:

"I've 'spected it a long time, and now I'll claw him if I die for it!"

She walked up and down the depot with her teeth hard shut and her eyes growing brighter all the time, and when she finally took the train for home, the bill of expenses tightly clutched in her hand, the officer looked after the receding train and mused :

"Now why did he give himself away in that manner? Why didn't he tell her right out that some one picked his pocket?"

————•••————

THE RETURN OF THE MULE.

You could see that she was innocent and confiding by the way she held that big brown, toy mule under her arm as she jogged along Woodward avenue, and no old woman's face ever wore a more satisfied look than hers did when she finally entered a store and placed that mule on the counter, and said :

"La! sakes, but I'm nearly tuckered out! This is the place where I bought this mule three days before Christmas."

"Yes, that toy came from our store," replied the clerk.

"I gin a dollar for it; bought it for my grandson. He's such a boy for horses and mules and wagons and whips, and so on, that I thought it would tickle him 'most to death."

"Yes."

"But it didn't. He's the disappointedest child you ever saw. Like to cry himself to death Sunday."

"What is wrong with the mule?"

" Everything. In the first place my grandson wants a mule which opens his mouth and can be stuffed full of hay. This mule's jaws are sot."

" Yes, but——"

" And he wants a mule which will roll his eyes and drop his ears."

" But we haven't any such mules."

" No, I suppose not, but the boy wants one just the same. This mule don't even kick."

" Of course not."

" And he hasn't got any harness on."

" No."

" Then what's the good of him? If he won't eat, nor bite, nor kick, nor roll his eyes, what's the boy going to do? Haven't you got a toy horse which runs away and smashes things?"

" No."

" Nor a lion which paws and roars?"

" No, ma'am."

" Nor a cow which bellers when you squeeze on her?"

" Sorry to say we haven't."

" Well, I've got to trade this mule for sumthin' or other to amuse that boy. If you had a tiger which frothed at the mouth I—"

" But we haven't got."

" Have you a goose which flaps her wings?"

" No. The only toy of any account we have left is a black boy who rolls his eyes and utters a squeak when you hit him on the back."

" That'll do—that's jist the thing, and we'll trade

even ! He'll put in to-day punching the black boy between the shoulders, use up to-morrer digging out his eyes, and next day he'll cut him up and string him over the back yard, and by that time his father will be home from New York with a drum, four mouth-organs and a boy's chest of tools. Here's your mule—gimme the blackamoor!"

COULDN'T STOP HER.

The gates at the passenger depot which shut out all people not having tickets for the trains were yesterday closed at the Union depot against an elderly woman wearing spectacles and using an umbrella for a cane.

"Can't pass without a ticket," said the man at the gate as she came up.

"I wan't to see if there's anybody on that train going to Port Huron," she answered.

"Can't pass without a ticket, madam."

"I've got a darter in Port Huron, I have."

"Can't help it, please. My orders are very strict."

"I tell you I want to send word to my darter!" she exclaimed, adjusting her spectacles for a better view of the official.

" Yes, but we can't help that, you see. Please show your ticket."

" I want this 'ere railroad to understand that I've got a darter in Port Huron, **and** she's got a baby four weeks old, **and** I'm going to send her up word in spite **of all** the gates in this depot !"

" Please show your ticket, madam."

" I tell you once more——"

" Please show your ticket, madam."

She gave the old umbrella a whirl and brought it down on his head with **all the vim of** an old-fashioned log-raising, and as he staggered aside **she** passed him and said :

" There's my ticket, sir, and I've got **more behind it !** Mebbe **one** man and a gate can stop me from sending word to my darter to grease the baby's nose with mutton taller if the weather changes cold, but I don't **believe** it !"

And she walked down to the train, found some one going to Port Huron, and came back **carelessly** humming the melody of " The Three Blind **Mice.**"

WANTED—A PEACEMAKER.

It has always been a wonder to me that there was not a professional class between the lawyer and the clergyman—a class to be called : " Peacemakers ; all kinds of Quarrels made up at the Shortest Notice and at Reasonable Rates."   If you go to a clergyman with a quarrel he talks and advises, but leaves you as mad as before.   If you go to a lawyer he hears you out and replies :

"Sue him, sir; you've got all the points to beat him, and it won't cost you over ten dollars to make him wish he'd never been born."

Take it in my neighborhood, for instance.   The man who lives in the cream-colored brick house got a new piano the other week.   The widow who lives in the cottage with a stone dog in the yard wasn't a bit envious over the fact.   She didn't care if he had a new piano in every room in the house, and a three-ply, warranted fast color organ down in the basement, but she couldn't resist saying to one of her friends :

" Well, it is curious to me how some folks will starve their stomachs and pinch their souls for the sake of buying an old horse-fiddle to torture their neighbors with !"

She didn't mean anything wrong, I assure you, but the family in the cream-colored brick heard of her remark, and they replied to it :

" And it is curious to us how a widow can take her husband's life insurance and squander it in velvet carpets, when she never had a rag one on her parlor floor during his lifetime."

They didn't mean anything, of course, but after that there seemed to be a coldness between the two families. Chickens were killed, cats poisoned, dogs clubbed, and windows broken, and only yesterday both were down to see the lawyers about slander suits and damages.

How easy it would have been for a peacemaker to have explained that the piano was a present from a rich old uncle to his cousin, and to have excused the widow's remarks by saying that insanity was hereditary in her family, and that one of her spells was just coming on ! She would have been invited to go over and pound on the instrument, and she would have pressed the family to run over and play circus on her new carpet, and peaches and cream would have cemented ancestral friendship.

The family living next to the corner, and the family in the house with a stone horse-block had been friends for years. A year ago the wife of the stone horse-block man came out with a fur-lined circular. She bought it without consulting the other woman. Indeed, she did not let on that she had it in the house for a week after it came home. Some one told the wife of the man next to to the corner that the stone horse-block woman had a fur-lined circular.

" I don't believe it !"

" But I've seen it !"

" It isn't silk !"

" Oh, yes it is !"

" Then the fur is cheap !"

" Oh, no ; the fur is splendid !"

" It must be her daughter's !"

" It can't be ; in **fact, she said** it was her own."

" Then she **never came** honestly by it, and I know it. My husband earns as much as hers, and I know we can't buy such things !"

She didn't mean anything, **but** her remarks **were carried to the** other, who **replied :**

" Well, **I** want her to understand that **I don't sit** up nights to watch my neighbors, **and I never stole a** hymn-book out of **a** church pew."

She didn't **mean** the least thing—I assure you **upon** my solemn word she didn't—but the fat was in the fire. Up went a fence twelve feet high be-**tween the** houses. Complaints were made to the **police of** smoking chimneys, howling dogs, bad smells, and a dozen other things. They are mad yet. They hope each other's children will **have** diph-theria, scarlet fever, measles, chicken-pox, and vari-ous other good things, and they **no** longer attend the same church, **nor** buy tickets for the same Sunday-school excursion.

How nicely a peacemaker could have patched things up. He would have been told that the circu-lar was bought with the $50 received from a grand-**father's** will, **and that** the wife of the man next to the corner had **the** jumping-toothache the day she spit out her criticism. He would have had them shaking hands and kissing and wiping their eyes inside of five minutes, and the stone horse-block wife would have said to the next-to-the-corner woman:

"I got it a little large through the shoulders so that you could wear it when you went to visit your sister in Dayton!"

And I am mad at the man on the southwest corner of the block, and he is mad at me, and it's all on account of nothing at all.. We bought a mantel and grate just alike and costing the same price. We had tiling of the same pattern, laid down by the same man. For five years we were like brothers. If I had a sick horse I consulted him. If his dog seemed a little off he consulted me. We went over to his house to play old sledge, and his family came over to my house to play croquet. I'd have turned out of bed at midnight of the darkest night you ever saw, and walked twenty miles through mud thirty feet deep, to bring a doctor in case of sickness, and I'm certain he'd have done fully as much for me.

In an unfortunate hour my brother-in-law from Chicago paid me a visit. He said the mantel was very handsome, and the grate a perfect beauty, and added :

"But you want a brass fender."

"No!"

"Certainly you do. It will be an immense improvement."

A day or two after he returned home he sent me a brass fender from Chicago. He not only sent it

as a present, but paid the express changes. Some one
told the man on the southwest corner that I had a
fender.

" It can't be !"

" But he has."

" I'll never believe it !"

" But I've seen it."

" Then he is a **scoundrel** of the deepest die !
Some folks would mortgage their souls for the sake of
showing off a little !"

When this remark was brought to **me I** turned
red, clear **back** to the collar-button. **I called** the
southwest corner man **a** liar **and a** horse thief. I
said that his grandfather was hung **for murder, and**
that his oldest brother was in State prison. I advised him to sell **out** and go to the Cannibal Islands,
and I offered to **buy** his house and turn **it** into a
soap factory.

The usual results followed. **He** killed my cat
and I shot his dog. He complained of my alley, and
I made him **put** down a new sidewalk. He called
my horse an old plug, and I lied about his cow and
prevented a sale. He got my church pew away by
paying a higher price, and I destroyed his credit at
the grocery. He is now maneuvering to **have** the
city compel me to move my barn back nine feet, and
I **have** all arrangements made to buy the house next
him and rent **it to an** undertaker as a coffin ware-
room.

A CORNER ON ICE.

THE first man to strike the coroner where the porter had thrown a pail of water over the flag-stones and produced a glare of ice was an insurance agent. He slid to the right, clawed to the left, clutched at a sunbeam, and went down with the exclamation: "Hanged if I don't!" He rose up to jaw and threaten and collect a crowd and almost lick somebody, and he went away stirred up for all day.

The next man was a tailor—tall, spare and solemn. His toes all of a sudden turned out, his left leg was lifted, and he spun once and a-half around before he went down with the remark: "I knew 'twould happen!" He got up to hurry along out of sight, and it was easy to see that he had calculated on about so many falls for the winter.

The next was a fleshy man with a smiling face and an air of good-nature. He didn't lose any time going down, and when he struck he realized that he had hit something. And yet what he said was: "Is it possible!" He got up slowly, forced a grin as the boys chaffed him, and looked back three times to make sure that he hadn't made a hole which would prove a man-trap for other pedestrians.

The next was a bank clerk with a pencil over his ear and a preoccupied mind. He was swinging his right hand and rushing right ahead when he suddenly saw billions of stars shining in the morning sky. His first thought was that somebody was celebrating Fourth of July; his next was to scrabble up and search for an asylum where he could hunt up his collar button and splice his suspenders. Not a word escaped him until he was a block away. Then he remarked: " At six per cent. it would be $854.17."

The next man was a strapping big fellow with an ulster on and a red silk handkerchief hanging out of a pocket. He began a sort of a shuffle as he struck the spot, increased it in a minute to a regular "breakdown," and finally went down with a whoop that was heard half a block away. He was up in a moment. Diagonally across the street he saw a man in an express wagon. The boys called to him that he had lost his red handkerchief, and that his nose would sadly miss it, but he would not wait. He strode across the street and up to the wagon, and as he hauled off and hit the driver a stinger on the ear he growled out :

" There, hang you! That makes us even ! "

" What even ! " shouted the victim as he rose up and adjusted his cap, but the other was gone.

3*

THE FOURTH FLOOR.

It was on the fourth floor. The occupant of an office sat reading his paper, when the door opened and a queer-looking old chap, having a very old hat and a very bad pair of boots, and making a very thin coat do a great deal of duty, entered and bowed and said :

" They wouldn't let me come up in the elevator, and so I clumb the stairs. Is it proper to say clumb ? "

The occupant looked up, and then returned to his article on " The Salt Industry of Michigan."

" Well, never mind whether it is or not," continued the man as he shut the door and leaned against it. " I clumbed, and here I am. I struck the town last week. I am not certain as to the properness of the word struck, but I arroved here and have had an infernal hard time of it. My friend, I am nigh onto 60 years old.

The occupant looked up, refolded his paper, and went on with his article.

" Nigh on to 60 and clean discouraged," said the old man. " Fact is, I kinder think if somebody don't gimme a quarter or sunthin' as a present I'll precipitate myself into the river. I believe precipitate is the word, though I wouldn't swear to it. Would you like to warm an old man's heart with a gift ? "

The occupant turned around and punched the fire, and then his eyes sought the paper again.

"Twenty-five cents would buy me a handsome present and save my life, but if you haven't got but fifteen I'll let you off. Avarice is not the predominating trait in my character. I believe predominate was properly used there, though I'll leave it to you."

There was deep silence in the room for sixty seconds.

"Well, we might say ten. That would buy a plug of tobacco, and as long as I had anything to chew on I shouldn't think of drowning myself. Yes, ten cents would kinder entitle me to mingle in with the joyous festivities of the occasion. You needn't be in any hurry about handing it over; I've got all the time there is."

This time the silence continued for 120 seconds, and was thick enough to knock down oyster soup.

"I presume you have a nickel about your person," whispered the old man after a while. "I won't agree to cut much of a figure in the festivities for that sum, but I'll make it go as far as possible."

There was more silence. Not a leaf stirred nor a bird chirped.

"Good-bye!" said the stranger as he opened the door and backed out. "When I am fished out of the river next spring please attend the inquest and identify me as the man whose life wasn't worth five cents! I go to precipitate! Precipitate may not be the word, but I go—I'm gone!"

BUYING A LOAD OF WOOD.

Bright and early the other morning a farmer arrived at the eastern market with a load of four-foot wood, and the first person to accost him was a woman, who asked ?"

" How much for the load ?"

" Four dollars."

" Have you got over a cord on there ?"

" Yes."

" I'll give you $3.50."

" Can't do it."

" I'm a widow with six children."

" Can't help that, ma'am—the price is $4."

She disappeared, but it was a dull day in the wood market, and at the end of an hour when she returned the man was still there.

" Is this the same load ?" she asked.

" The very same."

" All dry wood ?"

" Every stick of it."

" No rotten chunks in the center ?"

" If there is a single one I'll give you the whole load."

" Then I'll give you three and a half."

" Can't do it."

" I am a widow with a sick husband and seven children to support."

" Yes, I know, but four dollars is the price."

" At noon she came again and offered him the same price, and although he still refused a bright idea popped into his head. He drove around the corner and unloaded nearly a quarter of a cord, re-arranged his blankets on the load, and drove back to the stand. In about half an hour the woman passed by and called out:

" Haven't you sold yet?"

" No."

" I'll give you three and a half in silver—all in quarters."

" Well, I guess I'll take it, and I'd as lief have silver as anything else."

He drove six blocks through the mud with a grin on his mouth, and he cackled and chuckled over the joke as he unloaded the wood. She placed four-teen quarters in his hand as he finished, and he hur-ried off as he saw her looking over the pile. That might have ended the transaction, but it didn't all the same. In the course of the next twenty minutes a man closely resembling the wood seller was seen to halt a policeman on Gratiot avenue, go down into his pocket fourteen successive times after quarter dollars, and when he had fished up the last one he was heard to shout:

" Every durned one of 'em has got a hole in it half as big as my fist, and I'm a villain if I don't carry the case clear to the Supreme Court."

IT WASN'T FLY-SCREENS.

SHE knew he was the fly-screen man by the samples under his arm, but she held the door open and permitted him to say :

" Madam, I notice that you haven't a fly-screen at any door or window."

" Not a one," she answered.

" You must be overrun with flies ?"

" We are."

" Flies are a terrible nuisance ?"

" Yes, indeed."

" And this seems to be a good locality for mosquitoes ?"

" Oh, yes, sir."

" I presume they bother you nights ?"

" Very much."

" And a great deal of dust blows into a house not protected by screens."

" A great deal, sir."

" And how many windows have you in the house ?"

" Sixteen."

" Each one ought to have a half size."

" Yes, sir."

" And I can make them cheaper to you than any other man in the business."

" I think you can."

" Do you prefer plain green or figured ?"

"Well, I always did like plain green."

"Very well; I will measure the windows and take your order."

"You needn't trouble yourself any farther," she quietly replied.

"What! Don't you want screens!"

"No, sir. The other day the woman across the street had ten minutes' conversation with a tin peddler, and she's had her nose in the air over me ever since. A fly-screen man is about three times as high as a potato man, and I've been talking with you to let her see that she isn't the only lady in town who can put on airs. She's mad as a hen by this time, and now you get up and dust or I'll have my dog run you clear to the river."

STRIKING A SOFT JOB.

A MAN sat writing in a basement office on Griswold street. An old man with a snow-shovel on his right shoulder and his boots covered with snow entered with a great racket and two or three "whews," and placing one of his snowy feet against the hot coal stove he said:

"First there was the creation of the world. I presume you admit that?"

The man who sat writing did not even look up-

"Of course you admit it. Snow was created along with other sorts of weather, and according to the laws made by man snow must be cleaned off the walks within six hours after the storm ceases, providing there is any storm to cease. Are you following me ?"

The man at the desk kept scratching away for dear life.

"Of course you foller. The next great event was the deluge. All the snow was soaked up for the time being, but we've had heaps of it since, and some men are too stingy to pay fifty cents to have their walks cleaned. I presume you catch on ?"

If the gentleman even knew that the old man was present, he did not betray the fact by a gesture. The visitor changed feet against the stove and continued :

"Then there was the Drift-Period. Icebergs, ash-barrels, snow-drifts and old hats went drifting around the country at the rate of forty miles an hour. The man who wants to keep out of the poorhouse, and is willing to shovel off snow at the rate of a dollar a day drifted too, and finally brought up in Detroit. I presume you twig ?"

If he did there was no sign.

"Then came the Stone Age," resumed the old man, as he hunted through his pockets for some tobacco dust. "Good many stones around, I reckon, and there have been hearts of stone ever since. Yes, sir, there are men in this very City of Detroit who wouldn't pay thirty cents to clear off their forty feet of side-walk if the snow thereon was up to their chins. I presume you tumble ?"

The man rose up from the desk without a word, walked over and seized the old man by the collar, and without even looking into his eyes, he opened the door and " lifted " him to the sidewalk at two motions and flung the snow-shovel after him. The ejected stood and stared around for a minute, rubbed the top of his head gently, and was a minute more in fully realizing the situation. Then he descended the stairs, opened the door, and walked out :

" It isn't the two kicks I care about, for I'm used to that, but it hurts me to think that I went and posted up such a man as you are on the Biblical history and solemn facts that you would never have heard of in all your born days !"

<hr>

HANDLING A TENNESSEE CROWD.

A Michigan man who has a patent windmill went down to Tennessee last fall to see what he could do among the farmers of that State. Reaching a town in the central part of that State, he went to a dealer in agricultural implements and stated his desire to erect his machine and call attention to it.

" Well, it can be done, I guess," was the reply.

" But how had I best proceed ?"

"Well, you kin put her up over on the hill thar. I don't know who owns the ground, but if you treat the crowd I guess no one will object."

"Very well."

"Next Tuesday is market-day, and there'll be heaps of folks in town. You want to be around early and treat the crowd."

"Yes."

"Set the old thing going and ask the boys over to drink something."

"Just so."

"You want to stand on a bar'l and make some explanations, of course, for it will be new to most of 'em. But don't talk too long. Make it about ten minutes and then treat the crowd."

"Yes."

"If you have to talk any more, tell 'em there's another drink ahead."

"I see."

"If the old man Jones comes in with his boys there'll be a row in the crowd. They shoot on sight. Keep your eye peeled, and if you see any signs of a row ask the whole crowd out to drink."

"Yes, but—"

"Look out for dog fights. If one takes place you can't hold the boys a minute. Keep your eye on the canines. If you see a yeller purp begin to bristle up ask the crowd to step over and moisten."

"Yes, but by that time the whole crowd will be drunk," protested the agent.

"Sartin it will, and that's what you want, of

course. That will **give** you a chance to skip out and take your life along **with you, and if you make a stop** anywhere within a hundred miles **I'll send** the windmill by freight—provided there's anything left **to send!** Nothing like knowing how to handle a Tennessee crowd, my friend. Did you ask me out **to** take sunthin'?"

----◆◆----

THE MAN WHO WAS WARNED.

DURING the uncertain days following the **close of the** war there **were certain** localities in **the** South where **a** man who **had a** grudge against **a** neighbor **got rid of him by** writing him an annonymous letter warning him **to** leave the State inside of ten days, **or** prepare to fill a grave over which no one would feel particularly interested in keeping the grass green. One day Col. Blank, who had removed to Arkansas from Southern Michigan and was attend-**ing** strictly to business, received such a missive. It **was** the rule to turn pale as death, rush home and pack up, sell **ont for nothing** and skedaddle **on the** wings of chain lightning, but the Colonel didn't **fol-**low it. It struck him that he knew the handwriting, **and he** went home, buckled on a knife and revolver, **and took a** ride of three miles into the country. He **dismounted** at the cabin of a long-haired, long-legged, old swamp owl, named Patterson, who was in the back yard mending a harness. The Colonel approached him to within three feet, and after they had seated and discussed the weather, the Michigander remarked:

"Patterson, I am going to leave Arkansas."

"Shoo! Anything wrong?"

"I've been warned away."

"You don't say!"

"Yes, I've been given five days to leave the State."

"And you calkerlate you will go!"

"Yes, I'll have to or be waylaid or hung up."

"Yes, I reckon that's so," chuckled the old man.

"But I want to take something with me to remember Arkansas by," continued the Colonel, "and I came out after your scalp!"

"My what!"

"Sit still, old man, or I'll bore you through! That's it—up with your hands! If I go back to Michigan and tell 'em I was warned out of Arkansas, and that I got up and dusted without firing a shot, they'll call me a coward. If I carry your scalp back I've got something to show for the two years I've put in here and the $6,000 I've laid out. Old man, if you know the Lord's Prayer you'd better repeat it quick, for I'm in a dreadful hurry to get back."

"Say, Kurnel, don't you like the kentry down here?" asked Patterson.

"Yes."

"Is the climate all right?"

" First rate."

" Chance to make money ?"

" Good chance."

" Then, Kurnel, don't go back ! I don't keer two cents about my scalp, but somehow I've got attached to you and it will rip up all my tender feelings to see you go ! Let my old scalp-lock stay right whar' she is, and you stay right whar' you be, and if any of the boys look cross-eyed at you fur the next ten years I'm a kyotte if I don't drive 'em into Mexico or make 'em lose themselves in the ground !"

The Colonel is down there yet, and old Patterson never meets him without anxiously inquiring if he's got over being homesick yet.

THE WONDERS OF SCIENCE.

IT is curious how narrow-minded some men are, and how little they care about subjects calculated to broaden and benefit their mental faculties. Such a man was half-asleep on a bench at the Union depot yesterday, when a very tall stranger with a very short linen duster on sat down beside him and said :

" Have you calculated the pressure per square inch which you exert on this bench ?"

The sleepy man scowled as he looked up, and then turned away as if he didn't want to hear any more.

"Do you know," continued linen duster, "whether it is dead weight or force of gravitation which permits you to rest on this bench?"

"No, sir," was the emphatic answer.

"What is the attractive power of earth? What force is exerted by the law of gravitation on feet the size of yours? Let us figure a moment."

"I don't want to hear you talk!" snapped the other as he sat up. "I am waiting for a train!"

"So'm I," said linen duster, "and that opens a subject for new thought. Do you know the weight of air displaced by a train moving at the rate of thirty miles an hour?"

"No, sir, nor I don't care! I'm in no mood for talking!"

"Suppose," remarked linen duster as he squinted his left eye at the sun, "that you are walking at the rate of six miles an hour, do you wish to know what pressure the air exerts upon your forward movement? Lend me your pencil and I will figure."

"I won't do it; and I tell you again I don't want to be talked to!" was the fierce reply.

"Do you know how long it would take a locomotive to reach the moon, running at the rate of a mile a minute?" softly asked linen-duster.

"See here, I'll knock your head off if you don't go away from me!"

"You, sir, weigh about 160 pounds, and have well-developed muscle; but do you know how much force is exerted in knocking down a human being, aud the force of atmospheric pressure to be overcome before your fist reaches his face?"

" I've stood your sass just long enough, and now you leave or I'll mop the ground with you !" shouted the narrow-minded man as he jumped up and spat on his hands.

" Are not the wonders of science interesting to you ?"

" No, sir !"

" And don't you care to know that the heat of the sun is 256,000 times——?"

" No, sir ! no, sir !"

" Or that the moon exercises an influence——?"

" No, sir—go off—I don't care—go away—you're a liar and a fraud !"

The man with the linen duster withdrew a few feet to lean against the wall, and the other went back to his narrow-mind and selfish interests. While the latter dozed and thought of nothing higher than ham and eggs, the former picked up an old nail and softly figured out the distance traveled by a father's arm in giving his son an old-fashioned whaling.

THAT FLY-PAPER.

Now is the season when the druggist hangs a
dozen sheets of sticky fly-paper in the windows to
show the folly of investing in mosquito-bars. The
said sheets are covered with flies, dead and dying,
sometimes artistically arranged and sometimes dropped on in a reckless though captivating manner.
There is no sham about this paper. It will catch
any fly who takes a sheet of it for a skating-park, and
it will hold him long enough for you to run to the
wood-pile and bring the ax and knock him in the
head. The only trouble is to work up the fly. He
sometimes knows his business, and you can't beat it
into his noddle that a sheet of this paper represents
a cool and grassy valley into which he is privileged
to meander in search of lumps of white sugar. He
will sit on the edge of the window-sill and wonder
and think, and kick out his legs in the sunshine, and
if you think he has got so hard up that he must come
down to molasses and pulp, you keep right on trying. Visions of the thousands of flies captured at
the drug store " since Monday noon " will rise up
before you, but only to make you more down-hearted.
If you spread out ten sheets on the chairs and table
and floor, you run more chances of catching a fly
than with one. Any arithmetic will tell you this.
It may be an hour or two before some reckless old
reprobate of a fly will start out to see what you have

been doing. Back into a corner and don't breathe while he is making for the table. He may light down. Flies have their tired moments the same as three-year old steers. He will slide to the east—then north by east—then southeast—then wheel to the west and look around to see if anybody has a broom trained on him. Give him time. If the molasses is up to his grade he will find it sooner or later. When he finally slides up to the paper you can bet you've got him. Taking hold of the table with his legs he will reach his head out, nibble a little, smack his lips, and then make a dive for the center of the sheet, calculating to fly off with it to his knot-hole in the ceiling. If you have tacked the sheet down you've got a fly. If you haven't, away goes a cent. You may catch a second fly before the summer is gone, but if you are impatient and want to make a show you must order you dead flies by the box from New York, spread out your paper in a quiet place, and put 'em on with the machine used by all respectable druggists.

"SUMMER BOARDERS."

He came to this office yesterday to see about getting out an illustrated catalogue. He was a nice old man, and honest in his convictions. He lives out from the city about eight miles, on Napoleon Creek, and it suddenly occurred to him the other day that his place was a beautiful summer resort, and . that his facilities for taking a few boarders should be published. -

" Fust," he began, as he removed his ancient tile, " Napoleon Creek flows right by the door, and there's allus at least a foot of water in it all summer long. Nicest place in the world for women to learn to swim. No sharks, alligators or snakes to bother 'em, and they kin splash around in harmless glee."

" Any fish in it ?"

" Yes sir-e-e, there be. They are small, to be sure, but all you've got to do is to catch more of 'em in a day. Napoleon Creek can't be beat, sir, for an attraction, and it furnishes the best kind of water for washing clothes. We save six bars of soap every week by using this water."

" Well ?"

" Wall, then there's a hill in the distance—over on Squar' Fuller's farm. I tell ye that hill looks lovely to a boarder sittin' on the back verandy ! It's kinder bold and defiant, and kinder soft and pleadin', and the sight makes a man feel sort o' awed, and humbled. The hill's a big thing, sir, and it's going to be a draw."

" Yes."

" Then there's the medder and a white school house beyond. Then, on 'tother side is the big stub that was struck by lightning. Boarders can take home all the splinters they want to, and my boy Dan can tell 'em all about how the pieces flew.

This **stub is** goin' to git 'em, sir—can't help it. It combines romance and **the power** of lightning together, **and boarders will stand around** thar' with their mouths open and tongues hanging out."

" Anything else ?"

" Anything else ?" he repeated in an **injured** tone. " Well, I should say **there** was ! **There's** sheep gambling o'er the lea, and they are going to draw ; there's cows wading through Napoleon Creek, and that will fetch 'em ; there's **an old fanning-mill** which the children kin **turn, and they'll cry to sit** up all night ; there's **a grove with more'n** forty birds in it, and boarders **kin take the kitchen chairs** right out **thar'** ; then I'm going **to break two colts** this summer and have a lightning-rod put up, **and** 'tween me'n the old women we'll **make it** a perfect paradise around **thar."**

" And your prices ?"

" **Wall,** bein' that this is the fust year, we shan't b'ar down very heavy. I want to git folks in the habit of comin' out there, and kinder advertise **her** up, and bimeby we kin make sunthin'. Don't **forget** to say that we have family prayers twice a **day.** That'll be another big draw, you see. Dan he sings **bass, my** wife sings **a** sort **of** soprano, I sing awlto, and Sophia Jane she accompanies us on the melodeon, **and I** tell you it's sweet. That'll get 'em hard ; and on extra occasions **I kin** prevail on the Edson boys to come over and help us. One plays the brass-drum and the other a mouth-organ, and they can't help but draw. You jest orter hear 'em play ' Baby Mine' once !"

" Beautiful, is it ?"

" Beautiful ! **Why, it just** melts you right down, **and you** don't care whether there's flies in the milk or not ! Wall, good-by. **Work 'er** up strong, and don't **forget** Napoleon **Creek and** the women **in swimming."**

" WHO SOLD DOT **COAT ?"**

ONE morning a tall young man of 20 landed at the Union Depot with a bundle under his arm, and after three or four minutes spent in getting his bear- ings he walked **up Jefferson** avenue and turned into **a clothing store.**

" Do you vish to try on some coats and wests for **a dollar,"** asked the proprietor as he rushed from behind the counter.

" No, **I** guess not. **Do you deal** on the square ?"

" My frent, dot is exactly vhat I does. I vas **so** square dot I lose $3,000 last year. Can I sell you an oafercoat for ten dollar ?"

" No, I guess not. Here is **an** overcoat that **I** bought of you four weeks ago."

" Bought of me ?"

" Yes, I think you are the man. When I got it home we found **that** it was moth-eaten. **I can** pick it to **pieces in a dozen places."**

" Is dot **bossible** ! **Und** how much you pay ?"

" Eight dollars."

" **My** sthars ! And vhat you want now ?"

" I want my money back."

" Vhell—vhell. My frent, I am sorry for you. You seem like an honest poy, and it vhas too bad."

" Yes, it was a swindle, and I want my money back."

" Dear me, but I vish you vhas here yesterday ! Let me oxplain **to you.** **You** bought dot coat four weeks ago ?"

" Yes, **four** weeks to-day."

" Vhell, I had sold oudt to my cousin **Philip** shust one day before. Philip ish not a square man."

" What have **I** got to do with Philip ?"

" Let me oxplain. In dree days Philip makes assignment to **my** brudder Louis. Dot Louis is a leedle off. **He** would sheat your eye-teeth away from you."

" Yes, but I haven't anything to do with Louis."

" Let me oxplain. Louis kept der place a week, und he gif a shattel mortgage to my fadder-law, and vhas bounced out."

" I don't know anything about **that.**"

" **Let me** oxplain. My fadder-law vhas took mit **a** fit and died, and he **leaf** dis blace to my wife. My wife vhas gone to Europe for two years, and she leaf **me** as agent. Now you see how **it** was. I gannot **tell** you who sold you dot coat. Maybe it vhas **Philip,** maybe Louis, maybe my fadder-law. It **couldn't** haf **been** me, for I vhas in Shicago. If you leave dot coat I vhill write to my wife. She is square, shust like me, and maybe she writes back dot you can take a linen duster and two white wests and call it all right."

" Say, this is a sneaking swindle," exclaimed the young man.

" Maybe it vhas. Philip vhas a great liar."

" I'll go to the police !"

" Vhell, dot is all right ; maybe der police vhill help me catch Louis. I shust found oudt last night dot he cut all der hind buttons off all der coats in der store before he left."

"If you'll step out-doors I'll mash you !"

" Vhell, I like to oblige, but you see I vhas only agent for my wife."

" Well, you'll hear from me again, and don't you forget it !" said the victim as he went out.

" I hope so—I hope so. I like to make it all right. I vhas only agent for my wife, but I feel so square dot I take dot coat back for three dollars if you vhant to trade it out in paper collars !"

AROUSING HIS SYMPATHIES.

" I SEE you have a lot of misfit pants," observed a stranger as he halted before a Jefferson avenue clothing store.

" My frendt, **vhalk in.** I haf more misfits ash would fit half der State of Michigan."

" What do you call a misfit ?"

" Vhell, somedings ash doan' blease somepody who orders 'em, and somedimes der cutter makes a mistake in der figgers."

" You keep a tailor, **I** suppose."

" Six tailors, my frendt, and all **dey do is to** make mistakes and misfits **in** order to keep up my stock like you see."

" **Is** that so ?   Well, now, what ails this pair."

" Dot pair," replied the dealer as he shook them out, " vhas made for a young man who vhas to be married last week.   Der gal she dies mit a fever, and so he doan' come after his cloze.   I lose shust four dollars on dat pair."

" And these ?"

" Vhell, dot pair vhas made for a deacon in der shurch who vhas sparking up a vidder vomans.   Der left leg is smaller ash der right, and he doan' take 'em.   I sell you dot pair for tree tollar."

" **Here's** a stylish looking pair which would **about fit me.**   Whom were these made for ?"

" **My** frendt, dot shtrikes **a** sad chord in my

heart.　He vhas a young man who vhas to wear dose pants at a bridal.　Der color vhas selected to match der bride's complexion, but shust one day pefore de marriage she changes complexions und dose pants vhas no good.　Dot vhas a loss of ten dollar to me, und der young man vhas so mortified dot he shump in der rifer und vhas drowned."

"Whom were this blue pair made for?"

"For a shudge, my frendt—one of our leading shudges.　Der cutter makes a mistake, you see? Der shudge vhas a man who vhalks mit his toes turned out, vhile does pants vhas cut for a man who vhalks mit his toes turned in.　I lose seven dollar on dot pair."

"Well, I declare!　You'll lose all of $500 on this lot, won't you?"

"My loss vhill be oafer $1,000, und last week I haf a fire and no insurance, my vhife breaks her leg, and der landlord raises on my rent almost half."

"Great ginger?　Why, I should think you'd shut up shop!"

"If I do dot den where you get some misfit pants?"

"That's so—that's so.　You are what they call a human—a humanitarum, I reckon."

"Vhell, I vhas human, I s'hpose."

"You bet you are!　And so am I, and when I meet a man with a soul like your's I'm his mutton and he's my chicken!"

"Vhill you vhalk in?"

"Sartin I will, and you can paw over that pile of

misfits and **hand me about thirty** dollars' worth **and** do 'em up and take your **cash!** A man who allows himself to be paralyzed, pulverized **and** smashed to **a jelly** to accommodate the public deserves to be patronized, and you needn't be a mite particular whether them pants match my complexion or are built to fit bow-legs or straight. Shut **the** door, keep the children out, and **lemme** jump into five or six pairs."

HE WAS CALM.

" Feel of **my** pulse !" he suddenly exclaimed, as **he** thrust his hand out to a policeman on the avenue.

The officer instinctively laid his hand on the butt of his self-cocking revolver, and drew back.

" Well, then, listen and see if my heart thumps— look me in the face, and see if I am pale," continued the stranger.

" What sort of a circus **is** this ?" growled the officer as he jingled his handcuffs.

" There you go—there it is again ! I'm fully prepared to be called a crank or run in as a lunatic ! Heap insult upon injury, but I'll be calm—terribly calm."

" **Who** are you ?"

" Bronson—Bronson of Indiana."

" And what's happened ?"

4*

"I arrive in Detroit this morning. I lend a stranger $45 and take a check for $500 as security. Check proves N. G. I prove to be a greenhorn who ought to be rubbed down with a brickbat and fed on nails. I find myself dead-broke in a strange city, but I am calm—wonderfully calm. Pulse is regular at about sixty-eight, and no excitement around the heart."

"Well?"

"Well, I go to a hotel. I register and take breakfast and report my financial condition. **Result:** Contumely and kicks, but more kicks than contumely. I am lifted into the street in front **of a** No. 10 boot and in the presence of 150 speculators, **but I am** calm—grimly calm. Not a hair rises on end—not **a** flutter under the left arm."

"That's good—go on," encouraged the officer.

"I select my bank from the dozen in the city, **and draw a** sight draft on my brother in Indianapo-**lis.** Result : No bank pays a sight draft till after collection, and I walk out. 'Nother bubble busted, but my calmness solidifies—no weakness **in** the knees—no wild thoughts of suicide. Simply a dreadful, icy calmness."

"And then?"

"And then **I** go to the telegraph office, and dispatch my rich uncle in Chicago to telegraph me $25. There is no anxiety while waiting. I lean against a lamp-post **like a man** carved of stone. The **answer** comes. He advises me to go to Halifax."

"**He** does, eh?"

"Exactly; but am I perturbed? Do my teeth chatter? Do my legs wobble as I glide around? Not a wobble nor a chatter. I am adamant itself. I am dead-broke—strapped—gone up—busted and cleaned out; but would you suspect it to look at me?"

"No; I wouldn't."

"Of course not. On the contrary I remind you of a calm, still summer morning—the waters without a ripple—the cows chewing their cuds in the green meadows—the plow-boy sitting on the barbed wire fence to kill time. I am repose. I am calmness. My dear sir, good-by—a calm good-by!"

And as he walked off he carefully scrutinized the windows for a sign of "Free lunch from 10 to 12 A. M."

"PEESNESS VHAS SHAKY."

One day a clothing dealer in one of the cities up the lake shore opened the door for a customer who laid a bundle on the counter and began:

"Two months ago I bought this 'ere suit of clothes of you."

"Oxactly, my frendt, und it doan' fit"

"I bought it to bury my brother in. Perhaps you remember the circumstance?"

"Oxactly—mit der greatest pleasure. Vhell, did you dig him oop und take off der clothes?

" No, sir ! My brother lay in a trance for four days and then came to life andis now perfectly well."

" Vhat a shame to act like dot !　Und so he doan' vhant der clothes ? "

" No ; they are too small for him.　Being as he never wore them we thought you might take the suit back and return the money."

" Dot vhas ompossible, my frendt."

" Why ? "

" Vhell, dot vhas not only against all de rules of commerce, but such a practice would bust a peesness all oop."

" I paid you $15 ; can't you give me twelve ? "

" Ompossible."

" Say ten."

" My frendt, you doan' know how dis clothing peesness vhas.　You bought dot suit eight weeks ago ? "

" I did."

" Vhell, right away after dot dere vhas an awful decline in wool.　Next comes some big failures in Rochester und New York.　On top of dot I sell oudt to my brudder.　Den my brudder assigns to my wife.　Den cotton goes down und my vife assigns to me.　Shust now der clothing market vhas shaky, und only an hour ago I gif my brudder a shattel mortgage to secure a loan of $300."

" Say eight dollars for the suit."

" I couldn't do it.　If you like to leaf it und take a four-dollar ofercoat I shut my eyes so dot I doan' see you take it avay und haf to tell my brudder dot we doan' make enough profit to pay our gas-bills."

" I'll never do that—never ! "

" Vhell, dot vhas for you to say. If your brudder vhas a man he dies vhen his time comes und not make all dis confusion. I doan' keep sthore for men to go into trances und come to life. Good-by ! I like to oblige, but peesness vhos too shaky."

IT WAS A JUG.

He seemed to be in perfect possession of all his senses as he walked out of the store with a jug in his hand, marched up to the corner, and there deliberately let the jug fall to the pavement. It was, of course broken into many pieces, and, of course, the oil splashed over the stone sidewalk. When this had been accomplished the man waited. In two or three minutes along came a citizen who halted all of a sudden, stared hard at the spot, and called out :

" Ah ! somebody broke a jug !"

" Yes."

" Oil in.it, wasn't there ?"

" Guess so."

" Probably let the jug fall ?"

" Probably."

" And the oil was wasted ?"

" It was."

" Well, I declare," he gasped, **as** he passed on. He had been gone only a minute when a lawyer **came** along. He, too, brought up with a sudden **jerk,** and asked :

" Something happened ?"

" Yes."

" Somebody broke a jug ?"

" **Yes.**"

" Had something in it, eh ?"

" Yes."

" Might have been **turpentine, but** smells **like** kerosene."

" It was kerosene."

" Ah ! then I was correct."

He lingered until the third man came up. The **new** arrival picked up the handle of the broken jug **and** remarked,

" Bless me, but this must have been a jug ?"

" **It was.**"

" **And it** has kerosene in it," he continued as he rubbed his finger on the walk and sniffed at it.

" **It** did."

" **Well,** by George, but that's queer."

He **also** waited, and a fourth man came up **and** went through about the same performance. Then a **fifth,** sixth and seventh came, and by and by there **were** thirty men in the group and more coming **every** moment. **Each** one picked up a piece of the **jug** looked it all over, snuffed at it and put on an ex- pression of interest, and one man had asked if the coroner had been notified, when a policeman pushed his way in, and asked :

" What's this all about ?"

" Why," answered the man who had started the affair, " I put some kerosene in a jug, and let the jug fall onto the walk."

Some of the crowd tried to laugh as it suddenly broke up, and some said they would pound him if they had to wait a whole year, while the officer went away muttering :

" This will **bear** looking into. **Where** was he going with that jug ? How came it to break ? **What** was he doing with kerosene ? Why didn't the jug contain molasses ? I'll have an eye on **him**."

SCALING HOTEL FIGURES.

An old lady, with a jerky voice and a great display of snuff-box and spectacles, got left by a train the other night and had to go to a hotel for lodgings and breakfast. A few minutes before train time the clerk went up to her room to notify her, and found her sitting in a chair as stiff as a major. As soon as he entered she broke out with :

" How much a day in this hotel ?"

" Two dollars, madam."

" How much where you don't have supper ?"

"Twelve shillings."

"How much where you sit up all night long, expecting to be murdered every minit."

"Just the same—twelve shillings."

"How much where you don't eat any breakfast for fear of being pizened!" she continued.

"Just the same, madam. There is your bed, and breakfast has been ready these two hours."

"Well, I don't pay it!"

"But, madam."

"No, not if I die fur it! Here I've sot in this blessed cheer all night long, hearing whistles and bells and folks running, and men whooping, and expecting every minit would be my last on airth!"

"Has that gas been going all night?"

"Every minit, sir. I've allus made a practice o mindin' my business, and I didn't propose to set fire' to myself by fooling with that thing. How much is it where you sot and tremble like a leaf, from 8 o'clock at night till next morning, wishing to goodness you hadn't been fool nuff to start for Illanoy alone!"

"Just the same, madam."

"Not by a jug-full, young man! Here's fifty cents, and you can take the rest out in a lawsuit! I haven't mussed the bed nor touched breakfast, and fifty cents is plenty for having a roof over my head. Git out o' the way, for I'm going!"

He had to move aside or be run over, for she picked up her satchel and put on steam until nothing could stop her. She made her way down stairs and started for the depot, and when a boy asked if she would have her baggage toted she wheeled on him and replied:

"You meander! I've bin swindled out o' fifty cents already, and if there's any more fooling around somebody will git hurt!"

------◆◆◆------

NO SUCH PERSON.

He had a fly-screen under one arm and a bundle of sticky fly-paper under the other as he entered a Michigan avenue saloon yesterday and said:

"Why don't you keep 'em out?"

"Who vosh dot?" asked the saloonist.

"Why, the pesky flies. You've got 'em by the thousand in here, and the fly season has only begun. Shall I put fly-screens in the doors?"

"Vhat for?"

"To keep the flies out."

"Why should I keep der flies oudt? Flies like some shance to go aroundt und see der city, der same as beoples. If a fly ish kept oudt on der street all der time he might ash vhell be a horse."

"Yes, but they are a great nuisance. I'll put you up a screen door there for $3."

"Not any for me. If a fly vhants to come in here, und he behaves himself in a respectable manner, I have nothings to say. If he don't behave I bounce him oudt **pooty queek, und he don't forget her !"**

"Well, try this fly paper. Every sheet will catch 500 flies."

"Who vhants to catch 'em ?"

"I do—you—everybody."

"I don't see it like dot. If I put dot fly paper on der counter somebody comes along und wipes his nose mid it, or somebody leans his elbow on her and vhalks off mit him. It would be shust like my boy Shake to come in und lick all der molasses off, to play a shoke on his fadder."

"Say, I'll put down a sheet, and if it doesn't catch twenty flies in five minutes, I'll say no more."

"If you catch twenty flies I have to pry 'em loose mit a stick und let 'em go, und dot vhas too much work. No, my frendt; flies must have a shance to get along und take some comfort. I vhas poor once myself, und I know all about it."

"I'll give you seven sheets for ten cents."

"Oxactly, but I won't do it. It looks to me like shmall peesness for a big man like you to go around mit some confidence games to swindle flies. A fly vhas born to be a fly, und to come into my beer saloon ash often ash he likes. When he comes I shall treat him like a shentleman. I gif him a fair show. I don't keep an ax to knock him in der headt, und I don't put some molasses all oafer a sheet of paper und coax him to come und be all stuck up mit his feet until he can't fly away. You can pass along— I'm no such person like dot."

IT WASN'T A MASH.

Soon after we left Meridian, on the way across to Vicksburg, a solemn-looking old chap came into the smoker and groaned and sighed and took on like a man terribly distressed, and when we asked him where he seemed to feel it the worst, he replied :

" Gentlemen, there is a powerfully good-looking young woman in the next car, and she has fallen into the hands of a human hyena."

" No!" shouted three or four voices at once.

" Yes, indeed. He's a wicked-looking wolf in sheep's clothing. If I mistake not, he represents some New England machinery house. He's a squeezing of her hand, and a whispering of his love, and the giddy thing has fallen right into the trap. I couldn't bear to see it any longer, and so I came in here. Gentlemen, some of you have daughters !"

Yes, there were three of us who had daughters ranging from 2 to 7 years old, and we were honest enough to admit it.

" Just think of your daughters being kayjoled by a Philistine !" he continued. " He's talking and flattering and promising, and she's somebody's daughter. Gentlemen, something orter be did !"

We agreed. We all lounged in and saw that she was a good-looking, happy-faced girl of 20, and we returned and held an indignation meeting. After a fine display of eloquence and oratory it was unanimously agreed that if the masher got off at Jackson, where we were to wait twenty minutes, the good old man should go in and tell that girl what was what. Jackson was finally reached, and sure enough the human hyena got off and ran into the hotel. He was not out of sight when we all entered the car, and the philanthropist took a seat beside the girl and began :

"My dear young lady, my heart is sad—oh ! so sad !—for you ! You are on the road to destruction !"

" W-what do you m-mean ?" she faltered.

" I mean that the villain who left you a moment ago is seeking to ensnare you."

" The v-villain !"

" Yes, ma'am, the wolf in sheep's clothing—the hyena in human form—the scoundrel whose very look proves the vileness of his heart. I warn you to beware of him as you would of a serpent."

" Why, he's—he's my husband !" she shouted at the top of her voice, and next instant she had her fingers playing through his venerable locks and excavating channels down his wrinkled cheeks.

All of us got away at last and found hiding places in the baggage and mail cars—all but the old man. When he managed to get clear of the bride he slid off the car and took a bee-line up town, and though he met several people while in sight of us, we couldn't see that he stopped to answer any questions.

ALWAYS HIS LUCK.

HE boarded the St. Clair River boat yesterday morning with his wife and five children, and the family were not yet seated when he began :

"Now, Sarah, I'll bet $50 you forgot to hook that woodshed door."

"Mercy on me, but so I did!" she gasped.

"Just· as I expected—just exactly ; we'll get home to find the house cleaned out or in ashes. Never mind, though, it would serve us just right."

The boat had not yet started when one of the boys who insisted on some gymnastics with a chair fell to the deck and set up a great squall.

"Broke both arms, or I'm a sinner!" shouted the father. "I told you he'd do it if we let him come along, and now he's a cripple for life !"

It was, however, discovered that the youngster had sustained nothing more serious than a skinned nose, and peace was restored and continued until the wife suddenly discovered that she had lost her watch.

"Of course—of course!" growled the husband. "There goes $125 of my hard earnings! I knew you'd have it stolen before you had gone a rod !"

"But perhaps I left it on the bureau."

"Well, it will be lugged off before night, just the same. Serves you just right for bulldozing me a whole month to make this infernal excursion. What ails that woman's baby !"

" I declare if it hasn't got the whooping cough !"

"Of course—of course! and not one of our children ever had it ! You'll have business on your hands for the next six weeks !"

The next half hour passed peacefully enough. Then somebody observed that a man whose gaze was fixed on the water probably contemplated suicide.

" I expect nothing else !" exclaimed the disconsolate husband, " but maybe he will listen to reason."

Going over to the stranger, he laid a hand on his shoulder, and brusquely inquired :

" Sir ! do you mean to jump into the lake ?"

" Yes, sir !" was the reply, as the man looked up.

" Just so—exactly—I suspected as much. You'll utter a yell as you go over and kick up all the bobbery you can, I presume."

" Yes, sir."

" And my wife will faint away, and every young 'un howl like an Injun ! I'll give you a dollar to go over on the sly."

" No, sir—not for a thousand "

" Haven't you any feeling for a man who has had steamboats and fish and rivers and lakes and flats pounded into him for three months ?"

" None, sir."

" And won't five dollars bribe you ?"

" It won't."

" Then go ahead with your oration and death-yell ! Make all the fuss you will ! Splatter around in the water as long as you possibly can, and fix your eyes on my family when you go down for the last time. I never had **any** other **kind of luck,** and I'm going **down to** the saloon and **get drunk** preparatory to **a** biler explosion! Good-by, old feller; **serves** me right, **and** I don't complain!"

When he was helped ashore at the **Flats** he was **weak** in the knees and limber **in his** spirit. Gathering his family around him he counted :

"Sheven, eight, **nine, ten,** 'lezen, twelve. Why, bless my stars! I only had five shildren when we left Detroit, **an now** I've got **ten! Juss** my luck— juss zi 'spected! Los' watch—whoopin'-cough—suicide—ten shildren—whoop! Sherves me jus' rize!"

———•◦•———

FISHING AT THE FLATS.

THEY have **every** data about fish at the St. Clair Flats. The boatmen have got it figured down so fine that nothing is left for the imagination **to** work on. I asked one **of** them how many fish he imagined passed up **the** government canal per hour, **and** he promptly replied :

"**I** don't imagine anything **about** it—I know. The number is exactly 3,267 per hour. Twenty-four **times that** gives **you** the correct figures for **a day,** **and if you** can multiply that by 365 **days** you have the number for a year."

"**But** won't those figures vary!"

"No, sir, not a vary. If you think they do, prove it."

"What is the average catch *per capita* of people who come up here to fish?"

"Seven three-pound bass and three four-pound pickerel."

"That is, if they hire one of your boats and go out?"

"Certainly. Under other circumstances they never catch a fish."

"Do you believe that fish ever sleep?"

"No, sir—not if there is any biting to be done. If you should stand on the wharf here and fish I presume the fish would go to sleep all aronnd you."

"If I should go out and catch a hundred pounds of bass and pickerel could I dispose of fifty or sixty pounds anywhere up here?"

"Yes, sir. We always pay ten cents per pound for all over fifty pounds' weight. I would give you a draft on New York."

"How large a fish did you ever see caught up here?"

"He weighed exactly thirty-four pounds. That is, I don't mean the sturgeon hauled in here every day or two. We don't count them. This was a pickerel."

"Do those who go out to fish ever catch any small ones?"

"Never. The limit is two pounds."

"I suppose people sometimes go out and do not get a bite?"

“Never heard of such a case, sir.”

“Is there such a thing as good or bad luck in fishing?”

“No, sir.   It is always good luck.”

“If I should bring my own lines and bait and boat, would I catch anything?”

“No, sir.   You could count on being upset and drowned.”

“Do fish bite out of curiosity or from hunger?”

“From a sense of duty, sir.   They desire to see our investment here grow and build up.”

“You were speaking of sturgeon.   If a sturgeon is hooked will he make a run for it and tow the boat?”

“He will.”

“Would I be certain of a tow if I went out with you?”

“Certainly.   We couldn’t do business here if we could not guarantee such a trifling matter as that.”

When we returned at dark, and I charged him with the fact I hadn’t even had a nibble, he coolly replied :

“Certainly not.   I supposed you went out simply to see the country, and therefore didn’t go near any of the fishing grounds.   The wind was also in the wrong direction.   It was also too late in the day. Fishing !   Why, if you want to catch fish come up here to-morrow !”

5

LOVE IN THE DEPOT.

A WOMAN arrived the other forenoon from the East with seven children in tow, and at almost the same hour a man reached the same depot from the North with five offspring of various ages and sizes. She was a widow, and he a widower, and the children had not been whipped more than once around before there was a sort of mutual sympathy that begot admiration and then friendship. One of the widow's boys offered one of the widower's girls a bite of his fried cake, which was accepted in the spirit tendered, and a 10-year old girl belonging to the man made up to the 2-year old belonging to the woman and soon secured the privilege of wiping its nose and combing its hair. Presently the widower made bold to inquire :

"Madam, am I wrong in believing that you are a widow ?"

"I have been a widow fourteen months to-day," she answered.

"Great Scott! but it's just fourteen months to-day since my Hanner died! Which way be you going ?"

"To Illanoy."

"That's just where I am going, too. Did you promise your husband never to marry again ?"

"No."

"And I didn't promise my wife, either. Fact

is, I believe I shall **unite as soon as I find some good** woman."

"**And** my children need a father's care," she sighed as she pulled little John Henry **off** the window sill and bumped him into a seat.

The man got up and walked around the waiting-room and took a closer look at the children. Then he returned and said :

"I suppose you've got a few hundred dollars, belong **to** some church, can **wash** and bake and mend, **and are of a** mild and forgiving disposition ?"

"**Yes,** that's **me.**"

"**Well, I'm** kinder religious, **even-tempered, and** am worth about $2,000. I'm sort **o' struck on you.** There's something about your **eyes that reminds me** of Hanner."

"**And** you look like Alonzo around the mouth," she sighed.

Then he bent **over** and whispered something about Chicago and getting married, and she nodded **her** head. He gathered his children under his wing, took them into a corner, and, solemnly and impressively observed :

"Children, I'm going to git married to that woman over there and give you a new mother. If any of you is going **to** kick and boo-hoo about it, begin now, so that I can tune ye down before the train goes. Henry, you are the oldest. Are **you going to** declare you'll run away or commit suicide **Let me** know, right now, for this is a good cool place to prance ye around with a shingle."

Henry said he guessed it would be all right, **and** the rest of the crowd seemed to agree, **and** ten minutes later the widower and widow sat holding hands and trying to eat peanuts, and the twelve children were biting and pulling hair and kicking to see who should **have a** seat on the steam heater.

"This is kinder the work of Heaven!" chuckled **the** widower as he hitched **a** little nearer.

"You bet, love," she replied, as she shucked **another** peanut with her teeth.

DIDN'T MEAN HIM.

"**TAKE a** square look **at** me!" he commanded as he halted in front of a policeman on the avenue yesterday.

The policeman looked him all **over.** He was a pretty good chunk of a man, carrying a florid face, a prominent nose, **and an air** of general innocence.

"I don't see anything wrong about you," said the officer.

"Do my clothes fit? Do I wobble when I walk? Do I wipe my mouth on my coat-tails? Does the sight of me remind **you** of cabbages and other green things?"

"Well, **no.** You **look to** me like **an** honest, good-natured fellow."

"Then," said the stranger as he brought his fist down with a thump, "there's going to be bloodshed in the town. I came in this morning with an excursion. We had scarcely landed when a man called out: 'Did you bring along the keow?' 'Did you mean that for me?' says I. He said he didn't, and I passed on."

"He might not."

"Then, as I was going up the street a chap in a door says he: 'Ah! smell the carrot crop!' 'Do you mean that for me?' says I as I walks up to him. He says he didn't, and I passed on."

"I presume he didn't."

"Well, I got up to Griswold street, and I was looking for the Post-office, and a man calls out: 'I'll bet he brought along raw onions and turnips for his dinner!' 'Do you mean that for me?' says I as I walks up to him. He says he didn't, and I passed on."

"He must have referred to some one else."

"Well, I walked through the Post-office and started for the City Hall, and I was almost there when a young fellow in the door of a barber shop calls out: 'There goes the biggest cabbage-head of the season?' 'Do you mean that for me?' says I as I walks up to him. He says he didn't, and I passed on."

"He could not have meant you."

"Well, as I was walking through the City Hall a great big overgrown chap sings out through his nose: 'Behold the second crop of dandelions! Oh, my!'

' Do you mean that for me ?' says I as I **walks up to** him.   He said he didn't and I passed **on.**"

" That's right."

" Mebbe **so, but** you look a here ! I'm going down **to the** ferry dock. The first man or boy who calls out **carrots,** pumpkins, onions, turnips, scarecrow, **green-horn,** pig-weed, or **huckleberry** blossom to me won't have no **chance to lie about** it. I'll **turn on** him and rend him, and slay him and hammer him stone blind ! Mebbe nobody means anything, and mebbe its simply their way, but **I've got** my dander up, **and if** you hear a roaring **sound like a** cyclone you may know that I'm climbing **for a** man who has called out 'summer squash !' **to me !"**

NOT RICH, BUT INDIGNANT.

AMONG the excursionists was a **fat** man encased in an immense linen duster, accompanied by a scared-looking wife whose weight would not have balanced 100 pounds. As they came up Jefferson avenue, the man wiping off his heated brow and limping on his sore corn, they turned **into** a store and the fat man said :

" We are excursionists. We have **come** to view **the** points of interest in your city. Can you direct me to the State House ?"

"**We** have no **State House** here, **sir.** Lansing is the capital, you know."

"Ah! **so** she is—of course. Wife, why didn't we go to Lansing? I expected some such trickery **all the way in. Well,** we want to go to the morgue and see the dead bodies."

"There **are** no **dead** in there now."

"No! Wife, what do **you** say to that! If that isn't downright robbery on us then I'd like to know! Where is the grand aquarium?"

"I guess it's down in Lake Erie."

"You have no public aquarium! Wife, how does that strike you after coming eighty miles? Maybe you can put with **it,** but I won't!"

"Maybe they have catacombs **here?**" she tremblingly suggested.

"**No,** ma'am."

"No! of course **not!**" growled the old bear. "**Not a** catacomb in the city, and we expected to see **at least** forty. My whole county shall hear of this swindle!"

"I suppose there are no mountains around here?" she queried.

"No, ma'am."

"Just as I expected!" blurted her husband as he mopped his red face again. "They haven't got a mountain, precipice or avalanche in **the** whole town! Mary, we've **been** outrageously swindled!"

"There might **be** some grand ruins, Richard."

"**I** don't believe it!"

"No, ma'am. All **the** ruins we have at present

are undergoing needed improvements, and **won't be** in running order for sixty days."

" Didn't I tell you so, Mary !   I knew the minute we landed that they hadn't a consarned ruin in **their** old town !   Let's go home."

"**The Cooper** Institute **isn't** here, is **it?**" **she** asked, **as she** rose up.

" No, ma'am."

" Just as I expected—just exactly !" roared the enraged lion.   " When you woke me up at **2** o'clock this morning and said we must not forget the Cooper Institute I knew you were preparing a disappointment for yourself.   Come on ! "

" We have **a** beautiful river," suggested the citizen.

" Is it **the Bosphorus?**" she asked.

" No, ma'am."

" No! of course not—come along !   We've been cheated and tricked and swindled and mopped in the gutter !   The Pyramids ain't here, they hain't got no volcanoes, and I'll bet a hat agin ten cents they never had an earthquake !   We'll go back to the depot ! **We** hain't rich, but we know when we are swindled ! "

LETTING A DOG LOOSE.

Some days since a saloon keeper on Gratiot avenue paid certain parties in Chicago $25 for a stuffed lion to add to the attractions of his saloon, and the other morning as the place was being scrubbed out the lion was placed at the front door to keep him out of the wet. Half a block down the street a farmer was having his wagon repaired, and a big bulldog was chained to the hind axletree. He grew uneasy the minute the lion was rolled out, and it needed only a few encouraging words from the boys to render him half frantic. He growled and plunged and tore around and attracted quite a crowd, among which was a man who remarked :

"That's a purty brave dog of yours, stranger."

"Brave! I'd like to see the man or beast he wouldn't tackle!" replied the owner.

"I dunno about that. Never saw a dog yet who'd stand before a lion."

"Well, here's one who'd stand before two lions. See how anxious he is to get there."

"Yes, but he puts that on because he's chained. If he was loose you couldn't get him within a rod of that specimen."

"Couldn't, eh? Maybe you want to hear yourself talk."

"Well, I dunno. I'm opposed to betting, card-playing, dancing and all that, but seeing you are rather sassy about this, I've got half a dollar here which says that you can't get that dog to go within six feet of that lion."

"Put up the money—put up the money!" shouted the farmer as he went down into his own pockets after the coin.

The money was put up, the crowd fell back and the farmer's face wore a smile of triumph as he still further excited the dog, and then slipped his collar. With a yell of rage the "canine" made a bee-line for the king of beasts, and in another moment there was reason for a terrific yell of applause. Dog and lion filled the air, so to say. The lion was rolled over and over, grabbed by the throat and shaken around, drawn across the street and back by the car, and when the dog finally let up on the corpse the battle-ground was covered with hair and hay and sawdust and glass eyes. At that moment the saloon keeper rushed out, a policeman came up, and for five minutes the air was rent with shouts and exclamations and expostulations.

"It was all in fun," explained the farmer.

"Dot lions cost me $25 in Sheecago!" protested the saloon man.

"Who put up this job?" demanded the officer as he glared around on the crowd.

By and by a deep silence fell upon the crowd, and in a voice which had only kindness in it the owner of the lion said he must have his $25 or he would start for the Police Court. The policeman said it was certainly a case for the courts, and the crowd said the farmer might **have known what would** happen. He protested, but finally came to time, and when he had passed **over** a $10 bill **and given his** note for the balance, he had **only one sentence to** utter. **That was:**

"Now, then, I'll give any of you five acres **of** land to put me face to face **with** the outlaw who put up this job on a hard-working, innocent man!"

THE BOY AND THE FAIRY.

ONCE upon a time a fierce and ugly **old** woman who lived at the edge of **a dark** forest in which wolves were thicker than candidates for the Legislature stole a boy who had wandered from home and took him to her hut to become her slave. The parents of the stolen boy had thirteen others, and **as** they were not in the habit of counting the drove **at** night this one, who was named Billy, **was not even** missed.

When the old woman reached home with the boy she tossed him into a corner and proceeded to lay down the law and to beat it in with **a strap.** She put Billy through such a lesson in **the art of** skipping and dodging as no other boy ever **took,** and **when** she had tired herself out she warned him that **if** he did **not** humbly obey all her orders his hide would be taken off and hung on the **fence** and sold **to** a tin peddler for fifteen cents.

Next day the old woman locked Billy in the hut and went away for an hour, and when she returned she had the body of a peasant whom she had killed. The **boy** was commanded to salt the body down in **a** pork barrel, **and** to save the ears for bangles to be worn on the old ogre's bracelets when she went calling. Every **day** for the **next week the** old **woman** went out **and** killed **a** man **and had him** salted down ; **but at** the end of that time, men **having become rather** scarce and the supply of **meat abundant, she** rested from her labors to have some fun with **Billy.** She obliged the boy to dance a jig on a hot **stove,** and when he called for his pa and ma she laughed in derision. Then she stuck him full of pins and needles and called him her dear little pin-cushion, and **this** was followed by forcing him to hold a red-**hot silver** half dollar with a hole in it in his mouth and sing the Star-Spangled Banner twice over.

The Chinese language utterly fails to depict a hundredth part of the cruelties practiced by that old ogre on that innocent boy, and in the course of six or eight weeks he had a sorrow-stricken appearance, and his clothes were too big for him. When she was home she was constantly pinching hunks of flesh from his legs and arms and throwing them out-doors for the wolves to eat up, and when she was absent on **her** raids, the boy could do nothing but howl **and weep** and call for oysters fried in crumbs and currant-**jelly** spread on bread and butter.

One day, soon after the old wretch had gone out to hunt up a fat girl and have her baked for dinner a little old man came rattling down the chimney and wanted to know if all the back counties had been heard from. Billy thereupon related his mournful fate, and the old man, who was a first-class fairy in alligator boots, laughed a sort of a buzz-saw gurgle and said he had been aching for a fuss for the last two weeks.

The stolen boy was hidden under the bed, where the splinters wouldn't hurt him, and the minute the old Ogre entered the door the Fairy killed her by a stroke in the eye with his umbrella. The great blue chest in which she kept all the money received for laundry work was then broken open, and Billy was sent home loaded down with $50 greenbacks and $20 gold pieces. He reached the door just as his father's farm was about to be sold on a mortgage, and of course bid the place in and saved it. He then put a barbed wire fence all round the farm, bought a windmill, put up three lightning rods, and was elected to Congress by such a majority that the infernal opposition hasn't been heard of since.

Thus you see, my dear children, that although you may be called upon to suffer for a time, and you may pass through afflictions thick enough to cut up cold and warm over for supper, you will eventually triumph over all and come out of the big end of the horn.

P. S.—Although Billy went to Congress he did not vote for the River and Harbor steal.

WANTED AN ESCAPE.

THE man with the patent fire-escape, patent applied for, is to be encountered on every corner. Some of him have a knotted rope, others a canvas tube, and others yet a rope ladder **worked** by a crane, a pulley and block. **Each one** is warranted to save everybody from the sixth-story in time of fire with the utmost promptness and dispatch, and without even a bruise on the shin, and the cost is **a mere** nothing. On Brush street there is a carpenter-**shop on** the first floor of an old house. The carpenter occupies only the first floor, while the garret is empty.

A fire-escape man dropped around there the other **day** and pointed out the dangers of a holocaust in **such** graphic language that the carpenter could almost **most** feel blisters raising up on the back of his hands. **He** realized **the** need of a fire escape, and he laid down **his saw and** paid a call on the owner of the place **and** asked him **to** have a hole cut through the floor and roof and **a** rope ladder put in.

"Let's see," mused the owner. "How **large is** the room you occupy?"

"About fourteen feet square."

"And you work there alone?"

"Yes."

"How many **windows?**"

"Three."

"**And** double doors?"

" Yes."

" Well, of course, I don't want you to burn up in there," observed the owner; " but I wish you would do me a favor. In case of a fire I wish you would open the three windows and the double doors and see if you can't possibly squeeze yourself out far enough for some outsider to catch hold of your hair and pull you through !"

"ANOTHER MERCANTILE FAILURE."

Out on Michigan avenue a man near 70 years of age started a small confectionery store some months since, and the other day sent word to his three creditors up-town that he had failed and desired to compromise. The trio went down to the store, which they found in full blast, and the four sat down for a talk.

" You see, shentlemens, I do no peesness, und my family eats up all der brofits," explained the tradesman by way of excuse.

" You owe me twelve dollars," replied one of the creditors, " and each of these others fifteen a piece. That makes forty-two dollars."

" Shust forty-two," sighed the old man.

" Now, then, how much money have you on hand ?"

"Shust zixty tollar und **no more.**"

"Very well, as you have had **bad** luck we will settle with you for one hundred and twenty cents on the dollar, and you can go on as before."

"Yaw, I will **do dot,** sheutlemens, und I am much obliged for such kind treatment."

He got out his money, the twenty per cent. was **added to the** claims and paid, and before the creditors **retired he** insisted on treating them to ice-cream. They had **been** gone **an** hour before **the** old man rushed out **and** halted a policeman and said :

"If I fails in peesness und bays 120 **cents on der** dollar vhat does it mean ?"

"It means that you don't understand how **to** fail," was the reply.

"Ish dot bossible ?" whispered the old man.

"I should say so."

"Vhell, I go pack to der shoe peesness again. Vhen I fail in dot peesness I makes everytings. Vhen I fails in dis peesness I pays more as I owes."

BEGINNING EARLY.

THEY are traditional. They walk out of the station hand in hand, and they stop at the first confectioners and buy soda-water and red **balls** of pop-corn **and a** quart of peanuts. They ride **on** the street cars and squeeze. They wander through the corridors of the

City Hall and squeeze harder. They sit on a bench in the Grand Circus Park and yearn and sigh and lock fingers and look as foolish as two boys caught in a melon-patch.

Just such a couple left the train at the Union Depot and walked up Jefferson avenue yesterday. She had long curls and a pink dress and a yellow sash, and he had a standing collar sawing his ears off, a button-hole bouquet and a pair of new boots freshly greased and one size too small. They hadn't walked two blocks when they came to a man sitting on a box in front of a store, and as he caught sight of them a grin crept over his face like molasses spreading out on a shingle.

" Grinning at us, I 'spose ?" queried the young man as he came to a halt.

" Yes," frankly replied the sitter.

" Tickles you most to death to see us take hold of hands, don't it ?"

" It does."

" And you imagine you can see us feeding each other caramels, can't you ?"

" I can."

" And you shake all over at the way we gawp around and keep our mouths open ?"

" That's me."

" Well, this is me ! I'm not purty, and I haven't been cultivated between the rows, nor hilled up nor fertilized. I ain't what you call stall-fed, and the old man looks twenty per cent. worse than I do, but it won't take me over a minute to jam you seven feet into the ground! I told Lucy **I was** going to begin on the first man who looked cross-eyed at us, and you are the chap. Prepare to be pulverized!"

"**Beg pardon, but I didn't** mean——!"

"**Yes, you did! Lucy**, hold my hat while I mop him!"

"Say—hold **on**—say——!"

He took up the middle of the street like a runaway horse, **and** the young man took after him, but it was no use. After a race of a block **the man who** grinned gained so fast that **the** other stopped **short** and went back to his girl and his hat. Stretching forth his hand to the innocent maiden he remarked :

" Lucy, clasp on to that, and if you let go for the next two hours, even to wipe your nose, I'll never call you **by** the **sacred** name of wife."

THE **ROSY NORTH.**

WE had to wait for half an hour between **Charles**ton and Savannah for the Waycross train, and during this time a black man came up **to me** and inquired :

" Say, boss, doan **you lib** up Norf ?"

" Yes."

" Dat's what I reckoned **on.** Kin I ax a **few** queshuns ?"

" You can.'

" Wall, sah, does ebery cull'd man up dar own a brick house with a cupulo on top ?"

" Oh, no."

" Does he walk aroun' with a bag of gold in one han' an' a bag of silver in de odder ?"

" I never saw any of them taking such a walk."

" Do dey all own hosses an' kerridges?"

" No."

" Do dey all have diamonds an' pearls an' welvets ?"

" No."

" Say, boss, my name's Jones, an' I lib ober beyand dat pine woods. My ole woman am all de time stirrin' me up to go Norf, an' she really believes dat if we once git up dar we can go out befo' breakfast an' pick up a pailfull o' diamonds. Now, sir, tell me de solemn truf 'bout it! Could we do it ?"

" No."

" Could we pick up a peck ?"

" No."

" Fo' quarts ?"

" No."

" Two quarts ?"

" No."

" Dat's nuff, boss—dat settles me! I reckon if I axed 'bout one quart you'd say yes, but if anybody 'spects I'm gwine to fool aroun' wid any sich small 'taters as dat dey am sadly tooken in. I'ze kept house long 'nuff to know dat a quart o' diamonds a day wouldn't keep a fam'ly in co'n cake an' bacon half de time. 'Bleeged to ye, boss. Mebbe I'll git up dat way arter a while, but I shan't 'spect to own no brick house wid a cupulo on top till I've been dar a hull week or longer."

DISCOURAGING THE TRUTH.

HE had a stub of a pencil in one hand and a sheet of paper in the other, and he walked up to a citizen who was about to go aboard a ferry boat and said :

" I have a document here for you to sign."

" But I never sign any petitions," was the speedy reply.

" This is no petition. This is an agreement to the effect that none whose names are signed below will either swear while fishing or lie about the size or number of the fish afterwards. Please write your name on the blue line there."

" But I never go fishing."

" Well, you can't tell when you may. Besides, I want the the influence of your name."

" I guess I won't sign."

" Let me hope that you will. Are you not willing to eschew profanity for an hour or two once or twice a year ? "

" I never swear anyhow."

" But perhaps you lie ! If so I only ask you tell the truth in just this one instance."

" I'm in a hurry to catch this boat."

" **Never** mind the boat.   Isn't your soul of more consequence than a ferry-boat. **Please sign right** there."

" **I** won't do it."

" **You** won't, eh? You refuse to bind yourself not to rip and cuss **and jaw** and howl because you don't get a bite.   You refuse to enter into an agreement not to come **home** and lie like a trooper and lose your **soul for the** sake of making somebody believe you caught **a** bass weighing six pounds! That's the kind of **a** Detroiter you are, is it?"

" **I've a good** mind to **spoil your nose**," growled the passenger.

" Of course you have.   **Just because** I want to bind you not to lie and swear **you** want my heart's blood.   If I had asked you to agree not to cheat and steal and burn buildings you'd have wanted to cut **my** throat.   **Go** on, sir!   Take your old ferry-boat and go to Windsor with it!"

" I'll see you again."

" That's it—more threats.   But you have tackled the wrong man, sir!   I'll have an eye on you for the next ten years, and the first time I know of your going out to fish I'll **follow you.**   Yes, sir ; I'll be **on** your track, **and if** you utter one profane word or tell one single lie I'll put you behind the cross-bars **of** the cooler.   Go hence, marked man!"

DE CIRCUS OR HEABEN.

AFTER the circus had opened to the public yesterday a gray-haired colored brother, who held the hand of a boy of 14 as both stood gazing at the tent, shook his head in a solemn manner and observed :

"It's no use to cry 'bout it, sonny, kase we am not gwine in dar no how."

" But I want ter," whined the boy.

"In course you does. All chill'en of your aige run to evil an' wickedness, an' dey mus' be sot down on by dose wid expeerience."

" You used to go," urged the boy.

"Sartin I did, but what was de result? I had sich a load on my conscience dat I couldn't sleep nights. I cum powerful nigh bein' a lost man, an' in dem days de price of admishun was only a quarter, too."

" Can't we both git in for fifty cents?"

"I 'speck we might, but to-morrer you'd be bilin' ober wid wickedness an' I'd be a back-slipper from de church. Hush up, now, kase I hain't got but thirty cents an' dar' am no show fur crawlin' under de canvas !"

The boy still continued to cry, and the old man pulled him behind a wagon and continued :

" Henry Clay Scott, which had you rather do— go inter de circus an' den take de awfullest lickin' a boy eber got, or have a glass of dat red lemonade an'

ADE
PHOTO-ENG CO.N.Y.

go to Heaben when you die? Befo' you decide let me explain dat I mean a lickin' which will take ebery inch of de hide off, an' I also mean one of dem big glasses of lemonade. In addishun, I would obsarve dat a circus am gwine on in Heaben all de time an' de price of admishun am simply nominal. Now, sah, what do you say?"

The boy took the lemonade, but he drank it with tears in his eyes.

MAKING A PASSENGER "GIT."

A JUSTICE of the peace in the interior of Michigan had a case before him some days ago in which the defendant, who had been arrested as a suspicious character, and plead guilty to vagrancy, was sent to the Detroit House of Correction for six months. A constable took him in charge to deliver him here, and as the man seemed rather pleased at the idea of securing board and lodgings for six months he was not handcuffed. As the train was about ready to go the constable moved across the isle to talk politics with a friend, and pretty soon they were having it hot and heavy. When the conductor came in for tickets he held out his hand to the prisoner, and the latter shook his head and replied :

" I don't pay fare."

" Aha ! You don't eh ?"   Well, **now, you pay** or git !"

" I won't pay !"

" Then you'll git ! When we slow up at the crossing **you** jump off. **If** I find you on **the** train after we pass there I'll give you a bounce **that you won't forget !"**

In two minutes the train began to slow, and the **prssoner walked** to the **door and** picked a soft spot **and** dropped **off.**   When **the train** had made another mile the conductor **held out** his **hand to the constable and** received two tickets.

" **Who is the extra one for ?"** he **asked.**

" For that prisoner **over** there."

" What prisoner ?"

" **Why,** that fel——!"

Then there was raving and gnashing of teeth and hurrying up and down, but it **was** no use.

·   " Sorry," said the conductor **as** he passed along, " but when a passenger says he won't pay fare on my train I give him **the** drop. The only thing that surprised me was **to see** how willingly he obeyed orders."

OBLIGING A PREACHER.

Just back of Missionary Ridge, Chattanooga, while following the highway to reach Tunnel Hill, I came across a little church half hidden in the woods. The building was primitive, and the old darkey who sat on a log by the door was more so. After I had made inquiries about the route and was ready to go on he said :

"Better git down, boss, an' come in to meetin'."

" Do you hold services this afternoon ?"

" Yes, sah. We am gwine to open in 'bout five minits, an' I 'spects de sermon will be a powerful one."

It didn't seem just right to be riding around the country on Sunday and so I got down and took a seat beside the old man. After a few minutes spent in general talk, he said it was time to go in. I followed after him, and found myself the sole audience. I next found that he was the preacher who was to deliver the powerful sermon. He opened services in regular form and with all due solemnity, and then announced his text and began preaching. I stood it for fifty-five minutes, and then as he had only reached "second G," I waited until he closed his eyes and then made a slide for the door. It was no go. I hadn't gone six feet before he stopped his sermon and asked :

" Stranger, must you be gwine ?"

6

"Yes, I feel that I must"

"An' you can't heah the rest!"

"No."

"Den I'll chop off right whar' I is."

"Oh, don't **do** that.   You can **go on with your** sermon just the same."

"But you see dar' mus' be a colleckshun tooken up arter de sermon," he protested in anxious tones. "If you'll obleege me by takin' a seat I'll sing a hymn an' pass de hat."

I sat down, and when he had read and sang a hymn, he passed the hat, transferred the quarter to his vest pocket and observed as we went out :

"**I** didn't git down to de moas' powerful part **of de** sermon, but if you happen 'long dis way nex' Sunday I'll giv' you de odder half.   Dat quarter **comes** jist in time to encourage me **to** keep de good work bilin'."

THE WOLF AS A REFORMER.

NE day a Wolf who had been pondering deeply for a whole week started out on a walk through the Forest. Meeting a Jackal, he said :

"My Friend, pause for a little time while I give you a **few** words of advice. You are a cross, snarling **creature,** hated by men, and despised by all the **Creatures of** the Forest. Let me hope that you will mend your ways and reform."

"Ho! ho! ho! but you are a pretty specimen to give me advice!" sneered the Jackal. "Why, it isn't a month since you devoured an old woman and chased a Professor of Elocution into the River!"

The Wolf passed on until he met a Hyena. By that time he had recovered his cheek, and he worked up a sad, sweet smile and observed :

"My dear Mr. Hyena, you would be an ornament to society if you would cut your nails and clean your teeth. Let me hope that you will cease your depredations and become an honest, conscientious animal."

"That's nice talk from an old wretch who lies in ambush for children!" replied the Hyena. "Why, if I was half as mean as you are I'd want some dying Jack-Rabbit to kick me to death!"

The Wolf next met a Fox, and after the usual salutations regarding the backward condition of the crops the Reformer began:

"My Friend, I feel it my duty to advise you to quit stealing spring chickens and get your living in an honest manner. Show the world that you want to be good and respectable and you will soon be beloved and honored."

"Taffy!" grinned Reynard—"taffy on a chip! You old villain, you'd better own up to some of the dozen murders you have committed!"

The Wolf next met an Owl, and when they had compared notes on the Malley trial the Reformer said:

"My dear Friend, why is it that neither the Jackal, the Hyena nor the Fox will receive my advice to reform?"

"My venerable fellow traveler," slowly replied the Owl, "reform should begin at home. Wash up —get rid of your bad breath—clean out your den— quit stealing and murdering—drill some decency into your own family, and then come and see us."

MORAL:

It is the men in State prison who most lament the wickedness of outsiders.

WHAT OF IT.

A Clam who was taking a ramble over the Meadows one day met a Hare, and after remarking that winter would soon be here, he added:

"Oh, by the way, I wanted to say that I don't believe in Christianity."

"You don't?"

"No, nor in the Bible."

"Is it possible?"

"And I may as well add that I have become an Infidel."

"Dear, dear me!" gasped the Hare, and with tears in her eyes she argued and coaxed and pleaded and reasoned with the Clam to change his views. She was still wasting her breath when along came the Coon and called out:

"Good-day to both. Why these tears, Mrs. Hare?"

The Hare explained, and the Coon turned to the Clam and inquired:

"Is it true that you do not believe in God or a hereafter?"

"Strictly true," was the reply.

"And what if you don't?" continued the Coon. "You are simply one Clam out of billions. What you believe or don't believe won't affect even one blade of grass nor disturb one grain of sand.   Please shoulder your opinions and move out of the path."

MORAL :

Let 'em Infidel, if they want to.

P. S.—Suppose they don't go to Heaven—what of it ?

THE FISH AND THE **HOOK**.

A FAT Bass was swimming around with her plump young daughter one day when a hook, temptingly baited, was dropped before their noses.

"There's a good dinner for us," whispered Miss Bass, as she started for the bait.

"Hold on, my child," cautioned the mother. "The bait is tempting, but beware of the hook which it conceals."

"Oh, I'll risk that."

"It will be death to you. Take a mother's advice and hunt for frogs."

But the giddy young thing could not be convinced, and taking advantage of the first opportunity she rushed forward and grabbed the bait, and—

MORAL :

You may think the fisherman caught her, but he didn't.   He fished all that afternoon and didn't even get another bite.

DIDN'T CARE FOR THE GODS.

A PEASANT who was driving a cart along a country road had the misfortune to get "stalled" in a mud-hole. In this emergency he slammed down his hat, cracked his heels together and loudly called for Hercules to aid him. Old Herc. leisurely appeared from the nearest corn-field, and when he saw what the row was he bit off a piece of plug and observed:

"Put your shoulder to the wheel and boost her out. The gods help those who help themselves."

"I'll see you in Texas first!" replied the Peasant, and he sat down to wait for the mud to dry up. While waiting for this event he made $7 on a dog trade, put up three lightning rods, sold a washing machine for $6 and got his board for nothing. At the end of four days his old mule walked off with the cart without any boosting, and the Peasant figured that he was about sixteen dollars ahead of that community.

MORAL :

Don't break your back for Hercules or any other old moss-back.

THE DOG IN THE MANGER.

A Dog lay in the manger when the Ox came to eat his supper, the canine snarled and snapped and tried to rush him out.

" Are you going to eat that hay ?" asked the Ox.

" No."

" And you won't let me eat it ?"

" No."

" Bet my last dollar I do !" exclaimed the Ox, and he gave the Dog a horn which sent him up among the rafters.

MORAL :

If your neighbors don't like the way you pound your old piano let 'em git.

THE BOY AND THE WOLF.

A Shepherd Boy, who tended a flock of sheep near a village, cried " wolf !" one day, and all the old moss-backs rushed out with pitchforks and pokers to find that the dreaded beast was all in the boy's eye. For three or four successive times the lad played this trick on the villagers, and they finally came to the conclusion that he was a liar who deserved to be made an Indian agent.

One day the Wolf really came, but when the boy mounted the fence and gave the alarm the villagers refused to move off their nail-kegs at the corner store, saying to each other:

"William Henry can't work that string on us again."

As no one responded to the call the Wolf set out to devour the flock, but before he had secured a taste of mutton the Boy laid him out with a bullet from his little toy pistol.

MORAL:

If you feel like lying don't let a whole village discourage you. It often pays 200 per cent.

----•◦•----

THE WOUNDED OX.

An Ox who was one day passing along the highway fell and broke his leg. In a short time along came the Horse, who halted and called out:

"Mercy on me! but what has happened?"

"I have broken my leg."

"Too bad—too bad! I assure you that you have my heart-felt sympathies."

When the Horse had disappeared along came the Mule and inquired:—

"How now, my old friend—what's the trouble?"

"Broken my leg."

6*

"Dear me! but **that's** unfortunate! You were always an honest, hard-working Ox, and I am deeply grieved that this accident has come upon you."

The Mule **pursued his** way, and the next animal to stop was the Hog.

"Hello! What **does** this mean?" he grunted as he checked his pace.

"Broken my leg."

"Is that possible! It isn't six **months** ago that you **had** a lame shoulder, and to have this misfortune come upon you is enough to discourage the best Ox in the world. If you don't recover from it **al**-ways remember that you had my warmest sympathies."

After the Hog came the Goat, who halted at **a safe** distance and called out :

" Anything contagious !"

"**No** : I have broken my leg."

"**Oh,** that's it? Sure it's broken?"

" Yes."

" And you'll probably be laid up for months even if **the** Master doesn't knock you on the head and make **beef** of you ?"

" Yes."

"Well, I'm sorry for you, and if you happen to get well I shall be highly delighted."

The Goat had passed out of sight when along **came** th Rhinoceros on his way to the pool.

"Hello! What's up now ?" he asked as he **looked** over the bank.

" Broken my leg."

"Is that so. Well, I never even had an introduction to you nor heard your name spoken, but here goes to help you. I'll get you up, help **you** home and see you through as far as I can. It **is** sufficient **for** me that you are in distress and need help. Have you no friends?"

"Oh, yes. They **have** all extended their heartfelt sympathies, **but** left **me lying** in the ditch."

MORAL :

"Sympathy, my friend," said the Rhinoceros as he aided **the Ox** to stand up, "sympathy sticks in the ear and lets the stomach starve. **Depend** upon your friends no longer than **they can** depend **upon** you. Come, now—here **we go**."

LAYING THE LION.

A M ouse who was taking his evening ramble through a great Forest, encountered **a** Lion under a Tree, and at once called out :

"Hi ! there—stand out **of** my **path or** I will demolish you !"

"But I **am** not in the path," meekly replied the old Beast.

"Then get down out of that Tree !"

"Yes, but I am not up the Tree."

"Who said you were ? I tell you to get out of **my** sunshine or I'll break every bone in your body !"

" Would it be impudence on my part **to call your** attention to the fact that the sun has been **down for two** hours ! " replied the terror-stricken Lion.

" Yes, it would, and impudence must be punished!" **roared the Mouse ;** and he sailed in and pounded the King **of Beasts** until the forest was filled with lamentations.

MORAL :

He that by the plow would thrive must sit around the corner grocery and talk politics.

———•••———

THE FOOLISH HARE.

A HARE who had long concealed himself in **a dense** jungle, and rendered his presence a terror to **the** neighborhood by raiding the sheep-folds and calf-pens, one day entered the house of a Peasant and said :

" **Base** caitiff, I have come to complain of your inhumanity ! The wool of your sheep sticks in my teeth, and **you** don't know how much **bother** I have with the bones of your calves."

" But what **can I** do ? " protested the Peasant.

" Dress **the meat** for me," continued the Hare.

The Peasant meekly agreed, and when the gory **old** Hare sailed out that night to make things trem-ble, he found a shoulder of mutton hanging against the sheep-fold. **He carried it to his lair,** and made his meal, **but it was** hardly finished when **he** found his hind legs trying to tie a knot around his neck. He fell down and got up and keeled **over, and as** he realized the situation he gasped out:

"**Alas!** the Peasant not only dressed my mutton, but he will dress my hide as well! What a fool I was to complain when I got **both** the meat and the wool! Farewell, my countrymen—I'm a goner!"

MORAL:

Don't stand a creditor off till to-morrow when **you can pay** him to-day. Tell **him** to call next week.

ALL IN THE FAMILY.

A YOUNG Alligator who was traveling across the **country** was suddenly seized in the jaws of an old Crocodile, when he cried out:

"Lands alive! but has it come to this? Why do you prey upon me?"

"Because I am hungry," was the calm reply.

"But there **is** really no difference between us. We both belong to the same family."

"All the more reason why I should eat you, for **you'll** be sure to agree with me," muttered the old **Croc.**, as he chewed him down.

MORAL:

If a first you don't succeed try him again. He'll finally lend you $5 to get rid of you.

A GOOD DEAL AFTER THE STYLE OF THE PERSIAN.

A Fox who was making a Journey across the country to see his Grandmother once more before she died discovered a Wolf burying something beside **the Highway.** He slipped into **a** fence-corner and waited until the Wolf had passed on, **and then crept** forward and unearthed the Object, which proved **to** be a dead Chicken.

" Ah, ha !" chuckled Reynard, " this comes from Keeping one's Eyes open as one travels. The Hare would not have seen the Wolf at all, and the Oppossum would not have had the Patience to wait for him to move on. It's a Big Joke on the Wolf, and here **goes for a** square meal."

The Fox devoured his dinner with much smacking **of** lips, but had scarcely finished when terrible **pains began** to rack his frame and he fell down in **tha** greatest torment and was soon breathing his last. When the Wolf returned and saw the dead body of Reynard and the feathers of the Chicken scattered around, he scratched his ear and wrote in his diary :

" MORAL :

" Came to his death by being too smart."

THE HARE AND THE FISH.

The Hare and the Fish, having borrowed tobacco of each other for several months, and agreeing perfectly well on politics, set out to make a journey together and see the sights of the World. They had not proceeded many miles when a Wolf was discovered in pursuit. The hare at once started off at the top of his speed, but the fish called out:

"Do not leave me thus—I cannot run!"

"A Fish who cannot run has no business to make a journey," replied the Hare, and away he flew to save his bacon.

The Fish hurried after as fast as possible, and both found themselves on the bank of a river, while the Wolf was yet a furlong away. The Fish at once rolled into the water and darted away, but the Hare shouted after him:

"Do not leave me—I cannot swim!"

"A Hare who cannot swim has no business to make a journey," and he sailed away and left the Hare to be eaten on the half shell.

MORAL:

An owl who had overheard the affair from his perch in a persimmon tree drew down his left eye and said:

"You don't know a man until you have traveled with him."

THE WOLF AND THE PEASANT.

ONE day a Peasant who was laboring in his field was surprised at receiving a visit from the Wolf, and he was about to rush for his gun when the Wolf called out :"

"Hold on, my friend—my visit is one of peace. I have come to have a serious talk with you."

"But you killed one of my sheep only last week," protested the Peasant.

"So I did, and that is the very matter I have come to talk about. I have felt conscience-stricken ever since that event, and have firmly decided to kill no more sheep."

"Well, I am glad to hear it, and I hope you will stick to your resolution."

"Oh, I certainly shall, and I hope you will give me due credit in the future."

The Wolf took his departure with a sweet bow and a melting smile, and the Peasant softly scratched the back of his neck and did a heap of thinking. That night he placed a large trap at the weak point in his calf-pen, and next morning he found the Wolf held firm and fast.

"Excuse my embarrassment," began the Wolf as the Peasant appeared, "but why did you move this trap from the sheep-fold ?"

"Because," replied the Peasant, as he hunted around for a club, "experience has taught me that a

Wolf who is tired of mutton is simply working up an appetite for veal."

MORAL :

Don't put your foot in it.

EVERY DAY PHILOSOPHY.

A HORSE owned by a Peasant one day refused to draw his load, having become tired of the tyranny of man.

" Perhaps I have been too hard with him," soliloquized the Peasant, " and I will now make his burdens easier for a time."

The Horse was therefore given lighter loads, his supply of provender increased, and his master never appeared at the stable without a lump of sugar in his fingers.

A Fox who had observed how the thing worked paid a visit to a Mule owned by the same Peasant, and asked :

" Do you want more oats and hay ?"

" I should murmur," replied the Mule.

" And would you like to loaf half your time away in the clover field ?"

" I'm blessed if I wouldn't !"

" And have some one rub you down with a piece of velvet and feed you cut loaf sugar ?"

"It makes my mouth water to think of it," said the Mule, as he nibbled at the fence.

"Very well then," continued the Fox. "All you have to do is to refuse to budge when hitched up. The Horse played that game, and the result is that he has become sleek and fat."

Next day when the Peasant hitched the Mule to his cart the animal refused to move.

"What! rebellion in my old Mule, too!" shouted the Peasant. "Indeed I cannot permit both animals to defy my authority. Having exhausted my kind words and Sugar on the Horse, I will try the virtues of a club on the Mule."

He thereupon pounded the animal until he was glad to speed faster and draw a heavier load than ever before.

MORAL :

The Fox had been watching the affair from a fence corner, and as he saw the result he chuckled to himself :

"A rich man may have his fence in the street, but a poor man must keep his sidewalk in repair to escape the Law."

SYMPATHY, BUT NO CASH.

A Jackdaw one day made its appearance in a grove where a number of birds had assembled **to talk** business, **and as** soon as he could secure the floor **he** began :

"**My** dear friends, **I desire to call** your Attention to one of the saddest cases it has been my Lot to know. Some of you will remember that Mr. Blue Bird was killed by a stone **thrown by** a Boy some six weeks **ago.** His Widow was left without any means of Support, and in addition to her great grief she is now in need of the necessaries of Life."

" Hear ! hear !" cried the Partridge and the **Loon** in chorus.

" It has quite melted my heart," continued **the** Jackdaw, "and I have taken it upon myself to see if **something** can't be done. Let us be charitable. Let us open our purses. Let us go at it and at least soften the pangs of poverty, even if we cannot dry the tears of grief."

" That's my style, and here's an ' X ' for the hat," said the Fish Hawk, **as** he drew **a** roll of wealth from his hind pocket.

The Turkey Buzzard followed suit, the Nightingale, Robin, Mocking Bird and others chipped in what they could spare, and when a good fat purse had been **made up** the Heron arose and inquired :

" I—I—that is—you know—I'd like **to ask how** much Mr. Jackdaw chipped in ?"

"Just what I was going **to ask,**" added the Owl.

"Gentlemen—I—I didn't contribute anything," replied the Jackdaw—"I'm **the** one who draws up **the** Resolutions **of** Sympathy instead of chipping in Cash.

MORAL :

Resolutions of Sympathy **should be** baked for **two hours** before being eaten.

THE CAT DIED.

A Cat which had just settled herself between the sheets for a nap was aroused one night by howls and yeowls on the roof of a shed near **by.**

"For the land's sake ! but what is that !" she exclaimed **as** she rose up on end. The howls continuing she got out of bed, raised the window, and called out :

"In the name **of** mercy, what is wanted, and who are you ?"

"I'm a Free Citizen," was the reply.

"But why those howls ?"

"I'm singing. In fact, I'm serenading you."

"But I don't **want** it. Go away or I'll injure you for life !"

But the Man refused to move **a** foot. Hairbrushes, bootjacks, water pitchers and bedsteads were heaved at him in quick succession, but he dodged each missile and continued to sing until the Cat cut her throat in desperation.

MORAL :

Turn about is fair play, and the chance is sure to come.

———◆◆———

THE WOLF AND THE GOOSE.

A Goose who was prowling through the forest one day in search of prey, observed a Wolf sitting on the limb of a Tree and called out,

"Good morning, my Dear. You are looking unusually well this morning."

"That's all Taffy," replied the Wolf.

"'Pon honor, but I'd give a thousand dollars to have your complexion."

"Would you ?"

"Indeed I would. And such eyes as you have got ! Yum ! yum !"

"Do you really think so ?" grinned the pleased Wolf.

"You bet ? Why, if I had your form I'd go on the stage and make my fortune."

The Wolf put his finger in his mouth and looked silly and felt flattered, and the Goose licked her chops and continued :

"Please come down and let me take the pattern

of your coat-tails. Such a graceful set I never saw in my travels."

The Wolf came down with his ears working with delight, and had only reached the earth when the Goose sprang upon him and chewed him into dish-cloths.

MORAL:

Beware of the Goose.

———•••———

THE WISE PEASANT.

A WEALTHY Peasant, who felt that his hours were numbered, called his sons around his bedside, and began: "James, you are the eldest, and I bequeath you my blessing."

The second son came forward, with bowed head, and the father said: "John Henry, you have been a good boy, and I bequeath you my good name."

The third son showed up, and the old man kindly remarked: "Andrew Jackson, you are my youngest, and I bequeath you the care of my grave. Good-bye, my dear sons. Each of you press my hand for the last time, and then skip back to the field, for this is glorious weather for corn."

"But, dad, you are worth $20,000!" they protested in chorus.

"That is true, boys, but I have tried to make an equal division. I have let fall the honor to you, and all the money to the lawyers. They would have got the sugar, anyhow, and in the getting would have left you nothing, and proved your mother a fool and your father a lunatic; besides I die happy and full of peace. Bury me just to the left of the old cow-shed, and pay for my tombstone on the monthly installment system."

MORAL:

The Lawyers were of course dissatisfied with the will, and carried the case into court.

THE WRONG BLOOD.

A PEASANT took great pains to sharpen up his Knife in anticipation of an opportunity to strike down a Doe which came every day to drink at a certain spring. As he crept through the forest the Knife was accidently thrust into his own leg. Dancing around with the pain, and angered at the sight of blood, the Peasant cried out: "Base ingrate! You have stabbed me!"

"It is true that you have been stabbed," replied the Knife, "but had you not sharpened me for the purpose of drawing blood this would not have happened."

MORAL.

Lies and scandals sent out of the kitchen may come back home through the front door.

THE GOOSE AND THE HARE.

A HARE which was running away from pursuit came to a stream, and was hesitating about making the plunge, when a Goose alighted near him and inquired : "Pray, what is the matter, to put you in such a tremble?"

"I am pursued by the dogs!"

"Oh! that's it! Well, the dogs won't touch me."

"But they will soon devour my meat unless I cross the stream. Please give me a lift on your back."

"You should have been born with less legs and more wings," chuckled the Goose, and she flew away and left the Hare to get across as best he could.

A few days subsequently the Hare was crossing a meadow, when the Goose came running and fluttering and cried out : "For mercy sake! aid me to escape!"

"What's the trouble with you?"

"I am pursued by a man who seeks my quills and feathers, and unless you help me away I am doomed."

"Oh! that's it? Well, I have no quills or feathers to lose!"

"But you will help me to get away?"

"You should have been born with less wings and more legs!" replied the Hare, and off he galloped.

MORAL :

It's a long lane which has no turn.

THE OLD WOLF AND HIS SON.

A Wolf who had arrived at a good old age and no longer felt able to go out and play the string-game on the Innocent and Unconfiding, called his Son to him one day, and said: "My cantankerous Offspring, I am growing old, I am stiff in the joints, troubled with Dyspepsia, and no longer have the sand to out and tackle anything bigger than a yearling Lamb. I feel that it is time for me to hang up."

The Son humbly agreed, and the Old Wolf continued: "I have managed, as you are aware, by strict attention to Poker, Faro and a few other Family Amusements, to lay by some Sugar for my old age. I shall turn over everything to you, Beloved Offspring, and depend upon you to care for me during the few brief years of my stay on Earth."

"Excellent idea, Governor—very excellent," replied the Son, and he went out behind the house to crack his Heels together and poke himself in the Ribs.

That same evening the Old Wolf sat down for a Smoke, but before he had drawn six whiffs from his Pipe the Beloved Son remarked: "That habit is both disgusting and expensive, and I'd advise you to quit."

The Pipe was laid aside, and the Old Man went to the cupboard to take a Nip of Red Eye for his Stomach's sake.

"And you also want to chop off on that," observed the Beloved. "Whisky not only costs Money, but Degrades the Intellect."

The Old Man **replaced the Bottle** with a heartfelt sigh and humbly **inquired if there** was any Cold Chicken left **from supper.**

"Cold Chicken! Well, you have got Cheek, and no **mistake.** If Codfish isn't good enough for you you'd **better Travel!**"

"You will, at **least, permit me to** stay in the House over night, **I hope,"** said the Father.

"Why, I have **no objections to your** sleeping on the floor **to-night, but you'd better Dig Out** pretty early in the **Morning."**

Then the venerable Parent fell upon the **Beloved** Offspring and **made** his Heels break his Neck, and flung him **out doors** and **over** the Fence, and gave him to Understand **that** henceforth he was a Wanderer and **a Horse Thief.**

MORAL :

Don't begin on the Old Folks too soon.

THE HARE AND THE FOX.

A **Fox** who was gamboling about had **the** ill-luck to fall over **a cliff,** and as he lay **on the** ground, unable **to rise, and** suffering great pain, along came a Hare.

"Well," said the Fox **as he** looked up, "the tables **are** turned, I am your bitter enemy and have often pursued you with intent to murder, but now I am helpless and you can take your revenge.”

“ Do you expect me to kill you ?”

“ Naturally I do, and I ask the favor that you kill me with a club instead of slowly torturing me to death by singing: ‘Only a Pansy Blossom.’ ”

But the Hare determined to heap coals of fire on his head and prove her own forgiving spirit. She therefore brought him water and food and nursed him until he was quite able to take care of himself. The very next day after they separated the Hare was crossing a field when she found herself pursued by a Fox. After running a long distance she was overtaken, and as she was knocked over she recognized in her assailant the very Fox whose life she had saved.

“ Why, you are the Fox whom I nursed !” she cried out.

“ Is that so ?”

“ Of course it is ! How could you fail to recognize me ?”

“ Well, fools look so much alike that it is hard to tell who from who. For fear of making a mistake I shall eat you and let the next one go.”

THE LION AND THE JACKALS.

ONE day two Jackals were having a hot dispute as to the origin of man, and were about to come to blows, when along came the Lion, and asked : "My friends, what seems to be the rumpus here ?"

"I claim that man originated from the ape," explained one.

"And I contend that he is descended from the fish," added the other.

"Have either of you any documents or affidavits ?"

"None."

"Then I shall claim that man is descended from the giraffe, and being able to roar louder than both of you together, shall carry my point. Be off with you, and as you go remember that arguments on theories test the wind more or as much as they appeal to the head."

"A BIRD IN THE HAND."

A CARP which had been hooked by a Fisherman looked up with Tears in its eyes and called out: "Pray, spare my life ! I am small and bony and shall not make over two bites for you !"

"I fully realize that," replied the Fisherman, as he tossed his victim into his pail, " but the man who throws away Carp in hopes to secure Bass, will go home to eat bean-soup."

DOMESTIC ECONOMY.

THE Wife of a Peasant who was in the habit of borrowing her Neighbor's Coffee Mill, one day broke the article beyond repair, and when her husband came in she cried out in Despair: "Alas! We are financially ruined for the excursion season! I have broken Mrs. Blank's Coffee Mill, and it will cost us thirty cents to replace it!"

"Ah! but you are indeed a poor Financier!" replied the Husband. "Send the remains home by the servant girl and get mad at the Lady. Then you will not be expected to pay damages, and she will not dare ask for your Flat-irons."

THE SELFISH HUNTER.

A WOLF having chased a Hunter across fields and through forests for several miles, at length had the mortification of seeing his Prey escape him by climbing a tree.

"Are you coming down?" he asked as he looked up and licked his chops.

"Not very fast!"

"I don't complain of that," panted the Wolf, "but what hurts my feelings is the fact that you didn't climb a tree on the start, instead of giving me this useless chase. Pray have some respect for other people's feelings hereafter."

THE HONEST CLERK.

A MERCHANT who felt that his Profits were not as large as his trade warranted looked over his books one Sunday and then interviewed his clerk with : "John Henry, you have taken $500 of my money since January."

"That's so. I used it to buy futures in cotton, and I lost."

" And I must send you to State Prison !"

" Oh, no ! Previous to January I took $800 of your money and bought wheat, and my profits have been so large that I can return all your money and have enough left to buy a race horse. But for my honesty you would have never known of the first steal. But for my business tact you would have lost all. You'd better go visiting and give me full charge !"

<hr>

THE MEETING ADJOURNED.

A LION who had long reigned with supreme power over the Forest, one day called a convention of all the beasts and announced his intention of abdicating.

" I am growing old and feeble, and I must soon pass away," he argued. " All things considered it is better that **my successor** be nominated and installed while I **am living** to give him **the benefits of my** experience and advice."

There was general joy among the Beasts, for the Lion had lorded it after his own fashion. The Elephant was **squinting** around, the Rhinoceros was **pushing** his nose into the crowd, **and the** Giraffe was **doing a heap** of thinking **way** down **his** throat when the Lion continued :

" After serious reflection and solemn consideration **I have** decided that my own **son** shall succeed me. The office will not only be kept **in** the family, **but** the family will be kept in office. There being **no** further business before the meeting we will adjourn."

" But why the need of this convention ?" **pro**-tested the Rhinoceros.

" Well, there wasn't any particular need of it," **replied** the Lion, " but it is customary to call one in **order to** collect the expenses of nomination. Brother Giraffe, pass the hat !"

MORAL :

" Attend the primaries !"

<hr>

A Wolf had the misfortune **to** break his leg, and being unable to hunt for his food, was soon reduced to the verge of starvation. One day as he was uttering lementation a Hare came along and inquired the trouble.

"**I am** almost **at** the point of death," was the **reply. I haven't** had a morsel to eat for days."

"Indeed!" exclaimed the Hare. "I'll go at once to the Hyena about it."

When the Hyena was consulted he stroked his chin reflectively and finally said:

"Are you certain that he is a Wolf of good morals?"

"No."

"Well, then, I'd better see the Lion about it before we do anything."

The Lion heard the story, winked in a wise way, and remarked:

"There ought to be a committee appointed to investigate his character. I'll see the Stork and mention the matter."

The Stork was informed that a Wolf lay dying of starvation, and she replied:

"Well, well, but that's bad. I'll see the Ox this very afternoon, and have him decide whether we ought to send in tracts or chicken-broth."

The Ox was duly informed, and the next day he walked over to see what should be done in the case. Arriving at the lair he found the Wolf dead, and the Owl had already been there and written on the rocks the

MORAL:

"Philanthropy is a thin tonic for an empty stomach."

THE HEN CONVENTION.

A Fox who found hard picking in a certain neighborhood one day visited a farmer's Dog and said:

"I have lately undergone a change of heart, and I wish you to make known the fact to your master's Fowls. They treat me as if I was a murderer, and it really hurts my feelings to see them hurry into the coop at sunset. The Farmer, too, seems to distrust me, for he has made the coop so tight that I cannot find a single knothole. What sort of a way is that to treat a Fox who is doing his best to earn an honest living?"

"I presume you would like to state your case to the Fowls in person?" observed the Dog.

"That's it—that's the very idea!" replied the Fox. "Say to them that I should like to meet them in convention under this tree to-morrow at noon. I will then explain my feelings toward them, and trust that the Fox and the Fowls will hereafter live in the greatest harmony. Indeed, the only difference between us is the fact that I have no wings, and they shouldn't hold me in suspicion on this account."

The Dog agreed to act as mediator, and at noon next day the Fox crept carefully through the weeds to the rendezvous and crouched down to await the coming of the Fowls. There was presently heard a great whirr and clatter, and two score hens alighted in the branches of the tree over the Fox.

7*

" The convention will now proceed to business," said an old Hen, as she peered down upon the Fox.

"Just so," grinned the Fox. "Please come down and we will proceed."

"Thanks; but if it's all the same to you we'd rather you'd come up here," replied the Hen.

" But I can't fly."

" And we are poor runners."

The Fox not being able to fly up, and the Hens refusing to fly down, the former was skulking off when he met the Dog, who said :

" My friend, the difference between undergoing a change of heart and desiring to undergo a change of diet and position is so obscure that many people never stop to fish for it. As a Fox you were respected for your cunning ; as a hypocrite even the old Hens despise you."

HE WAS DISCHARGED.

A Fox who had been dug out of his den by a Peasant, and was about to be knocked on the head, cried out : " Hold on ! Hold on ! You are about to murder an innocent Fox !"

" But here are the feathers of my missing hens."

" Yes, I admit the presence of hen's feathers, but deny the killing. Take me before the law. If I am guilty the law will punish me."

The Peasant **relented, and the** Fox was **arraigned** on charge of **murder.** The case seemed clear enough when the prosecution rested, but **the opposing counsel** arose and remarked : "Your **Honor, the** prosecution has failed to prove **that all of this occurred** in the County of Posey, and **I demand my client's** discharge."

" I discharge the prisoner," **said** the Judge, "and I would warn the prosecution that **it** further weakened its case by not showing whether **hens** have feathers **or** bristles."

MORAL :

The dog probably killed the hens, and it's **a wonder** the prosecution didn't think **of it.**

———•••———

THE OWL AND THE FARMER.

An Owl, who was reconnoitering a Farmer's hencoop, was caught by the leg in a steel trap, and held fast until the toil-hardened agriculturist came out **in** the morning to finish him.

"Sir ! What is the meaning **of** this outrage !" demanded the Owl.

" You were after my Poultry," was the reply.

"**W**e will let the Law settle that point. I will **see if a free born** American Owl **is** to be treated in this lawless manner !"

Being taken into Court, the Owl put in the defense that no Farmer had any legal right to keep Hens, and the Judge closed the case by saying: "While the presence of the Owl in the vicinity of the hennery goes to show that he would **prefer Fowl to Hash, the Farmer** has failed to prove whether the trap was **bought** of a man with **a squint in** his **left eye or a wart on** his nose. The **Owl is entitled** to **$100 damages** for his injuries, and the Farmer is jugged for **thirty** days for unlawfully obstructing the **United States** Mail."

MORAL:

Keep Owls instead of Hens.

———•••———

THE PEASANT AND THE ROBBER.

A PEASANT who **was abroad** at night **encountered** a highwayman, who called out: "Your money or your life!"

The Peasant wanted to live to see three days without **a** thunder-shower or a cyclone, and he therefore emptied his pocket of his loose change. But, behold, next day he **was** arrested for passing counterfeit money, **and** when brought into court he dis**covered** that his accuser **was** the man who had rob**bed** him.

"That **may** all be," replied the Judge to his state,

ment, "but do you know whether or not this man made a mental reservation to return your money as soon as he could get work in a Cider-Mill?"

And thereupon he cast the Peasant into jail and thanked the Robber for his prompt complaint to the Law.

MORAL:

Put your counterfeit money into the Sunday contribution-box.

* * *

LOOKING FOR TRUTH.

A PEASANT who had often heard that Truth was a Jewel lying at the bottom of a well, one day descended into his well to search for the treasure. He skinned his knees and elbows, barked his nose, run an old fork into his foot and shivered around for six long hours before his wife drew him up and asked:

"What in Goodness' name were you doing down there?"

"Looking for Truth."

"Why I could have told you before you went down that you were the biggest Fool in America!"

MORAL:

You can get more Truth than you want around any well-curb.

THE SAILOR AND THE SHARK.

A Sailor who had fallen overboard and was speedily interviewed by a Shark, cried out to his enemy,

"Have pity on a man who **is down !**"

"My friend," replied **the shark, "a man who** keeps himself above **water is of no use to me. Now is** my time."

MORAL :

The man who falls overboard in business can **expect** no **favors of the** sheriff.

THE FOX AND THE FARMER.

A Fox one day made a call upon **a** Peasant and bitterly complained of the custom of shutting poultry up nights in Fox-proof **pens.** "It isn't **because I** suffer at all," added **Reynard, "but think how** uncomfortable it must **be for** the poor Fowls. It is their condition I wish **to mitigate."**

The peasant took **the matter under** advisement, and next evening **he neglected to shut up** his Fowls. Next morning he **came across the** Fox just as he had **finished** feasting **on a fat Pullet, and cried** out :

"Ah! this is the way you take to pity my poor Fowls, is it?"

"Well, you see," grinned Reynard, "I feel very sorry for the Fowls, but at the same time cannot afford to miss an opportunity."

MORAL :

The man with ten acres of land to sell is the chap who first sees the need of an orphan asylum.

ON THE HALF-SHELL.

On the beginning of a certain New Year a motherly old Goose felt it her bounden duty to do something for the betterment of the World. She, therefore took a stroll down to the Swamp and sought an interview with the Fox.

"Well, what's on hand this morning?" asked Reynard, as he came to the front.

"To-day is New Years, if you remember."

"Oh, certainly."

"It is the day on which **all** Fowls and Beasts should solemnly resolve to break off some bad habit. I have appointed myself a committee of one to wait upon you and ask if you could not make at least one good resolve?"

"Well, y-e-s, I think I can," replied Reynard.

"That's nice. What resolve will you make?"

"Oh! I'll let up on the Hares this coming year and go for the Geese!"

And he ate her on the half-shell.

MORAL :

Don't ask a man to stop chewing tobacco and become a drunkard.

PLAYING THE HOG.

A Wolf and a Fox were travelling across the country in company when they discovered a piece of meat attached to a string.

"My eyes are the sharpest, and I saw it first," exclaimed the Fox.

"My nose is the best, and I smelled it long before you could see it," replied the Wolf.

"Well, we'll divide even up."

"Not exactly, my friend, I have the longest stomach, and must therefore have the largest share. I will eat what I want and what is left will be sufficient for you."

The Fox being the weaker party had to sit and lick his chops while the Wolf devoured every ounce of meat and sighed for more. He was sighing with satisfaction when a sudden pain racked his body, and in a moment more he knew that he had been poisoned.

" Well, well," mused the Fox, as he saw the other struggling with death; " one **doesn't always** miss **a** Good Thing by letting some one **else gobble up his** Dinner."

------●------

THE CLIPPED HORSE.

A **MAN** who owned a fine **Horse had** him **clipped** in midwinter, and the shivering animal turned around and asked him :

" Why do you deprive me of my coat **in such** cold weather ?"

" Oh ! **it's to make a** daisy of you," was the reply.

As soon as the Horse was attached to the cutter he began kicking, and did not stop until he had demolished **the** outfit.

" What **on** earth possessed **you** to **do that ?''** asked the owner.

" Because **a** daisy of a Horse would look bad before a cheap Cutter," was the reply. " And I may as well smash that; if you are going in for looks **you'd better get** your Hostler **to** hold the reins behind me."

THE HAWK AND THE HEN.

A FISH-HAWK who had a way of throwing three cards about in a dexterous manner, one day met a Hen and invited her to bet on his game.

"But I don't understand it."

"Why, all there is about it, I toss these three cards so, and so, and you bet that you can pick up the Ace of Spades, for example."

"I don't want to take you money," protested the Hen.

"Oh, as to that, you are quite welcome."

"Well here's an X that I pick up the Ace."

The Hawk smiled as he thought how easy it was to throw snuff in a Hen's eyes, but, lo! Biddy picked up the card she had named and raked in the sugar.

"I'll be hanged if I am not completely discouraged trying to make an honest living!" cried the Hawk, as he flung down the cards in disgust; and he thereupon not only turned Robber, but ate the Hen to boot.

MORAL :

Never discourage industry and integrity by taking money from a Three-Card-Monte man or a Faro Bank.

CARELESS PEOPLE.

A couple of Rats who were prowling around a strange house came upon a Jar of N. O. Molasses which could be reached from a shelf. One of them at once leaped into the sweet substance, and after a brief struggle to get out again he sank out of sight.

"Really, now," mused the other, as he hastened away from the dangerous neighborhood, "the person who left the cover off that Jar should be prosecuted for criminal neglect."

MORAL :

Of course the Cook didn't discover the Rat until she was pouring out the last of the Molasses.

THE PHILOSOPHER'S ADVICE.

A Merchant who found that he must either increase his sales or close his doors and beat his Creditors, hunted up a Philosopher and asked him what course he should pursue.

"Have you lived long in the Town?" asked the old man.

"Yes, for years."

"And you know everybody?"

"Every man, woman and child."

" Are the people all at peace with each other ?"

" They are, oh wise man. There has not been a word between families for years."

" Then you must return home and slyly provoke quarrels and hard feelings. Do as I say and your trade will increase four-fold."

The Merchant wonderingly obeyed the injunction, and in a week there were scarcely two families in the Town on speaking terms. Mrs. A. gave a card party and did not invite that stub-nosed Mrs. B., and Mrs. B. gave a coffee and left Mrs. A. to drink cold tea at home along with her monkey-faced daughter. Mrs. C. suddenly ceased to lend to Mrs. D., and Mrs. D. discovered that Mrs. E. was wearing dresses sent her by a rich sister in Boston.

The result was as the Philosopher had predicted. There was a sudden demand upon the merchant's stock for coffee-mills, flat-irons, fluters, axes, shovels, groceries and other things, and one woman ordered a set of cups and saucers, an eight-day clock and $10 worth of knives and spoons with the explanation :

" Being that one of my neighbors has started the story that I had to hire my husband to marry me, and the other has affirmed that we are so stingy that we starve a dog to death every six months, I will now show my independence by neither borrowing nor lending. You may also send me some quilt-frames, a new teapot, two stoves kettles, a steamer, a dozen fruit jars and a dish-pan."

Then the Merchant had to hire two extra clerks, build an addition and speculate in mining stocks to get rid of some of his money, and drummers traveled hundreds of miles to see him, and the Commercial Agencies rated him good for a million.

MORAL :

The howl of a neighbor's dog is unnoticed until the owner refuses to lend his wheelbarrow.

COULDN'T TELL A LIE.

A Fox who was being Pursued by the Hounds came upon a Hare sitting in the bushes and called out: "If anybody inquiries for me please say that you haven't seen me for a month Past."

"Oh, I couldn't do that," replied the Hare— "that would be Lying."

"Very well, then, suppose you take a run across to yonder fence and back and tell me if there is any snow on the other side ?"

"With pleasure," answered the Hare, and away she sailed.

The Hounds got sight of her as she sped along, and directly the whole pack were hard at her heels.

"That comes of being too good," chuckled the Fox as he saw her finally overtaken. "The skin of a Hare who died for Truth isn't half as valuable as the pelt of a Fox who lives to Lie."

SO KIND!

A Bear which had been caught in a Trap was moaning and sighing and wondering if every cloud had a Silver Lining, when along came a Cow and asked what particular ward caucus that was and who had been elected chairman.

"I'm caught in a Trap," moaned the Bear.

"Can't you get away?"

"No, indeed."

"Have you been here long?"

"Yes; for five or six hours."

"And you must suffer dreadfully?"

"I certainly do."

"Well, as there is no chance to escape, and you must continue to suffer until released, I will at once go and inform my master and let him come at once and knock you on the head.

THE OLD 'UN'S ESCAPE.

A Wolf who had grown old and gray and could no longer move about like a Farmer's Boy in front of a Bumble Bee, saw with Regret and Sorrow that his Son looked upon him as a Burden and wished him

Bounced from the Cabinet. He was one day wiping his Tearful Eyes on a Sheep-skin when the Son entered the Cave and remarked : " Dear Father, how would you like to take a walk with me this fine day ?"

" Do you really want me to ?"

" Of course I do. Your health is very dear to me, and I have been Pained for some days past to see how pale and careworn you looked.''

The Old Man felt as tickled as a hired man with the Boss gone and both Oxen too lame to Work, and the pair set out with smiles galloping across their faces. When they had penetrated the Forest a long distance a Lion suddenly appeared, and the Son called out : " King of Beasts, I have brought you a Dinner ! Eat him and tally one for me !"

" Stay !" roared the Lion. " This chap seems old and tough, and I am not the sort to eat poor meat when better can be had. You are the dinner I want to get hold of ! "

" Well, well !" mused the Old Wolf as he trotted homeward alone, " if it is sad to be old and tough it is likewise dangerous to be young and tender, and after all I will make the best of my lot. William Henry didn't get more than a rod ahead of me on that deal—not if I can see straight !"

WHY HE PROMISED.

A Fox who had gorged himself with three Fowls was sitting in a fence corner with a disgusted look on his Face when along came a Peasant, who said :

" The only thing I have against you is that you steal my Fowls."

" If that's all we can be Friends," replied the Fox.

" How ?"

" Why, I am ready to promise that I will never again disturb the peace of your Hen-Roost."

" Honest ?"

" Honest Injun," said Reynard as he laid his paw on his stomach.

Two days afterward the Peasant was crossing his fields when he suddenly came upon the Fox devouring one of his finest Hens.

" Ha ! but it is scarcely forty-eight hours since you promised to let my Fowls alone !"

" Yes, I know," replied Reynard as he gulped down a leg ; " but just then I was stuffed with Chicken and could hold no more."

MORAL :

Don't expect that what a man promises on a full stomach will be carried out on an empty one.

LOSS OF CONFIDENCE.

A SHEPHERD was eating his dinner beside a Spring when a **Wolf** walked out of **the Forest and** coolly inquired :

" Well, how is **the W**ool and Mutton business ?"

" Pretty fair," replied **the** astonished Shepherd.

" **I have** come to tell **you,**" continued the Wolf, " that the Hyenas have formed a plot **to** break into your Sheep-fold to-night, and **to offer** my services as a Private Watchman."

" You **are ever so** kind to give me this warning."

" And you just leave the gate open and go **to** bed feeling perfectly safe. The first Hyena **who** comes fooling around your Mutton will find his heels breaking his neck."

After some further conversation it was agreed that the gate should be left **open** and that the Wolf should stand guard.

Darkness was scarcely an hour **old** when a great outcry was heard at the Fold and the Shepherd ran out and discovered **the** Wolf **in a Trap** he had **set** within the Pen.

" Is this the kind of confidence you had in me ?" howled the Wolf, as he struggled to get free.

" I had plenty of confidence in you," replied the Shepherd, " but **more in** the Trap ! Prepare **to** die !"

MORAL :

Don't lend both horse and saddle to **the same** person.

8

THE WOLF'S DECISION.

ONE day two Foxes who were journeying together came across a Track in the dust which much astonished them.

" I believe it is the **Track of a** Rhinoceros," observed one.

"**I think it** is that of an **Elephant,**" replied the other.

" I say Rhinoceros !"

" And I say Elephant !"

" Then I travel no longer with such an **Idiot !**"

"Then you **can** travel alone with a Fool !"

They were cuffing each other about in a lively manner, **when along came a Wolf** and asked the cause of the trouble.

" Why, **that** Bigot sticks to it that this is not the track **of a** Rhinoceros !" shouted one.

" And he, the Narrow-minded Muldoon, won't **admit that it** is the Track of an Elephant," **added** the **other.**

" Gentleman," said **the Wolf as** he examined tho spot, " this is simply the place **where a fat man** struck a Banana Peel and sat down **to Reflect.** You are both wrong **and** both Fools."

MORAL :

Men are ever willing to fight in defense of what they don't know.

THE HEN AND THE FARMER.

A Hen having laid an Egg set up such a Cackle that presently the whole Barn-yard was in Confusion and the Farmer came running out to see what was going on.

"What is it?" he demanded as the Hen cackled louder than ever.

"Why, I've laid an Egg!"

"An Egg? Why, a single Egg isn't worth but two cents at the present market price."

"Yes, I know, but if I didn't do two shillings' worth of cackling over every two cents' worth of egg, the world would soon forget me."

MORAL:

Send a bundle of old clothes to an orphan asylum and then interview a reporter.

THE MAN WITH THE ACCORDION.

A Peasant having saved up a sum of Money by hard work and peeling his Potatoes close, went to the nearest Village and invested in an Accordion. On his way home he began playing the air of "My Grandfather's Clock," but scarcely had the echoes reached the Forest when out came a Chopper, who cried out:

"Man! Man! for Heaven's sake hang up on that! You will kill us all with your Racket!"

"Can't help that," replied the Peasant, as he pulled away harder than ever. "If what tickles me all over is Death to you that is not my lookout. I will now give you "The Empty Cradle," with variations."

MORAL:

"If our neighbor doesn't want our smoke let him move away.

———••———

THE LION'S ADVICE.

A WOLF who had a dispute with a Hyena determined to destroy him, and therefore went to the Lion for advice.

"Set a trap for him," was the reply, "and when you have caught him eat him."

The Wolf went away and laid a snare beside the path often traversed by his enemy, but just as he was cackling with satisfaction he blundered into the trap himself and was held fast. In this emergency along came the Lion, who called out: "By George! but what's all this!"

"I'm fast in my own trap," humbly replied the Wolf.

"So I see. I came out here expecting to help you eat the Hyena, but as the case now stands I shall help the Hyena eat you."

" But I set this by your advice," protested the Wolf.

" True you did, and I advised your enemy to set one for you as well. Odds is the difference to me whether I eat Wolf or Hyena."

MORAL :

The lawyer gets his pay, no matter how the suit goes.

------●●●------

THE TWO BRAGGARTS.

THE Woodchuck and the Opossum met one day near the den of the Wolf, and the first called out : " You should have heard me singing last night !"

" It couldn't have been equal to my great speech," replied the Opossum.

" And I am also a Poet."

" Well, I'm a Statesman."

" I can growl in four different keys."

" And I can conquer the Lion."

Thus they bragged over each other until their noisy voices disturbed the Wolf, who came forth and remarked : " Gentlemen, I take your word for it, that Woodchuck is equal to Chicken and Opossum sweeter than fried oysters, and you shall furnish me a dinner ! Come hence !"

MORAL :

One never loses anything by keeping his mouth shut.

THEY WOULDN'T SQUEEZE.

A **Hyena** and **a** Wolf met one day in a narrow path **in the forest.** By a little squeezing they could have passed each other and gone about their business, **but** the **Wolf** yelled **out:** " Ho! there! out of my path!"

" You **are no bigger** nor **better than I am!"** was the Hyena's reply.

"This is my path!"

" You're another!"

Thus they bantered and jawed until each was determined not to give way, and in the fight which en**sued both** rolled over the bank and were badly shaken **up.** They **were** still jawing when a Lion **came** along and cuffed them apart, and observed : **" That** path **belongs** to me alone, and if I catch either **one of** you using it I'll break your back!"

MORAL :

If you won't squeeze to accommodate, and if you will fight, don't fight over that which concerns your neighbor more than yourself.

THE VAIN PULLET.

A Fine, fat Pullet who was roosting on the limb of a tree safe from danger was saluted by a Fox with: " Good evening, Miss Pullet—I never saw you look better.   Your figure is perfectly lovely."

" Do you really think so ?"

" Certainly I do. I'd give anything if I could wear my hair done up in a French roll and have it become me as it does you."

" Aren't you joking ?"

"I was never more serious in my life. You small feet and pretty mouth are the envy of all the Pullets in the neighborhood."

" Dear me, but is that so ?"

" And everybody says you have such a tony air about you."

" Oh ! la !"

" I think if we were to walk out together we'd mash the whole town."

" Really, now ?"

The Fox gave her more soft solder, and in the end the vain Pullet flew down and furnished a square meal for the crafty Villain.

MORAL :

" Flattery," said an old Rooster, as he looked down at the few bones and feathers, " flattery is the soft purr of a cat. The sweeter the purr, the longer the claws and the sharper the bite."

THE NEWER ARITHMETIC.

IF it costs a colored family **eighty cents per** week **to** keep **four** dogs **and a** goat how much less will it cost if a policeman breaks the goats neck and two of the dogs **get** **in the way of a** street car ?

Six times seven girls **are** how many girls, and **what on** earth are they **good for?**

A lady bought a **hat for $12,** a set **of** frizzes **for** $4, a pair of shoes for $6, **and** a comb for $3. **How** much would **all** have **cost her** if the **man** hadn't told her that he had **quit** the trust system ?

A woman pays seventy-five cents **for** a shirt for her husband **and $9 for a** silk pair of hose for herself. What **was the cost of both?**

A man gave $3 **to** the foreign missionary fund and chipped in a nickel to buy a two-shilling Testament for a home murderer. How much did he give

[176]

in all ? Also, if the soul **of one heathen is worth fifty** times the soul **of an** intelligent **white** man, how much more valuable **is** the soul of **an** Indian than a Congressman's ?

A man who desires to move a cook stove weighing 200 pounds calls in a neighbor to lift 180 pounds **of the infernal** old thing, while he gets away with the remainder ?

A tramp has 200 feet to go to reach a gate, while the farmer's dog has 300 feet to go to bite the tramp. The tramp travels at the rate of twelve miles **an** hour and the dog at the **rate** of twenty. How near the gate will the **poor,** discouraged sufferer be when the canine catches on ?

A man who gulps down a five-cent glass of beer and tells the saloon-keeper to charge it is obliged to pay **a** doctor $2 50 for cementing a crack in his skull, while the saloonist is fined $3 for doing such a cracking good business. How much money was involved altogether, and how much would have been saved if the beat had waited until a candidate came along and asked him to take something ?

A housewife sold **a** coat to a peddler for a vase worth nine **cents, a** pair of boots for a china dog worth six cents and a vest for a glass bottle worth four cents ; how much did she receive for all, and

8*

how much over **$6** clear **profit did the peddler**
make ?

A grocer takes **twenty-eight** pounds of butter
worth thirty-two cents per pound, and mixes it with
fifty-six pounds of butter worth fourteen cents per
pound. He then hangs out a sign **of** " gilt-edged
butter," and sells the whole for twenty-nine cents per
pound. How much does **he make ?**

A soldier's widow in **the service of** the government has a salary of $600 per year and pays a polit-
ical assessment of two per cent. How much **does**
she have left ?

If the **Governor of** Missouri pardons State Prison
convicts at the rate **of** three for every nine days how
long will it take to pardon 528 convicts ?

A Wisconsin school teacher had nineteen scholars
and she figured up at the end of three months that
she had bestowed 128 lickings on the school. Allow-
ing that one boy received seventeen of them, and
that three of the girls escaped entirely, how many
lickings did each of the others receive ?

The average fisherman gets four nibbles to **one**
bite, and three bites to a fish, and half his fish are
not worth carrying home. At this rate how long
will it take a fisherman to exhaust the supply of
sheep-heads and dog-fish ?

The friends of a certain man chip in four cents apiece and purchase a sponge to present him on his birthday as emblematical of his daily life. The certain man lets himself loose on the donors and damages each one's head to the amount of $3 47. How much is each donor out of pocket?

———

A man pays fifty cents extra to take laughing-gas while having a tooth pulled. The dentist could have pulled six as well as one, and without any further cost. How much did the patient lose by being so stingy with his molars.

———

The candy eaten by a schoolgirl costs just as much as her school-books; the peanuts she devours cost more than her singing lessons; her ice-cream costs more than her French, and the gas and fuel she consumes while sparking foot up twice the cost of learning her to paint landscapes on old jugs and pitchers. Therefore, how many daughters must a man have to be rich.

———

A young man wagers fifty cents that he can put a billiard ball into his mouth, and he wins the bet. A surgeon charges him $7 for four hours' work in removing it. What was the exact gain in being smart?

———

An alderman pays a reporter $5 to write him a speech favoring the erection of a new school house, but after delivering eleven cents' worth of the oration he is informed that there is no question before the meeting, and he falls back and breaks a pair of suspenders worth thirty-five cents. How much is the great man out of pocket?

A member of the Common Council promises the **appointment** of **public** weigher to seven different **men**; that of City Hall janitor to eight others; that of wood inspector to six more. How many promises did he make in all, and how many men thirst for his blood?

Two men who regard their sacred honor as at stake go out to fight a duel. One shoots a calf in a field and the other pops a farmer sitting on a fence, and they shake hands and declare their sacred honors **freed from** all stains. How much sacred honor does **it** take to fill **a** flour-sack, and how long would it **take** one grasshopper to eat the whole business up?

A tramp hires out to a farmer for $14 per month. **He gets a boss dinner, works an hour** and skips. Counting the dinner worth thirty cents how much did he make? Counting the three bites he got from the farmer's dog at twenty-five cents each how much did he lose?

Jones sells his **farm for** $3,000 **and** invests the **money** in mining stock paying a dividend of sixteen per cent. How long will it take the company to absorb his capital and leave him as flat as a pancake?

A citizen who thinks it would be nice to have fresh eggs every day buys thirteen fowls at **sixty** cents each; lumber to the amount of $12; hires a man for $5 to build a park and in three months pays out **$4** 20 **for feed.** In the twelve **weeks** he gets four dozen eggs **and** loses five hens **by** death and mysterious disappearance. **How much** have his eggs cost him per dozen?

A father pays $200 to **educate** his daughter **in** music; $50 to enable her **to say** "good-day" **in** French; $100 to give her lessons in painting; $25 to learn her to dance. She then marries a man **who** is working on a salary of $14 per week. How much will she save by doing her own kitchen work for five years, estimating a girl's salary at $2 **50** per week?

A boy buys a harvest apple for a cent. He gives **a boy a** taste for **a** kite worth four cents; another **boy a** small bite for a marble worth a penny; a third boy a big bite for a jackknife worth six cents, and then has enough left to get up a case of colic worth $7. How much does he make by the speculation?

A servant girl works in a certain family for three weeks at $3 per **week.** She breaks four goblets at twenty-eight **cents each,** three tea-cups valued at **twenty** cents apiece, throws $1 20 worth of bread and biscuit into the alley and gets away with half a set of knives and forks costing $3. How much is the family out of pocket?

A druggist mixes two ounces **of water and** three cents' worth of powder together **and** charges fifty-six **cents for the** prescription. Estimating the water at eighty cents and his time at twenty, how much **does** he lose?   **It's** curious, but druggists lose money just that way.

At $6 per ton how **many** tons of coal can **be** bought for $24?   [The **greenhorn will** answer " four tons."]

A stage coach robber was enabled to lay up **$4,580** in ten months, but **a** Niagara Falls hackman salted down $5,265 in nine.   How much better is it to rob **at** Niagara Falls than out West?

A tramp gets a cold biscuit at one house, **a** piece of meat at another, an old vest at the third, and the owner of the fourth house runs him three blocks with a dog.   How much more does the tramp respect the fourth person than the other three combined?

A St. Louis daily paper steals four paragraphs from one exchange, six from another, five **from another** and three from a fourth.   How many does **it** steal in all, and how long will such a man be permitted to roam **the earth?**

It takes twenty blows of a hammer in the hands of a woman to drive a ten-penny nail three inches. She misses the nail twice where she hits it once.

How many **blows does she strike in all, and** how far can her voice be heard when she strikes her thumb?

A gentleman **who** has a library of 12,000 volumes, opens ten volumes **per year.** At this rate **how** long will it take him to reach the last book?

Only one newspaper man out **of** every sixty-four **ever has** a sharp knife, but only **one** lawyer **out** of every 120 carries a lead pencil. **How much better** is it to be a newspaper man **than a lawyer?**

In the vaults of a State **Treasury** are $500,000, and the Treasurer starts for **Mexico.** How **much** does he leave behind him?

In one month the **owner of** a three-minute horse lied **ninety-four times** regarding his speed. At this rate **how** many times would he lie in a year, and how **would it help** the speed of the horse any?

A school teacher gives a pupil fourteen paragraphs in the science of government, thirteen examples in arithmetic, three pages of history, one page of grammar, one of orthography, and half an hour **of writing as** a daily lesson and expects him to pass **75 per cent.** At this rate how long will it take her **to rush him** into a lunatic asylum?

If a lawyer charges a plumber $5 **for** advice, and the plumber charges the lawyer $5 50 for stopping a leak in **a water-pipe,** how much is the lawyer ahead?

A saloonist buys a barrel of whisky in bulk and draws two barrels from it by the drink. There is nothing to figure on this. The figuring was all done by the saloonist.

———

A poor man who has forty feet of sidewalk cleans it twenty-four times between December 1 and February 28, while a rich man who has 400 feet does not clean his once. Where does the poor man get ahead of him? and why is it that a rich man never falls on the ice and drives his coat buttons up to his shoulder blades?

———

In a school-room are twelve benches and nine boys on a bench. Find who stole the teacher's gad?

———

A laundress takes in twelve shirts and has four stolen from her line. How many are left and what are the losers going to do about it?

———

A farmer sold eleven bushels of potatoes and the product purchased two gallons of whisky at ninety cents per gallon. How much per bushel did he get for his tubers, and where did he keep the jug?

———

What velocity must a locomotive have to pick up a deaf man walking on the track and fling him so high that six cars pass before he comes down?

———

A boy earned twenty cents per day for eighteen days, and bought his mother a mush-rat muff costing

$2 10.   How much did he have left to go to the circus with?

A mother standing at the gate calls to her boy who is exactly sixty-eight feet distant. It takes two minutes and twenty-two seconds for the sound to reach **him**. Find from this the velocity with which a woman's voice travels.

A woman earned forty-two cents per **day by** washing, and supported a husband who consumed four dollars' worth of provisions **per week**. How much was she in debt at at the end of each **month** up to the time he was sent to the work-house?

A father agreed to give his son four and one-half acres of land for every cord of wood he chopped. The son chopped three-sevenths of a cord and broke the **ax** and went off hunting rabbits. How much land was he entitled to?

A certain young man walks five-sevenths of a mile for seven nights in a week **to** see his girl, and after putting in 112 nights he gets the bounce. How many miles did he hoof it altogether, and how many weeks did **it** take him to understand that he wasn't wanted?

Two men agree **to** build a wall **together**. One does four-fifths of the bossing, and the other three-tenths of **the work,** and they finally conclude to pay a man $18 **to** finish the **job.** Find the length and height of the wall.

A woman arrives at the depot three minutes ahead **of train** time. She has to kiss seven persons, **say** "good-by" to thirteen others, send her love to **twenty-two** relatives and see to four parcels. She accomplishes it all and **has** forty-one seconds to spare **to** tell **a** dear friend how to mix seven different ingredients into a mince-pie. How long **did it** take the train to reach Chicago?

It is twenty-six rods from Smith's house to the saloon where he takes a nip six mornings per week. In fifteen **years** how far has he walked?

If a college student tears down two signs, upsets four ash barrels, rips up five rods of sidewalk, breaks two windows and mashes the Professor of Latin all in one week, how would a charge of bird-shot affect his sacred constitution the following Monday night when girdling shade-trees?

A wise Arabian, who had $13 in his vest pocket, wanted to divide it among five beggars so as to give each one **$3.** How did he proceed? [This is the one that always keeps the boy after school and gets his jacket dusted.]

How many boys three feet tall will it take to climb over a wall five feet high and carry off half a

bushel of harvest apples? This must be figured by
the rule of three—two boys and the old man's dog.

During a courtship of three years a young man
writes his **girl 472** love-letters, calls **her an** angel
1,481 times, accompanies her to twenty-eight picnics
and seventy-two singing **schools, and then** walks off
on his ear **and** marries **a widow with six** children.
Find how much the **girl** loses, providing she lights
on the right kind of a lawyer to move a jury.

A peasant **who** had half **a cord of** wood **at his**
door desired **his** five sons to **saw it up in** such **ratio**
that the eldest should saw three-sevenths and **the**
youngest one-sixth. **How** did they divide the wood?
[**Key: For** the **teacher only:** They let the old man
saw it, of course.]

The average woman speaks 142 words per **minute. In a** conversation lasting sixteen minutes a ser-
vant girl with her ear at the key-hole catches 356
words. How many does she miss, and how did she
get that black eye?

If it takes a boy **12** years **of** age twenty-two min-
utes to bring in six small sticks of wood, how long
will it take him to walk **a** mile and **a** half to see a
circus procession?

A fond husband hands his wife $20 with which to
purchase a spring bonnet and—well, we don't re-

member the rest of it.　He probably **died** soon after handing over the money, or she discovered that the **twenty was a** counterfeit, or something **or other** happened to cut the thing short.　Come **to** think **of it, a** fond husband bought himself a $50 overcoat and gave his **wife** twelve shillings to get her fall hat clapboarded over for winter, and she thanked him kindly, and he smiled lovingly, **and** the mother-in-law went and hanged herself in the **wood-house.**

If a man **buys a** box **of strawberries with** the bottom **shoved** up half-way to the top **for twenty-five** cents, how many can he buy for $2?

Bought a horse 14 years old for $65 and sold him **to** an editor for $120 as **a** 6-year-old stepper.　How much did **I make?**

If it takes eighteen men to do the bossing and four **men** to **do** the lifting when a street-car horse falls down, how many bosses and lifters will **it take** to put five horses on their feet?

Julia has 5 beaux and Emily has 3, while the old maid next door has none.　**How many** beaux in all, and how many would be left if they should give the old maid half the crowd?

How many are $18 less the $5 you lent a Congressman's **son to help him** pay his fare to Iowa?

A certain city has a population of 420,000.　The census man can't find but 231,580.　What is the difference, and where **did the** remainder hide during the census taking ?

———

A. has an overcoat **for** which he paid $18, and his wife **trades** it off for two red-clay busts of Andrew Jackson worth thirty cents each. How much money will she get from her husband to buy a fall bonnet ?

———

If six men who talk politics and dispute on Biblical questions can build a wall in five days, how long will it take two men who whistle and flirt with the widow on the corner to do the same work ?

———

A man pays thirty cents for **three** pounds **of** evaporated apples and gets a $14 newspaper puff for sending them to an orphan asylum. Does he gain **or** lose, and how much ?

———

How many peck peach-baskets, each holding six quarts, will be required to hold seven bushels of peaches, each bushel of which is short four quarts ?

———

How do you obtain an abstract number ? Answer: Hire a strange boy to take a dozen oranges to your house.

———

How do you obtain a concrete number ? Answer : Mix **one** part Akron cement with two parts of sand and spread.

———

A citizen whose gas bill was $7 for the month of January shut his house up for two weeks in March and his gas bill was $7 75. How much did he make ?

If a butcher-cart **going at the rate of a** mile **in** three minutes strikes an Alderman **who** is walking at **the** rate **of four miles an** hour, what **is the** resisting power of **each ?**

A County Treasurer knows of a dead sure thing **in wheat, and he** puts in $3,000 of the people's cash. The **distance** from his town to Canada is 180 miles, and the average speed **of a** railroad train is thirty-five miles an hour.   Find—but they never find 'em.

A lady bought some tape for **eleven** cents, and some thread for two cents, and worked **off a quarter** with a hole in it on the peddler.   How much did she save to buy tracts for the heathen ?

A stone weighing twenty-two pounds is concealed **under** an old hat, and a man kicks it with such force **as** to send it nine yards.   As it takes two and one-half pounds of active pressure to move one pound of dead weight one foot, what force did he exert ?

A man spends eighteen **cents** for lager, ten cents for tobacco, twenty cents for cigars, fifteen cents for street-car fare, and loses **$1 50 at** poker ; he then permits his wife **to** purchase a button-hook **for** three cents, and figures that her extravagance will ruin him in **three** years.   What is his capital ?

A man **has** ninety-one sheep, eighty-seven calves **and** thirty-five pigs, and he desires to divide them equally among three sons and a daughter so that **the** daughter shall have nine more head than the **boys.**

What will be the share of each, providing three sheep are stolen, two calves get lost and five pigs follow a circus away ?

A citizen desires to move a cook stove twenty-four feet and put up sixteen feet of stove-pipe without using the ax or hammer. Find the exact divisor.

In one lot there are four calves, and in another two young men with their hair parted in the center. How many calves in all ?

An Alderman who has an official salary of $100 per year, spends $120 to be elected. How much would he lose if he didn't sell his influence to rings and schemers ?

Mary bought a comb for ten cents, a spool of thread for six cents, and a paper of pins for seven cents. She handed the clerk a fifty-cent piece with a stove-pipe hole through the rim. How many cents did she receive in change ?

A man ordered a ton of coal and received 1,800 pounds. How much more was due him, and how did he go to work to get it ?

A woman bought eleven yards of cloth and paid for it with butter, giving three pounds of butter for a yard. There was a stone weighing five pounds in the center of the crock, and the dealer cheated her a yard and a half in measuring the cloth. Who was ahead on that trade, and how much ?

A farmer's wife has twenty-two hens. A preacher comes to stay over Sunday, and she cooks a neck-piece of corned-beef. How many hens has she left?

A boy earns eighty cents a day and beats the old man out of his board at $3 per week. How much will he have after the first grand aggregation of gigantic wonders leaves town ?

Albert has nine marbles and Aaron steals four. How many are left? Aaron drops a dime from his pocket and Albert swallows it. What was Aaron's profit on the whole business?

A man trades a $70 watch for a $45 shot-gun pays $3 for repairs and then exchanges it for a $30 horse, which kicks a $28 cow to death and then dies of a broken heart. How much did the man lose ?

In a certain room there are eleven women sitting down. A lady passes the house with a new spring bonnet on. Find the number who got up and rushed to the window. (That's where you are fooled. One of 'em was too lame to get out of her chair.)

The distance from a roadside fence to a certain harvest apple tree is three times the distance from the ground to the first limb, which is two yards, one foot and nine and one-half inches. What is the distance from the fence, and how many harvest apples can a fat boy eat ?

A merchant has three clerks. Their united ages are five-sevenths of the number of herrings in a box. What are the exact figures?

———

A man died leaving property valued at $17,000 to a certain relative. Eight other relatives wouldn't have it that way, and contested the will. The property was then divided pro rata, and each one's share was found to be seventeen cents. What became— but, of course, you know that the lawyers got it.

———

A farmer takes four dozen eggs to town and exchanges them for two pounds of sugar at nine cents per pound, and when he returns home his wife gives him fifty-five cents' worth of "you infernal old saphead!" Figure it all in and find how much he received per dozen for the eggs?

———

A lightning-rod man sits down to try and remember how many farmers he has swindled. He can't begin to recall names and dates, and so he multiplies his eighteen years' of experience by two, adds five, subtracts one, and calls the result one-fourth of the grand total. What is the total?

———

The scholars in a certain county school set out to " lick " the teacher. The number of girls who, of course, don't take a hand in, is thirteen, and this is four-sixths of the number of the boys, who got the worst shaking up they ever heard tell of. What was the exact number, coming as near as you can without halving up anybody.

A fond father purchased a set of tools for his boy, paying therefor the sum of $3.25. In a short time the lad bored six holes in the piano case, sawed off six chair legs, split two door-panels and amputated the sofa's left arm. Find what the **exact sum** was, and also notify your friends that the **tools are for** sale at one-third off.

James has six apples and divides one among his five brothers and sisters. **How many has** he left?

If a quart box of strawberries holds a **pint and a** half, how many boxes will it take to make **a peck,** and how quick can a tramp get away with them?

If a farmer can **mow** six acres **of grass in one** day, how many liars **will it** take to **mow thirty-eight** acres of grass in **three days?**

A guest at the hotel **pays the** porter twenty-five **cents to** take his trunk **up** stairs; **ten** cents to a colored boy to bring him a pitcher **of water;** twenty-five cents to the waiter **to** bring his **dinner;** twenty-five cents further to the porter to **bring** his trunk down stairs; fifty cents to the omnibus driver, and $3 to the landlord as the regular **rate of** the house. How much **has** he been swindled, and what is he **going** to do about it?

A coal dealer **has a driver** weighing 185 pounds who is weighed **with 750** loads of coal during the

GRO
Nichols
PHOTO-ENG. CO. N.Y.

winter, what would have been the gain to the consumers had the driver only weighed 150 pounds?

If a policeman on night duty sleeps an hour and a half each night for thirteen years, how many years of such arduous labor will it take to reduce him to a walking skeleton?

In each county in the United States are seventy inhabitants who believe they would make good State Governors. Of this number only two per cent. ever get to be even a constable.

What is the exact number of constables, and how many law-suits can a wide-awake officer provoke in a year?

A grocer has a horse which he asserts can trot a mile in 2:40. He puts him on the track under a watch and finds his best gait to be 3:28. What was the difference between the grocer's estimate and the watch, and why did he whollop the poor horse all the way home?

A father at his death left $12,500 for the benefit of his only son, 14 years, 8 months and 12 days old, the money to be paid him when 21 years of age with interest at six per cent. How much money did the lawyers leave for the boy?

A merchant who has a stock valued at $8,000 advertises that he will dispose of it at one-fourth off. How much does he make?

A citizen has a cow which gives six quarts of milk per day, while his sales foot up nine quarts. There is nothing for the student to find in this case. Simply turn on the water.

A grocer buys a chest of tea weighing eighty pounds.   He sells twenty-seven pounds of it as " my unapproachable sixty cent tea," and the remainder as " our splendid forty cent Oolong."   How much did he receive in all and how much did he have to give to the heathen that year to quiet his conscience?

A plumber who does sixteen cents' worth of repairing desires to charge for four pounds of solder in his bill.   Please suggest how it can be done without injury to his system.

ARMY STORIES.

LEFT ON THE FIELD.

PERHAPS you knew what it was to have a bullet plow its way into your flesh, but were you ever left wounded on the field —left to wear away hours of daylight amidst groans and prayers and curses—to wear away a night which seemed years long, while men shrieked in agony and died—while wounded horses sighed and groaned and dragged themselves along—while ghouls prowled over the blood-red grass and wet their fingers in warm blood as they searched the bodies of dead and wounded for plunder?

"Forward!" came the order.

I looked up and down the line as we left the cover of the woods, and the regiment was dressed as if on parade. We were the battle-front of a brigade, and were going to charge a battery half a mile away. No skirmishers out—no firing. The battery was belching away under a cloud of blue smoke, and the ground was open and clear.

Tramp! tramp! tramp! No lagging—no forging ahead. Common time—march! march! It was a snail's pace, but we were to increase it. The left of the line was swinging ahead a little as the impatient men increased their steps, when suddenly the enemy discovered our manœuvre. There was a lull in the firing for fifteen seconds as the battery changed front, and then a shell tore through our center and battered six or eight men into bloody pulp.

"Double quick—charge!" and away we went, each man shutting his teeth hard as he entered the smoke-cloud, from under which the tongues of death leaped forward to scorch and wither dozens and scores and hundreds.

A grim veteran at my left raised a cheer. It was yet on his lips when a grape-shot tore a hole through his breast and sent him into a dry-ditch, dead before he struck the grass. Two boy brothers on my right halted for an instant as the grape and canister shrieked around them. I looked back and they were gone—dead under the feet of the second line.

How far it was! How long it took us to pass over that quarter of a mile! Now we see shadows around the guns—now the powder-flame burns our faces—now we are cheering and shooting and using the bayonet. The guns are ours! Men fall to the ground as they step into pools of blood. Every gun has its blood-stain—every wheel is covered with crimson spots. Men died before the guns—around them—behind them. We cheer—hip! hip! hu—!

Where am I? The afternoon sky is over-head—the roar of battle is in my ears—I am lying on my back on the ground. What does it mean? Heavens!

What a burning, blistering, gnawing sensation in my left leg above the knee? I am wounded, and I am lying where I first went down. The guns were here, but they are gone now, part of them captured, part of them dragged away by hand. The tide of battle has shifted, and over this meadow the dogs of war are tearing at each other's throats.

Is there any one else here? I lift my head. Any one else? Great God! but the field is covered with dead and wounded—with men writhing and growing—with fragments of bodies—with pale-faced dead—with blood-stained dying! I can touch the dead on either side, and close behind me a piteous voice calls out:

"Comrade, for the love of Heaven give me a drink?"

That pain again. Is the leg being roasted over a slow fire? I scream and shriek and clutch the grass, and keep company with thousands of others who are being tortured to insensibility by pain or driven to distraction by the still continued carnage.

Ah! it is night. The falling dew has brought more than one poor soldier back to life and renewed suffering. The batteries are silent, the muskets are resting after their deadly work. There is silence—no! From woods and meadows and knoll and valley, from almost every yard of ground on that long battle-front rise groans and cries and prayers and pleadings. A general prides himself on a strategic movement, a colonel will be promoted for bravery, a major is flattered by the cheers of the living, a captain is proud that his men stood like a stone wall, and the result is five thousand dead and **wounded** and mangled men—fathers, brothers, **and sons.**

This **is** glory. Scream and shriek, but some one **has won** fame. Pray **and** plead and rave and curse, but the telegraph is flashing the news **of a** glorious victory **over the** country. The enemy has not retired **as yet, but is** getting ready to fall back **when the night** grows older.

Hark! Is some one moving? Yes, **it** is a step. Is it some wounded man hobbling away under cover of darkness? Nearer—nearer—and some one looks into my face. It is the ghoul of the battle-field— the hyena who drags his talons through blood and gaping wounds to rob dying men's pockets?

" Go away—I am not dead !" I shriek in his face as he bends closer, **and he** leaps aside **to** growl and swear and search the body of one whose pale, up- turned face is just catching the silver rays of the new moon. I hear more steps. Ghoul meets ghoul and holds a whispered conversation, and they separate **with** hands full of plunder. Now comes a heavier **step.** A trooper's horse is dragging himself across **the** field, a shattered leg making him utter almost human groans. He is more merciful than the ghouls. He weaves and turns to avoid the bodies in his path—he even halts and puts his nose against the faces of the dead as if he would speak to them.

So and so until midnight comes and goes, and then lanterns flash, the ghouls speed away, and friends carefully lift up the wounded and carry white faces as they find comrades stiff and stark in pools of clotted gore.

And all this for—what?

FOLLOWING "GINERAL PICKETT."

A DUSTY, grizzly, crippled man of fifty, leaning a good share of his weight on a cane when he walked, sat on the post-office steps yesterday while he ate a dry crust of bread. He was nibbling away, trying to find the soft side, when he looked up and saw that he was watched.

"Say, Yank, do you call this tuff?" he called out as he chewed away.

"Well, dry bread isn't much of a meal," was the answer.

"That's so, but when rations ar' low and the commissary wagons in the rear, you've got to fill up on the best you have. I've been camping out, long-side of dry bread and water for a whole month."

"Going anywhere?"

"I reckon. I'm allus goin' somewhar' and never gittin' thar'."

"On the tramp?"

"Kinder, though I call it on the march. You see, I got flanked by hard times, and I'm changing my base, I'm looking for risin' ground now on which to form a new battle line. I've got a brother out here in Kent County, and I'm marching that way."

9*

"You were in the war?"

"Wasn't I! Can't I shet my eyes and see jist how Gineral Pickett looked when he led us agin your Second Corps down at Gettysburg on the 3rd of July? Wasn't it bilin' down thar' that day! Woof! but how one of us got back behind **Wright's brigade** alive is more'n I kin tell!"

"So you were under Pickett?"

"Right under Gineral Pickett, and I kin see the lay of the ground on that day as plain as that 'ere hoss. If I'd bin lyin' back under the wagons that day I wouldn't hev got two bullets in me nor bin jabbed with a bayonet. Lord, stranger, but I thought I was a goner in that fight! I can't talk about it 'thout chills sweepin' up my back."

"Yes, it was hot."

"Hot! Well, when thirty-nine men out of a company of fifty are killed dead, and six of the other 'leven wounded, you may reckon somebody was tryin' to hurt we 'uns! It was about four o'clock in the arternoon. All our guns had been boomin' away for three hours to break the **Fed.** center, and Pickett was to lead us as a stormin' party. The regiments fell in like clock-work, lots of the boys lookin' awful white around the gills, and no one but the officers speakin' above a whisper. We knew we were goin' to charge rifle-pits and old vets behind them, and that lots of us were goin' over to the Emmetsburg road to stay thar' forever. Wah! but I crawl when I think of it!"

He tossed the crust away with a look of contempt, grasped his cane with a firmer grip, and said:

"Pickett led, and behind us were Pettigrew's men. Attention! Forward! And we went down in steady lines, every company dressed as if on parade, and everybody waitin' for the ball to open. Boom! Boom! You 'uns opened on us with forty cannons, all booming at once, and it was awful, sir, to hear the screamin' of grape and canister. It tore men to pieces and sent their blood spurtin' on all sides. It took off legs and arms, and the poor fellows shrieked out in awful agony. 'March! March!' and by and by we rushed at the guns with a yell. Behind 'em were the rifle-pits, and beyond were lines of blue six or eight deep. Sich a roar! Sich screams and yells and shrieks! Stranger, I believe I got jist as near old Satan's headquarters that day as a live man can!"

"And you were driven back?"

"Yes, but the ground was covered with dead men first. They lay thar' in heaps. We trod on 'em as we surged up and fell back, and the wounded, driven to madness, caught at our legs or struck at us as we went past. We were among the guns when I got this bullet in the shoulder. Down I went, and I got this one in the leg. I was hangin' to the wheel of a gun and pullin' myself up, when somebody chucked a bayonet into me, and that laid me, and it was months before I got out."

"And now?"

"Well, I dunno. I ain't of much account, but,

mebbe sunthin' will turn **up** by-and-by. I'm marchin' on to see my brother, and like enough **I'll go into** camp out thar'."

" And forget your battles !"

" Forgit nuthin ! You 'uns and we 'uns ar' all right now—no more war to ever come between us, but **I'd rather** lose this right arm than to forget how Gineral Pickett looked **that day as** five thousand **men** behind him marched down **to** death. If ye fought on the Union side I'll divide **my** crusts with ye and give ye the biggest half of **my bed, but when** ye keep step with a man down to the jaws of death, and go back alone, if ye ever forgit him ye ar' a wolf ! That's me, stranger, and now—attention ! File right—march !"

And he moved away with slow and painful step, to pitch his tent again when his old wounds ached.

———◆◆◆———

THE CANNON'S STORY.

My name ? Well, I've had several. When I **was** taken from the navy yard, long years **ago, and** mounted in a battery on the Potomac, they called me " Pet." I was the smallest gun in the battery, and from the way I had of knocking the enemy about the gunners came to **love** me. Then I made **the** sixth **gun in a field** battery, and was with McClellan **on** his Peninsula campaign. I was **a** lucky gun from the start. Would you **believe** that I never even lost a **wheel** until my thirteenth fight **was almost ended?** Some cannon are always in trouble. **There** were two pieces in my battery which might better have been left at home. They looked handsome on review, but in action they had a hundred excuses for not standing up to their **work**. The ammunition was poor, the shells too large—the ground unfavorable—the range imperfect—something was the matter every time they were called to the front.

As for me, I like to see a cannon stand right up to its work. Ask any **one who** knows **me** and they will tell you that I was a fighter. If I had kept **a list** of the number of army wagons and ambulances I have knocked to pieces, and the number **of men and** horses I have killed, you would open **your eyes in** surprise. I have seen the time that I was the only gun left in the battery fit for service, and when the entire company rallied about me I felt a bit proud. **Let me** see? I have been attached to no less than **six** different brigades **of** infantry, three different brigades **of** cavalry, and have been posted in two forts and one earthwork. Ask any artilleryman if that isn't a good record. I have been struck over 100 times by bullets, grapeshot and pieces of shell, but you see that I am good for another campaign. I was personally acquainted with McDowell, Richardson, Kearney, Burnside, McClellan, Hooker, Custer, Kilpatrick, Sheridan, Grant, and several others, and I believe that I have received words of praise from all of them.

And yet I have a stain on my record. Sometimes

I am sorry about it, and again I am glad. I don't think any of the men laid it up against me, but yet it was a break in my record. They had sent me over into the Shenandoah Valley to fight with Sheridan, and I joined him only five days before the battle of Cedar Creek. When the men came to count my scars and look me over they agreed among themselves that I was a trusty piece, and they rejoiced that I had come among them. Such talk as this naturally made me anxious to prove true all they had predicted, and it was with a feeling of deep satisfaction that I saw the battle of Cedar Creek commence. In ten minutes after the first alarm I was throwing shell among the enemy, and the men around me were shouting :

"Give it to 'em, Beauty; you're shooting as true as a rifle!"

I don't care to tell you the part I took in that affair, but you can judge that I was at the front by the fact that I was hit by bullets no less than twelve times, and every spoke in my wheels had a stain of blood. As the fight grew hot I forgot myself in my desire to maim and kill. In my eagerness to slay I almost jumped clear of the earth, and I felt a thrill of delight when the shells were changed for grape and canister. I saw the enemy forming for a charge, but I did not move. I heard them say how much depended on me, and I was too proud to give back a foot.

Just in front of me, as that regiment came charging on, were three blue-eyed, beardless boys. I knew ·

they must be brothers. I knew that a good mother had kissed them good-bye at some farm-house gate, and that a gray-haired father had felt his old heart ache as they marched away. I was made to maim and kill. I had been called a trusty cannon. Aye! I had taken delight in war's horrid murders. But as the three fair-haired boys came sturdily on, and I saw that all would be wiped out at once, I faltered and grew weak for the only time in my life. I felt the tears of the mother—I heard her sobs of anguish above the roar of battle. I could not take them all. I held my grape against the pull of the lanyard. They pulled again and again, but the powder refused to burn. As the lines came near the brothers bore away to the right, and when they were out of range I sent my terrible missiles crashing into other faces and tore a score of men into bloody fragments. Thus, though I look grim and murderous, I have my weakness. Warriors would not look for sentiment in black-mouthed cannon, but if you come closer you will see that the birds have nestled in my throat and reared their young among the powder stains.

FINDING THE TRAIL.

HERE in the shadow of this grim mountain is a camp of cavalry—200 men in faded and ragged blue uniforms, every face sunburned and bronzed, every sabre and carbine showing long use, every horse lifting its head from the grass **at short** intervals for **a** swift glance up and **down the** valley.

Here at the foot **of the** mountain, the Apache trail, which has **been** followed for three **days,** has grown **cold. Aye,** it has been lost. **It is as if** the white men **had** followed a path which suddenly ended **at** a precipice. From this point the red demons took wings, and the oldest trailer is at fault.

The **men** on picket looked up and down the narrow valley, with anxious **faces. Down** the valley, a mile away, a solitary wild **horse paws** and prances and utters **shrill** neighs of wonderment and alarm. Up the valley is a long stretch of green grass, the earth as level as a floor and no visible sign of life. The pines and shrubs and rocks on the mountain side might hide ten thousand Indians, but there is not the slightest movement to arouse suspicion. **It is a** still, hot day. Not a bird chirps, **not a** branch waves. The eye of a lynx could detect nothing beyond the erratic movements of the lone wild horse adown the valley and the flight of an eagle so high in air that he seemed no larger than a sparrow.

For **an hour** every man and horse has looked for "signs," **but** nothing has been discovered beyond what has been described. It is a lost **trail. There** is something in it to arouse suspicion **as well as** annoyance. Ten miles away **the** trail was **as** plain **as a** country highway, and the Indians had no suspicion of pursuit. Five miles back there were signs of commotion. Here, in the center of **the** valley, every foot-print suddenly disappears.

Look, now! A sergeant with **grizzly locks** and fighting jaw rides down the valley, followed by **five** troopers. They are to scout for the lost trail. Every man has unslung his carbine, every saddle-girth **has** been tightened, and every man of the six looks over the camp as he rides out, **as** if he had been told that he was bidding a last farewell to comrades. They ride at a slow gallop. **Each man** casts swift glances **along** the mountain side **to** his right—along the mountain side to his left—at the green **grass** under his horse's feet.

What's that! Afar up the slope **to the** right something waves to and fro for a moment. Higher up the signal is answered. Across the valley on the other slope it is answered again. **Down** the valley, **a full** two miles beyond where the wild horse now stands like **a** figure of stone, and where the valley sweeps **to the right like** the sudden turn of a river, the signal is caught up **and** 200 Apaches, eager, excited and mounted, draw back into the fringe at the base of the mountain and wait.

The little band gallop straight down upon the lone horse. Now they are only half a mile away, and his breath comes quick and his nostrils quiver as he stands and stares at the strange spectacle. A little nearer and his muscles twitch and quiver and his sharp-pointed ears work faster. Only eighty rods **now, and with a** fierce snort of alarm and defiance he rears up, whirls about like a top, and is off down the valley like **an** arrow sent by a strong hand. The **sight may** thrill, but it does not increase the pace of those who **follow.** The men see **the wild horse** fleeing before them, **but the** sight **does not hold** their eyes more than **a second.** To **the right—to the left** —above **them**—down the valley—they are looking **for a hoof-print, for a** trampled **spot, for a** broken twig—for a sign however insignificant to prove that men have passed that way. They find nothing. The **signals up** the mountain-side were visible **only for** seconds.

After the first wild **burst of speed** the lone horse looks back. **He sees** that **he is not being** pushed, and he recovers courage. He **no** longer **runs in a** straight line, but he sweeps away to the left—swerves away to the right, and changes his gait to a trot. When he hears the shouts of pursuit and the louder thump of hoof-beats he will straighten away and **show the** pursuers a gait which nothing but a whirl-**wind can** equal.

Look! It is **only** a quarter of a mile now to the **turn** in the valley. The lone horse has suddenly **stopped to sniff the air.** His ears are pointed straight **ahead,** his eyes grow larger and take on a frightened look and he half wheels as if he would gallop back to those who have seemingly pursued. **Five,** eight, ten seconds, and with a snort of alarm he breaks into a terrific run, takes the extreme left **of** the valley, and goes tearing out of sight as if followed by lions.

" Halt !"

The grim sergeant sees " signs " in the actions of **the** horse. Every trooper is looking ahead and to **the right.** **The** green valley runs into the fringe, the fringe into dense thicket, the thicket into rock and pine and mountain slope. No eye can penetrate that fringe. The Indians may be in ambush there, or the horse may have scented wolf or grizzly.

" Forward !"

No man knows what danger lurks in the fringe, but the order was to scout beyond the bend. To disobey is ignominy and disgrace ; to ride forward is —wait ! There is no air stirring in the valley. Every limb and bough is as still as if made of iron. There is a silence which weighs like a heavy burden, and the harsh note of hawk or buzzard would be a relief.

Here is the bend. The valley continues as before —no wider—no narrower—level and unbroken. The wild horse was out of sight long ago, and the six troopers see nothing but the green grass as their eyes sweep the valley from side to side.

"Turn the bend and ride down the valley for a mile or so and keep your eyes open to discover any pass leading out."

" Halt !"

It is more than a mile beyond the bend. No pass has been discovered. No signs of a trail have been picked up. The sergeant has raised himself up for a long and careful scrutiny, when an exclamation causes him to turn his face up the valley. Out from the fringe ride the demons who have been lurking there to drink blood. Five—ten—twenty—fifty— the line has no end. It stretches clear across the valley before a word has been spoken. Then it faces to the right and 200 Indians **in war paint face the** grim old sergeant and his five troopers.

"Into line—right dress!"

It is the sergeant who whispers the order. Six **to 200, but** he **will** face the danger. To retreat down the valley is to be overtaken one by one and shot **from** the saddle or reserved for torture. Down the valley there is no hope; up the valley is the camp and rescue. The two **lines** face **each** other for a moment without a movement.

"Now, men, one volley—sling **carbines—draw** sabres and charge!"

A sheet of flame—a roar—a cloud of smoke, and the six horses spring forward. Then there is a grand yell, a rush by every horse and rider, and a whirl-**pool** begins to circle. Sabres flash and clang—arrows whistle—revolvers pop—voices shout and scream, and then the whirlpool ceases. It is not three min-utes since the first carbine was fired, but the tragedy has ended. Every trooper is down and scalped, half **a** dozen redskins are dead or dying, a dozen horses are struggling or staggering, and turning the bend at a mad gallop is the sergeant's riderless horse. **He** carries an arrow in his shoulder, and there is blood on the saddle. In five minutes he will be in camp, and the notes of the bugle will prove that the lost trail has been found.

CUT OFF.

Now stand and look about you. Here are the dying camp-fires of **a** company of soldiers. **To** the right the ground **is** broken into swells **like** great **green waves.** On the left is a scraggy plain. **Ahead,** seeming only **two** or three miles away, is a mountain range. The soldiers will have to ride a long ten miles to reach it. You can see their backs **as** they trot over the crest **of** a swell half a mile away.

Now look behind you. **Twenty** tufted heads **are** peering over the ridge, not 300 feet from a campfire—twenty pair of eyes glint and gleam and blaze hate as the cavalry disappear. Now twenty Indians rise up and peer and look. They were hiding there a full hour before the troop left, but they were not strong enough **to** give battle. They waited on in hopes that some one would linger behind and fall a victim. Like tigers they hugged the grass—like snakes they wormed themselves along—like devils they bided their time.

Hah! Every redskin has disappeared like a flash. The clank of sabres has almost died away in the distance, and no bird utters its note near the deserted camp. What is the alarm!

Thud! thud! thud!

It is the hoof-beats of a horse. **A trooper** returns at a gallop, searching the ground with his eyes. There it is—the iron pin with which he stakes his horse. He overlooked it in packing up, and has returned to make good his loss.   He gives one anxious look around him, and then dismounts.   The pin is in his hands when there is a rush of feet, and he straightens up find himself the center of a circle of demons.   **Not a** yell has been uttered—not a shot fired, nor a bow bent.

He is a brave old trooper.   He bears the scars of **arrows** and bullets, and he **has sent** more than one **redman to** his long home.   **See how pale** he grows as he looks about him and sees **the circle** complete. See the despair in his eyes as **the devils mock him !** The troop is two miles away and riding **ahead at a** trot.   He clutches the stout iron pin with **firmer** grip, but after a moment his fingers relax and it falls to the grass.   If he had raised it to strike a dozen arrows would **have** entered his body before the blow fell.   **He** is trapped, and there is no hope.

Before the troopers have missed their comrade he **has** been captured, tied to his horse, and is riding away at a gallop.   As he leaves the camp he turns and looks back over his trail.   Three or four miles **away he sees** a line of blue for an instant **as the** column sweeps over a ridge.   Now it fades out, **and** he is doomed.   There is a malicious **chuckle** from every savage throat, and the trooper feels a chill creep over him **at** the sound.

The gallop slackens.   There is no hurry.   The **cat** has the mouse and enjoys its sufferings.   Over ridges—across little valleys—skirting hills—and here **is a** lone tree beside a purling **stream.**   Behind it is a hill.

Between it and the creek is a level spot of ground a hundred feet square. **The red riders** dismount, pull their prisoner from his horse, **and the animals** are turned loose to crop the rich short grass.

Despair first nerves a man to take desperate chances. Then it unnerves him and chills the blood. An hour ago the trooper's face was like bronze. Now it is **as white as the snow** lying on **the** crest of that grim mountain fifty miles away. But he is no coward. A coward would lament and beg **and** entreat and demand mercy. The old man shudders as they bind him to the half-grown cotton-wood, but no **word** passes his lips. He does not look at the Indians, **but** over their heads at the green plain—the groves—the silvery thread winding around the glorious sun which is warming the heart of **every** living thing beyond that circle of savages.

Now an Indian leaves the circle and advances to **to** the tree. **He** laughs in the face of the prisoner. **He** peers into his eyes. With his keen knife he reaches out and severs an ear and waits for a scream of pain. **It** does not come. **The** teeth shut hard, the eyes grow stony in their gaze, and that is **all.** The swift sharp knife severs the other ear, and the fiends shout with pleasure at the ghastly figure before them. They hope to hear screams and shrieks, but they are disappointed. The blood trickles down —a chill shakes the old man—and then his white **lips are** pressed closer than before.

Not one Indian now, but the whole circle. They **crowd** around him with sharp knives, and each seeks some new torture. Fingers are unjointed, the nose is sliced off, **cords** and tendons are exposed, powder **is** poured upon the hair and fired, and after each hellish act they draw back and hope to hear his **screams of** agony. Not **a** sound escaped his compressed lips. His wide-open eyes were fixed upon a **distant** grove, and they never moved.

They had one more torture. With devilish glee they ran here and there in search of whatever would burn and a fire was kindled around and upon the bloody feet. The flames wavered and sputtered among the blood-wet grass, and more fuel was heaped **on.** The morning breeze fanned the blaze into brighter life, and as it mounted up the savages danced about the tree and shouted till the hillside rang.

The flames **take hold** of clothing and flesh, but the stony eyes look through the veil of smoke without a quiver. The horses scent the roasting flesh and stand with heads high in air. The Indians sniff it, and dance with greater energy. All of a sudden the prisoner straightens up, his head drops forward and the flames burn away at a corpse.

The sun mounts higher, passes its zenith, and when it is low in the west a troop of cavalry sit their horses around the lone and blackened tree. The soldier was missed, and here is the end of the search. An officer rakes over the ashes and uncovers a few **buttons,** the **heel of** a boot, two or three bones, and whispers to himself :

" And these red demons are wept over by philanthropists, prayed for in churches, made the wards of charity, and petted by a government which fondly dreams that they have souls! Attention, company! Forward—right wheel!"

SNAKES IN THE GRASS.

If you stand here and peer through the darkness you can see it all. There is the wagon of a lone emigrant family, its cover weather-worn and rent, to prove that the journey has been long and weary. Ten feet away are the embers of the fire on which the evening meal was cooked. Between the wagon and the fire is the rude bed of robes and blankets on which mother and children are sleeping. On the other side of the vehicle stand the horses, munching at the short sweet grass or listening to the far-off voice of the wolf.

That is the back-ground. In the fore-ground a sentinel sits with his back to the solitary cottonwood. At his right-hand runs a little brook—at his left is the boundless prarie o'er which night has spread her mantle. Forty feet away are wife and children trusting in his vigilance. Overhead gray-white clouds are driving across the star-light heavens, and the moan of the wind has an uneasy, nervous sound. Away out on the prairie the wolf gallops from knoll to knoll and snuffs the air, and the coyote gnaws at the bleached bones of the buffalo and utters his short, sharp cries of hunger.

Is there danger? All day long as the tired horses pulled the wagon at a slow pace, the emigrant has carefully scanned the circle about him, but without cause for uneasiness. He knows he is in the Indian country and for the last twenty-four hours his nerves have been braced to hear their dreaded war-whoop and to catch sight of a band riding down upon him.

It is midnight as we find him. His ear has been as keen as a fox's and his eye has not rested for a moment. The stakes are human lives—his life with the rest. The odds are ten to one against him.

"Ah! if we were back at the old home in Ohio! You remember the old farm-house hidden away among the cherry and pear trees? There is the highway, lined with dusty May weeds. Half a mile below is the quaint little school-house where the children learned their A, B, C. Half a mile above is the bridge across the ——"

The sentinel rouses up and rubs his eyes. It was the creek talking to him. As he listened to its monotonous babble it suddenly began to converse in plain tongue. For a moment he is thrilled and alarmed. He looks keenly about, and he listens with bated breath. There are the same sounds—the wail of the coyote—the munching of the horses—the babbling of the brook—now and then a half-groan from one of the children sleeping an uneasy sleep. And now the brook talks again:

"There was the big brown barn full of sweet-smelling hay—the pasture lot with **its** cows—the pond in which the bare-legged children used to wade —the orchard with its burden of fruit. Don't you remember how **yon** used **to** sit on the stoop at evening-time and smoke your pipe and watch the children at play on the grass? How peaceful everything was! There was a drowsy feeling in the summer air —the lazy hum of insects—the low songs of the good wife as she rocked baby to sleep—why, you sometimes fell asleep and let your pipe drop **from ——**"

The brook babbled and the man slept. **Aye!** the sentinel who had five lives in his keeping slept and dreamed, and in his dreams wandered back to the **old** home and heard the old familiar sounds.

"Sh! It was a rustle in the grass! Turn to the left a little more. There it is! Thirty feet from the sleeping man a rattlesnake rears its head above the grass and looks around. Its eyes gleam like stars. The neck swells, the tongue flashes in and out, and it coils and uncoils itself as if in fierce combat. Now it is advancing—now it swerves to the right—now to the left—now it halts and coils itself to strike. It might creep up and bury its fangs in the flesh of the sleeping man, and it will! It creeps again. It glides through the grass like a gleam—now to the **right—now to** the left—now straight ahead.

"S-s-s-h!"

The serpent halts. Twenty feet more and it could have struck the sleeper, but some movement of his has alarmed it, and it **glides** away for **fifty feet, as fast as a shadow** travels.

Now look beyond the snake! Is it a second serpent **worming** its way over the ground to **surround** the sleeper with peril? Is it wolf or panther creeping forward to make a victim? **Now** you can see **more clearly.** There is the scalp-lock and feathers—the dark face—the gleaming eyes—the shut teeth and bronzed throat of a Blackfoot warrior. A courier from one branch **of his tribe to another; he has** discovered the encampment, circled around it **twice,** and is now creeping upon the man, who sleeps instead of watches.

How softly he moves! A panther stealing upon **a listening doe** would not exercise more care. Almost inch by inch, and yet he is slowly approaching. **He was a** hundred feet away. Now he is ninety—eighty—seventy—sixty! He can see a dark mass **at** the foot of the tree, and he knows that the sentinel must be asleep or he would not be in that position.

See the rattlesnake! It has faced about. **If it was** daylight you could see a fiercer gleam in its eye—a tightening of the cords and muscles—a fiercer flash of the red tongue. A straight line of sixty feet drawn from **the** Indian to the tree would pass over the snake. Now the warrior creeps forward again—**not** a weed breaking—not a rustle to prove his presence. **Two** feet—four—six—! See the snake! Its head is thrown back—its eyes shoot sparks—there goes the deadly z-z-z-z-z of his rattle. The head of the **Indian** is not **three feet** away **as** he hears the ominous sound. He draws back, but there is a dart, a flash, and something strikes him full in the face and is not shaken off until he springs to his feet with a cry heard for half a mile around and rushes away in the darkness.

What was it? The sentinel is wide awake and upon his feet. Wife and children have been startled from slumber to grow white-faced and tremble. Even the horses have raised their heads and are peering into the night. There was a single cry—the wild scream of a human being suddenly terrified.

"It was nothing—nothing but the howl of a wolf!" whispers the sentinel, as he walks over to comfort wife and children ; and by and by all is quiet and peaceful as before. The night grows apace —the stars fade—daylight breaks. As the sun comes up the wagon moves on its way and the brook and the camp and the cotton-wood are left behind.

"Yes it was the howl of some wolf prowling about," whispers the emigrant to himself as he walks beside his wagon and cautiously scans the prairie.

Three hundred feet to the left is coiled a snake, which darts its venomous tongue at the rolling wagon. Half a mile beyond lies the dead body of the Black-foot—swollen, distorted—a horrible sight under the light of the morning sun. Overhead circle three or four vultures of the prairie, and creeping through the grass come the lank, hungry wolves to the feast. The wife laughs, the children frolic, the husband regains his light heart. Night wrote the record of the serpents in the grass, and he will never read it.

"A MAN AS WAS WRONGED."

IF it had been a pleasant day, and if we hadn't all been out of sorts with our luck, we should have had a word of welcome for the stranger as he entered our camp that wretched afternoon. As it was fifty of us saw him leave Chinese Trail at Dead Man's Elbow and walk into our camp, and never a man rose up to salute him.

The stranger seemed to expect just such a reception. That is, he didn't seem a bit surprised. He passed down the single street we had named Road to Riebes, turned to the left at the lone pine tree, and without once looking around him he staked off a claim and began to erect a shanty.

"Bad man, I'm afeared," growled Judge Slasher as he partly closed one eye and gave the stranger the benefit of the squint.

"Bin bounced out of some camp fur stealin'," added the big chap from Kentucky.

"Tell you, he's got a hang-dog look," put in the man known as "Ohio Bill."

Every man in the camp was down on the fresh arrival, and that without cause. Ordinarily we were a jolly set, and a stranger coming among us met with words of cheer, but that afternoon the devil was to pay. The three mules belonging to camp had strayed off and been gobbed by the Indians, and on the heels of this discovery came the announcement that we had only salt **enough to last two days, while** the sugar was entirely gone.

So we were cross-grained and out of sorts, and it was lucky for the stranger that he gave us no excuse to pick a quarrel. The next day was bright and fair, and if it hadn't been for Judge Slasher some of us would have gone over and excused our manners and asked the stranger to chip in and become neighborly ; but the Judge said :

"He's a bad un, he is. I kin tell it by **the way** his head is set on his body. Fust thing **we know a** committee will come along here and gobble **him up** fur robbery or murder."

Two weeks had passed, and while some of us had given the stranger a curt "good morning," no one had struck hands with him, or entered his shanty to smoke **a** friendly pipe. Then a climax came. The six of us occupying one shanty were working in common, and our bag of dust was buried in a corner of the fire-place. One morning this bag was missing, and you can imagine that there was a first-class row in no time. There was the hole where some one had dug under the stones and carried off our treasure, and whom were we to suspect ? **We** had faith in each other, and we could not suspect outsiders because none of them knew where our bag was concealed, and because this was the first case of stealing ever **known on** Betsy Jane Hill.

Yes, we were mad, and in the excitement **of** the first **discovery we** came near having a free fight among ourselves. It increased our anger to discover that we could not reasonably suspect any one, and this fact made every one of us try the harder to pick up a clue. At length Judge Slasher sprang to his feet with the exclamation:

"By the bones of Kidd! but I know the thief!"

"Who is he?"

"That hang-dog, sheep-stealing stranger! Hang me! if I didn't dream of this coming in here last night to borrow a shovel, and it was his digging under the stones which started that dream! He has held aloof from us, and that's proof enough that he came here for no good purpose."

It was a straw to catch at. We had lost in a night all we had gained by months of hard work, and we didn't stop to reason. It was decided to lay the charge at the stranger's door, and if he could prove his innocence so much the better for him.

The news that the White House, as we called our shanty, had been robbed, spread like wildfire, and as we started for the stranger's claim our crowd numbered a full hundred. He was outside at work, and as he saw us coming he was startled. The angry murmurs and black looks must have frightened him. You will say that an innocent man would have stayed and braved the storm. As the crowd swooped down on this man he started off at a run.

"Halt! Halt! Halt, or we'll shoot!" shouted a score of men.

"He's the thief——stop him! stop him!" roared the Judge.

Five or six shots were fired almost as one, and the

fugitive tumbled forward on the rocks. Three bullets entered his back, and as the foremost men bent over him and turned his white scared face to the heavens he gasped out :

"You have murdered me—God forgive you !"

"Now to search him !" said the Judge as he came up, and half a dozen hands made quick work of it. Resting on his breast, and made fast to his neck by a ribbon, was a package wrapped in oil-skin. There was a flutter of excitement as the Judge rudely snapped the string and held the package in his hand. It was our dust.

No! We formed in a circle around the Judge as he sat on a rock and opened the package, and in less than a minute there were white faces among us. What were the contents? A photograph of a fair-faced middle-aged woman, and on the card was written :

"Mary—died June 19th, 1857."

That was the dead man's wife ! There was a second photograph—that of a babe about a year old, and the Judge read aloud in a trembling voice :

"Our Harry—died April 4th, 1857."

That was not all. On a card were locks of their hair. There was a gold ring once worn by the wife, a faded ribbon which her fingers had touched, and a bit of plaid like the dress the baby wore when photographed. Relics of what? Of years agone—of a

10*

fond wife and beautiful child—of joy and happiness—of a husband's love and **a father's grief!**

And we were looking **down** upon these things and feeling **our** hearts swelling up and our eyes growing misty when up comes our good-for-nothing, half-witted cook with the bag of dust in his hand! **In** repairing the fire-place he had moved the bag, **and** in the excitement over its supposed loss what little wit he had was frightened away for the moment. The hole under the stones had been made by some small animal in search of food, and in our haste we had accused **and** murdered an innocent man.

It came to us in full force as we stood there, and men sighed and wiped their eyes and walked away with trembling steps. **The** Judge felt that he **was** most to blame. He was looked upon as **a** hard, **wicked man, but those relics of the** dead **broke** him **hp. He** sat **there** and wept like a child, and in a **voice** hardly audible for his great emotion, he **moaned:**

"Heaven forgive me for this awful deed!"

With sorrow—with tenderness—with hearts like children, we **dug a grave and** put the poor body into it, and with his own hands the Judge planted the head-board and **engraved** thereon:

"Here lies **a** man as was **wronged!**"

"DIED GAME."

T is morning on the prairie.

To the east is the rosy sunrise and the dim, far-away outline of a mountain range ; to the north a shadowy line which may mean hills or timber; to the west and south a broad, level ocean of green grass which has no limit. It seems as level as a floor to the eye, but it is cut up with dry ravines and ditches, and there are sharp ridges and dips and sunken spots.

The sun is warm, the air still, and every blade of grass is loaded with diamond dew-drops. There is no bird to chirp, and no crickets to call out, but there is no feeling of loneliness. One who faces that morning sun and feels the vastness of the prairie is lost in quiet amazement. There is an awe upon him akin to that which man feels when he sees the ocean lashed to mighty fury. The one is an exhibition of Divine anger—the other of Divine peace.

See! A rough-clad, full-bearded man, of iron muscle and fearless courage, suddenly rises from a hollow, tosses aside his blanket, and slowly turns his head in every direction to scan the green grass sea. At the same moment his horse emerges from a dip which has heretofore sheltered him, and, with a whinny of recognition and pleasure, advances straight upon his master.

Alone! Man and horse are the only living creatures in sight. They are as much lost to the world as two grains of sand washing to and fro in the Atlantic. The master's hand steals up until it rests upon the horse's neck, and the faithful animal crowds a bit nearer. Both are awed by the broad expanse. The mighty grandeur of Nature steals in upon the man's soul, and it seems to pass like an electric current to the horse. He raises his head. His nostrils expand. His eyes grow clearer and larger. Surely he must see the picture spread out before him there, and something of its beauty must be felt.

See that! The man's hand goes up to shade his eyes. He is looking straight to the west. He stands like a rock, and his eyes are as keen as an eagle's. The horse is looking in the same direction, ears pricked forward, lips quivering, and every muscle in his legs tightened up as if for a race. What is it? A flutter on the surface of the prairie caught the man's eye for an instant and then disappeared. It was two miles away. It was only a trifle; but on that trifle depends his life. A shipwrecked sailor catches his breath at sight of every white cloud creeping above the water-line. The hunter on the prairie feels his heart pound at the flutter of a bird's wing—the bark of a coyote—the hoot of an owl—at sight of a hoof-print or a **broken bush.** These **may** mean nothing, or they may **mean an ambush—a race** for life—capture and torture.

"Yi! yi! yi!"

The level seeming prairie is broken two miles away **by a dry** ravine deeper than a man's height. This curves and bends and leads on for miles. Scrambling out of its depths, **and** each one sounding his war-whoop as he mounts his pony, are a score of Indians.

For two days the hunter **had swept the horizon** in vain. He was alone **on** the great ocean. Night had been tranquil and full **of sound** sleep. Here, now, rising like specters from the earth before him, **is a band** of blood-thirsty demons raving for his life. The sight stuns him for **a** few seconds. Then, with **a** growl **of** chagrin and defiance, he flings the saddle upon his horse, picks up his rifle, and while yet the **Indians are a** mile and a half away, he mounts and heads for the **east.**

A race for life has begun.

The hunter's horse strikes into **a** long, steady gallop, which would keep him alongside of a train **of** cars. There is a chorus of yells from the redskins as they make the first rush. Then the silence of the prairie **is** broken **only** by **the** thud! thud! of horses' feet. **The very** silence **is** ominous, and speaks of a **grim determination to** run the victim down.

Steady, now! **The** hunter's horse devours mile after mile of the green prairie, now at the crest of a swell—now almost hidden in a dip—now for an instant out of sight **of those who** follow.   **They gain a little.**   The hunter plans **that they shall.** Every **yard they gain requires an** extra speed that will take ten **minutes off the race** after high **noon.   At 10 o'clock they have** gained half **a** mile.   Then the pace is even, **and** neither **loses** or gains.

There is something terribly grim **in following a man to his** death.   Not a shout—not a **call—not a rifle-shot.**   Thud! thud! thud! **over level and ridge** and always to **the** east.   **The sun mounts higher and** higher, and now and then **the hunter glances back** with a faint hope that the pursuit has been abandoned.   No!   He might as well expect a wolf to quit the pursuit of a wounded deer leaving its life-blood **to** stain the grass at every rod.

It is high **noon.**

The pursuit began over sixty miles away, but the breeze brings **to the** hunter's ears that same monotony **of hoof**-beats, and he glances **back to see** that same **dark** line strung out at his heels.   It has become **a question of** endurance.   If he can tire them **out he will** escape.   He shuts his teeth anew, reaches **for**-ward **to** caress his horse—

He **is** down!   A burrow caught **a foot as** the horse sped onwards, and man **and animal roll to** the ground.   The race is finished.   **The poor** beast whinnies an apology **for his** fall as he flounders about with a broken leg, and the exultant shouts of **the** redskins **hardly** reach the hunter's ears **before he is** down alongside the crippled horse and his **rifle aimed at the** approaching foe.

It is another bright, peaceful **day.** Here are the same pure air, the same blue sky, the same panorama of grass and flowers and dimly outlined mountains.

A band **of** hunters are crossing the prairie at a steady gallop, instead of a single man riding for his **life.** A vulture **rises up** with a hoarse scream—a second—a third, and the odor **of** decay reaches the nostrils of riders and horses. The band halts, rides to the left, and presently all look down upon a sight which tells its own story. The swollen carcass of **a** horse, the scalped and disfigured body of **a hunter**— trampled grass—spots of blood—broken arrows—the earth uptorn by hoofs.

One with stouter heart than the rest dismounts and picks up a dozen flattened bullets and a score of **arrows.** Than he circles round the spot and gathers up the empty shells thrown out by the hunter's Winchester. Bullets, arrows and shells are deposited in a heap by the corpse, and the man points out one— three—five—seven spots on the prairie where the trampled grass and stains of blood show the fall of horse or man. Then in a voice in which sorrow and pride were mingled he whispers:

"Poor Tom! But he died game!"

THE KING OF THE CANYON.

DRIVING square into the great mountain, as if human engineers had planned it and human hands blasted and **dug, is the** great, dark **ravine called a** canyon. Its floor is of rock and bowlder, with, perhaps, a tiny stream trickling down. Its sides are soil, and bush, **and rock** and gravel. Its roof **is the heavens.**

Stand here in the mouth and look up. **It** is mid-**day, and yet** it is twilight around you, and above you **can see the** stars twinkle. One falling from the cliffs above would pass through a thousand feet of space before striking the rocky bottom. You shud-der at the thought, and **the awful** stillness around you brings a chill.

The canyon is grim. It may echo your footsteps, but there is no squirrel nor chirp of bird. If living things tread this rocky path they leave no trace be-hind. It would furnish quarters for a thousand Indians waiting to pounce down upon the emigrant **or** prospector, but the savage stands here and feels the chains of awe clogging his footsteps. This grim-ness awes him ; this silence makes him tremble.

Push forward a few steps. The darkness deepens. Overhead the stars shine brighter, and you can **hear** the drip of water down the rugged and **moss-grown** rocks. The dark cell of the prison **has its** terrors, but the occupant feels that he can **almost reach out** and touch the sunny, bustling world around **him.** There is **nothing** to bring awe or **fear.** In this can-yon **it is ever** night. **It is e**ver terrible in its silence. It is ever chilly **in its** grimness. The intruder feels **his** heart jump and throb as he wonders what dangers may be concealed by the further darkness.

The miner never comes here. The prospector

looks in and hurries away. **The savage halts, wonders, and passes on. It seems** as if **a wolf would draw** back from such a retreat. **In the hottest day** of summer **it is** chilly here. In the brightest sunlight the shadows ever dance over the jagged rocks and rugged cliffs. When earth rent herself apart in some awful struggle and mountains were torn and seamed as they rocked **to and** fro, the canyon was made. It is one of the scars left behind by which **to** read the history of ages ago.

Fifty steps further up. **Now the blackness of** midnight surrounds us. The **trees, a thousand feet** above our heads, shade the chasm until the stars **are** lost sight of. The grimness becomes a burden which you can feel, and **as a** current of wind sweeps up or down the rocky defile you can hear groans and sighs **and** feel **your blood** run cold. The drip of the water has **life, but it** weighs **upon you.** In such stillness **that you** can count **the** beats of your own heart, the drip! drip! drip! of the ice-water trickling along the cliffs would drive you insane in an hour.

Hark! Thunder? No! Beginning with a low mutter, like the gathering of a terrible storm, and swelling and growing until the canyon seems to quiver and pebbles rattle down from above—it is the King **of** the Canyon—the Grizzly! Our footsteps have reached his **ear—he** sniffs the air with growls **which mean** death. Two hundred feet beyond us in **the pitch** darkness is **the** lair of the King. Nothing **that lives** and walks can pass his tollgate. Right there is the canyon narrows, and there is his home.

Listen!　**How the** rocks tremble under that roar! The scream of a whirlwind sweeping over the prairie **cannot** stun you like this.　The King rises up and moves about, and his feet fling the bones of his many victims against the rocks and down the dark path. **His** eyes have a baleful light, and he tears at the **cliffs** with his long claws.　He has the scent, but he cannot locate it.　If he could—if he does—!　Come away!" The King of the Canyon **is at** home and hungry.

A WOMAN IN CAMP.

No man of us who was there can ever forget the afternoon a party of hunters and Indian fighters rode up to our mining camp with a lone woman in their midst.

It had been twenty-two months since any **of us** had seen anything more resembling a woman than a **pair** of spectacles and a red cotton handkerchief, and to **say** that we were knocked down, stepped on and crushed into the hard soil with astonishment **is** saying little enough.

The woman was a widow who **had** been captured by the Indians from an immigrant **train** and then recaptured by **the** hunters.　She was about forty years of age, had taken the situation coolly, and **instead of** making an effort to restore herself to the train **and to** **her** relatives with whom she was journeying, had **asked to** be set down in our camp until she could make up her mind what course to pursue. This was the way the leader of the hunters turned her over to our care :

"Say, you diggers arter silver, here's a woman who wants to stop here for a spell till she gits rested. She's eddecated, and she sings like a south wind blowing over prairie flowers."

And this was the way we received her :

"Ahem—yes—ahem—jess so—hats off, boys—no swearing—glad to see ye—hope yer well—ahem—exactly !"

There were thirty of us standing around there, mouths open, hats off, knees wobbling, and more coming up from the diggings every minute, and something in the situation made the widow grin as she looked us over. I file my claims as follows:

1. I assisted her off the horse.

2. I said I hoped she was well.

3. I remarked that it was a melodious afternoon.

4. She accepted my arm as we walked to camp, and then accepted my shanty as her headquarters.

If a tidal wave six feet high had come rolling up the valley it wouldn't have produced half the flutter occasioned by the presence of the Widow Fleming. There were eighty or ninety of us, rough, brawny and more or less wicked, some married, some divorced, and some old bachelors, and to have a dumpy little black-eyed widow with a pretty mouth and a voice as sweet as sixty cent molasses pop in upon us at 3 o'clock in the afternoon was excuse enough to stop work and send the query up and down the lines :

" Well, isn't this the next thing to the judgment day ?"

Several curious things happened right away. Col. Taylor, who had never been known to wash his face or comb his hair, started out in search of a clean shirt and a pocket-comb, and offered up as high as $15 without being able to secure them. He then made a bee-line for the creek, washed the only shirt he was ever known to have, combed his hair with a stick, and in half an hour was back in camp and wanting an introduction to the widow.

Bill Goodhen, the ugliest looking man in camp, offered $5 for a piece of looking-glass two inches square, and not being able to find one he went and washed his feet as the next best thing.

There was a general washing up and combing and scrubbing and hunting out clean shirts and neckties, and the old man Payson, who had been sick in bed for a week, got up and began to chew tobacco and call for his clothes, and he observed :

" Gentlemen, who knows but what this widder heard that I had $60 saved up and she has come here to ask for my hand in marriage ?"

I have further claims to file, as follows :

5. I was chosen guardian to the widow by a unanimous vote.

6. The widow seemed perfectly satisfied with the choice.

7. I had the only clean white shirt in that whole camp, and only five buttons were missing from the garment.

Other claims were intrusted **to me to be filed, as** follows :

Seven different men had **their hair cut.**

Six others shaved themselves with jack-knives.

Over a dozen of our band let up a notch **or** two **on swearing, except** when on the other **side** of the camp.

Well, it was curious **what a** change that widow wrought in our camp, in our way of living, and **upon** the manners of the men. Each one made an **effort** to clean and slick up, and in most cases **with marked** success. Before her advent we could count **on two** or three quarrels **per** day. **After** her coming **such a** thing was never known. Indeed, one day when Peter White **so** far forgot himself as to insult Charles O'Gay, Charles took him aside and whispered :

" Peter, **I kin turn** ye wrong side out in six ticks **of a** clock, **but I'm** not the sort of a gentleman to kick up a row and upset a lady's nerves. I'll lay it up agin ye, and arter she leaves camp I'll wallop ye or die trying."

And the widow, she sewed on buttons and mended rent garments for the whole of us, and she taught this one how to cook, and that one how to patch and darn, and before we knew it she was a god-mother and an idol. **A** queen could not have commanded deeper respect, **nor** an angel greater reverence.

She was with us about six weeks, and then went away with friends who came for her. Each man was taken **by** the hand and given a good-bye word, and as she was lost to sight down the trail the awful silence among our crowd was broken by the thundering report of the Judge blowing his nose, followed by the husky observation:

"Wall I swam! Hanged if I've felt so much like crying in about forty-seven years!"

THE SKELETON STORY.

Ride closer!

It is two miles ahead to the foot-hills—two miles of parched turf and rocky space. To the right—the left—behind, is the rolling prairie. This broad valley strikes the Sierra Nevadas and stops as if a wall had been built across it.

What is it on the grass? A skull here—a rib there—bones scattered about as the wild beasts left them after the horrible feast. The clean-picked skull grins and stares—every bone and scattered lock of hair has its story of a tragedy. And what besides these relics? More bones—not scattered, but lying in heaps—a vertebræ with ribs attached—a fleshless skull bleaching under the summer sun. Wolves! Yes. Count the heaps of bones and you will find nearly a score. Open boats are picked up at sea with neither life nor sign to betray their secret. Skeletons are found upon the prairie, but they tell a plain story to those who halt beside them. Let us listen:

Away off to the right you can see tree-tops. Away

off to the left you can see the same sight. The skeleton is in line between them two points. He left one grove to ride to the other. To ride! Certainly; a mile away is the skeleton of a horse or mule. The beast fell and was left there. If he left the grove at noon he would have been within a mile of this spot at dusk. It is therefore plain that he did not leave until mid afternoon, or possibly at dusk. Signs of Indians may have driven him from his trapping-ground, or mayhap he had exhausted the game and was shifting to new fields.

It is months since that ride, and the trail has been obliterated. Were it otherwise, and you took it up from the spot where the skeleton horse now lies, you would find the last three or four miles made at a tremendous pace.

"Step! step! step!"

What it is? Darkness has gathered over mountain and prairie as the hunter jogs along over the broken ground. Overhead the countless stars look down upon him—around him is the pall of night. There was the patter of footsteps on the dry grass. He halts and peers around him, but the darkness is too deep for him to discover any cause for alarm.

"Patter! patter! patter!"

There it is again! It is not fifty yards from where he last halted. The steps are too light for those of an Indian. A grizzly would rush upon his victim with a roar of defiance and anger. A panther would hurl himself through thirty feet of space with a scream to unnerve the hardiest hunter.

"Wolves!" whispers the hunter as a howl suddenly breaks upon his ear.

Wolves! The gaunt, grizzly wolves of the foothills—thin, and poor, and hungry, and savage—the legs tireless—the mouth full of teeth which can crack the shoulder-bone of a buffalo. He can see their dark forms flitting from point to point—the patter of their feet on the parched grass proves that he is surrounded.

Now the race begins. There is no shelter until the grove is reached. Instinct guides the horse, and terror lashes him with such a whip as human hand never wielded. Over space, through the gloom, almost as swift as an arrow sent by a strong hand, but a dark line follows. A line of wolves spreads out to the right and left, and gallops after—tongues out—eyes flashing—great flakes of foam flying back to blotch stone and grass and leave a trail to be followed by the cowardly coyotes.

Men ride thus only when life is the stake. A horse puts forth such speed only when terror follows close behind and causes every nerve to tighten like a wire drawn until the scratch of a finger makes it chord with a wail of despair. A pigeon could not skim this valley with such swiftness, and yet the wings of fate are broad, and long and tireless. The line is there—aye! it is gaining! Inch by inch it creeps up, and the red eyes take on a more savage gleam as the hunter cries out to his horse and opens fire from his revolvers. A wolf falls on the right— a second on the left. Does the wind cease blowing because it **meets a forest?** The fall **of one man in a** mad **mob simply** increases the determination of **the** rest.

With a **cry** so full **of** the despair that wells up from the heart of the strong man when he gives up his struggle for the life that **the** hunter almost believes a companion rides beside him, the horse staggers—recovers—plunges forward—falls to the earth. It was a glorious struggle, but he has lost.

The wings of the dark line oblique to the center—there is a confused heap or snarling, **fighting,** maddened beasts, and the line rushes forward **again.** Saddle, bridle **and** blanket are in shreds—the **horse a** skeleton. **And now the** chase is after **the hunter.** He has half **a** mile the start, and as he runs the **veins** stand **out,** the muscles tighten, and he wonders at his **own speed.** Behind him are the gaunt bodies and **the** tireless legs. Closer, closer, and now he is going to face fate as a brave man should. He has halted. In an instant, a circle is formed about him—a circle of red eyes, foaming mouths and yellow fangs, which are to meet in his flesh.

There is an interval—a breathing **spell.** He looks up at the stars—out upon the night. **It** is his last hour, but **there is no** quaking—no **crying** out to the night to **send** him **aid. As the wolves** rest, a flash blinds their eyes—a second—a third—and a fourth, and **they give way before the** man they had looked **upon as their certain** prey. But it **is** only for a moment, he sees them gathering for the rush, and firing his remaining bullets among them he seizes his long

11

rifle by the barrel **and braces to meet** the shock. Even a savage would have admired the heroic fight he **made for life.** He sounds the war-cry and whirls his weapon **around him,** and wolf after wolf falls disabled. He feels **a** strange exultation over the desperate combat, and as the pack give way before his **mighty blows** a gleam of hope springs up **in** his **heart.**

It is only for a moment; then the circle narrows. Each **disabled** beast is replaced **by** three which hunger for blood. There **is** a **rush**—a swirl—and **the** cry of despair **is** drowned in the chorus of snarls as the pack fight over the feast.

*   *   *   *   *   *

The gray of morning—the sunlight of noon-day—**the stars of evening will** look down upon grinning skull **and** whitening **bones,** and the wolf will return to crunch them again. Men will not bury them. They will look down upon them as we look, read **the** story as we have read it, and ride away with a feeling that 'tis but another dark secret of **the** wonderful prairie.

WILLIAM TRIPP'S OLD MOTHER.

William was wicked.

When I pick out one man from a mining camp made up of 300 runaways, debt-jumpers, cut-throats, gamblers, horse-thieves and murderers and call him wicked, I mean for the **reader to infer that** he **was** right up and down bad.

Which was exactly the case with William Tripp.

Nobody seemed to know when or how William settled himself down in our midst. For all I know **he** was the founder of White Dog Diggings, and perhaps it was the rest of us who settled down in his midst. Be that as it may, he was there and there he remained, notwithstanding several broad hints to the effect that he would look handsome at the end of a rope.

Wicked! Well, he was that!

Such a swearer as William was! He would begin as soon as his eyes were open in the morning and keep up **a** steady fire until 10 o'clock at night. He spent more time in inventing new oaths than some of **the** men did in digging for gold. He swore by every saint ever heard of. He swore by the heavens and earth—the angels—whales—sharks—wild-cats—pirates—preachers and even pork and beans. I think his greatest anxiety was to find something new to swear by, but he found enough to make any man's flesh creep.

And he was a cheat and a liar.

There wasn't a man in camp who would believe him under oath, and no man ever played cards with him **and** escaped his knavish devices. He was quarrelsome, overbearing, hasty, and inclined to shed blood, and though shot at a dozen different times he always escaped without a scratch.

You wonder that **we didn't run him out or hang** him.

Well, somehow we always intended to, but always put it off to **a m**ore convenient date. The success **of** bouncing **a** man depends a good deal on who the man **is.** On our first gentle hint to William Tripp that **unless** he was packed up and out of camp inside of thirty minutes his anatomy would be riddled with bullets, he produced a couple **of** revolvers, backed up against **the** Red Eye Saloon, and calmly observed that he was aching for a little excitement. **I** think his actions **at** that particular time **had** something **to** do with our giving him rope, and seeking to get along with his eccentric traits of character.

"1 move," said Elder Beacon one night when we were talking about William's bad ways, "that the committee get the drop on him and then run him in-.to the hills."

Just so, but who were the committee? That was another point we could never satisfactorily deter-mine, and that was another reason why William **continued to** abide with us.

Shoot! Well, you never saw such an eye and such **nerve.** Just as far as **he could see** the bowl of a pipe in a **man's** mouth he could smash it with a bullet. Almost every hat in camp had an air-hole made by one of his bullets, **and** though I **was** prejudiced against William I had to admit that he respected men's heads in shooting at their hats. **No doubt** he would have felt real bad had his bullet carried **too low.**

RED EYE
PHOTO-ENG-CO-N-Y.

One day when a **sort of a parson** came over from Turkey Creek to wrestle with William and entreat him to turn from the wrath to come, what happened? Why, William backed off fifteen paces and cut every button off the parson's coat with bullets, and **as a** grand wind-up he made a long shot after the flying victim and left his mark on the man's ear in order to know him again.

But there came a halt in William Tripp's mad career, and it happened in a curious way. A fire in his tent one night burned up **a** lot **of** his traps, and he had to make a ride of thirty miles on Col. Cooper's old mare to replace them with new. The morning he rode out of camp was the last time we saw him, **but** we heard from a dozen different **ones just** what happened him. About twelve miles from our camp was the Overland Trail, and just where our own trail struck in was a pretty little valley with plenty of water and wood. It was a favorite camping spot with immigrants, and the day William Tripp reached it he found half a dozen wagons and as many families halted for a breathing spell.

The deviltry in William's nature bubbled over when he struck that valley and beheld such a scene of peace. Children were playing around, women were washing and mending, and the brawny men were repairing wagons and harness and whistling over their work. William drew rein and gazed upon the scene for a few minutes. Then he out with his revolver. Seated before one of the fires was an old woman with her knitting in hand and a pipe in her mouth. It **was a** long shot, but the **evil one urged** William to try **it,** and **try** it he did.

What happened ?

Something **even worse than** murder. The bullet went straight for the old woman's head and crashed **into** her brain. Then something awful followed. She **rose** to her feet, whirled around to face the **shooter,** and true as you live she seemed to look **at** him for thirty seconds **before** she **tottered** forward and shrieked **out :**

" William ! **Oh !** my son William !"

Then she pitched forward on the grass and **was** dead in a second, and the red blood oozed out and made a terrible stain on the green grass.

And William—what did he do? He was like **one** turned to stone. The woman's words plainly **reached his ears, and he** must have recognized her **face. In** the one awful moment in which he sat **gazing** at the corpse **on the** grass it must have flashed **across** him that his poor old mother had made that **long** journey with neighbors for no other purpose **than to** hunt him up—he, the boy who had left her years before and had been the subject of her nightly prayers ever since. Wicked as he was he must have felt her devotion and sacrifices.

And then ?

He sat there in his saddle, his eye fastened on his mother's corpse, and the revolver still in his hand. The situation had petrified him. While he sat thus **one** of the immigrants, who believed that the camp **was to** be attacked by a force leveled his rifle over the wheel of a wagon and sent a bullet plowing through William's heart.

Ah! well; it's years and years ago, and the twin graves in the valley have long since been trampled out of sight, and White Dog Diggings can be found no more, but the day the news of that awful tragedy came back to us we dropped spade and pick and could work no more for the day. And after a long period of silence among the men, who had instinctively gathered around Judge Desire to hear his opinion, the Judge arose and said:

"Feller citizens, the wicked don't live out half his days, and don't you forgit it!"

THE CIRCLE OF DEATH.

Take your stand here on this bluff and you can look down upon a spectacle as exciting as anything offered in the days of blood-thirsty Roman sports. Stretching away to the west is dip and hollow and broken ground for a mile. Then comes the grand prairie, sweeping clear to the north fork of the Republican before it surrenders to the hills.

Did ever human King have a grander throne? He stands on a knoll covered with rich, sweet grass, and even with the naked eye you can see the violets and blue-bells and forget-me-nots peeping between the blades. It is a throne of wild flowers.

Ten miles away are **a dozen** moving black specks. They are buffaloes. Nothing else with life in it is nearer. The King's domains are rich in food and drink, **and** the lazy sunshine tells of peace and harmony.

He stands with head elevated, and as he slowly **turns in** his tracks he sniffs the air for scent of danger. **Who** is our king? A buffalo bull—Nature's monarch **of Nature's** grand pasturage.

How came he here, alone and deprived of companionship? Men become cynics and world-haters and shake off all attempts of friendliness. So with animals. This monarch is here to pout and sulk and feel aggrieved and plan for revenge.

Ah! High above him, with every foot of ground under your eyes, **you** could **see no danger.** His **keen** scent warned **him of peril, and** a wolf breaks **cover** not **100** feet away in a manner **to** startle you. **He seemed to rise from the** very earth—not with **a bound and a yell,** but with **a** quiet coolness that **bodes evil.**

The bull lowers his head, and his eyes flash at the sight of the enemy who has come **to** disturb **his** reveries. Compare their size and strength, and you laugh at the **idea** of a wolf bringing **harm** to a buffalo. One blow **from a** hoof—one toss **from** the horns— and the wolf would lie crushed **and** dead.

Pooh! 'Tis **an** enemy not worth a second glance! The wolf may **look** with longing eyes, and lick his chops for taste of blood, but he is wasting time. **In** that grove to the left a party of Indians camped **last** night. He had best shamble across the broken **ground** and hunt for bones and scraps.

What! another! **As** the quail rises from **cover,** so that second wolf suddenly shows himself above the **grass.** **You** cannot say that the beasts even suspect each other's presence. They are fifty feet apart, and both sit and stare straight at the monarch of the plains. The bull gives his head a toss as he sights the second arrival. Wolves hunt in pairs. Here is the pair. Nothing strange in that.

Yes, rub your eyes to see if they are clear, **and** you will find they haven't deceived you. Up pops a third, fourth, fifth and sixth wolfish head, followed by a body which is ever gaunt and lean—ever **the** synonym of hunger. One wolf created nothing **beyond** momentary surprise; the pair bred a feeling **of** contempt; the six of them may bring peril.

And so the monarch evidently reasons. He paws **the** ground, shakes his head, and that low bellow expresses anxiety as well as defiance. He could wheel and rush away, and in an hour he could be feeding with the herd. But there are pride and obstinacy and jealousy to be consulted. No deputation **has** come from the herd to coax and reason with him, **and** he will do battle for his life rather than give in. **It** is both manlike and brute-like.

What! Have the six multiplied so fast? Just a moment ago **we saw** only the half dozen; now there are ten—twelve—sixteen—they are rising from the earth all around him! The bull turns a if on a pivot. Wolves to the north—the east—the south—the west. Tht circle is complete. Watch him!

When a man must die in the presence of his enemies let him die like a warrior. The monarch knows what this gathering means. He sees the lolling tongues, and hears the gnashing of teeth. There is no help for him. He must die like a craven or prove his courage.

See the head go up! Hear the roar of defiance! Is there anything craven in that attitude?

The wolves have been sitting as quiet as so many blocks of stones placed on the grass. That roar of defiance put life into them, and they move nearer.

Curious pantomime! A grand old buffalo turning slowly 'round and 'round in his tracks to eye each separte wolf and watch every motion. A score and a half score of gaunt, grim, waiting beasts— every eye fixed upon a common center—every fang sharpened for a feast.

Swish—swirl—rush!

The circle closes in at the signal, and for fifteen seconds the eye is confused. It appears as if some one hidden in the grass was tossing and waving strips of gray and white cloth. The roars of the bull are almost drowned in the yelps and growls and howls of the assailants.

Good! There is game there! The monarch has used his horns and hoofs to such good purpose that the circle has opened away from him. Legs and flanks and shoulders have been bitten, teeth have drawn blood where a bullet would hardly penetrate, but he is not disarmed. Under his feet are two dead wolves, two more limp around outside the circle.

Um-m-m-m! Paw! Toss! Come again if you dare!

There is the rush, the swirl, the strange spectacle of gray-white bundles jumping over each other and the circle falls back again to breathe.

Ho, ho! There are long tufts of hair on the grass, more dead wolves, spots of blood. The bull shakes his head and seems weak on his legs. A spyglass would show you blood trickling down from a score of savage bites while he barely touches the grass with one hind foot. There is a low bellow, and something in it smacks of fear. Bah! If you must die why not prove—— !"

That's good! That is a roar of defiance, grandly loud and deep, and the monarch gathers himself and makes a rush. He has turned assailant. With lowered head and blazing eyes he rushes at one spot in the circle, and a gray-white body rises high in air, to come down without life.

There is such a circling and swirling now that you can see nothing but the mass—now and then breaking away for a second, to reveal the bull fighting for his life.

It is over? He is down and his blood is smearing the grim jaws of the wolves as they tear at the hot flesh. Ah, well! but there was game and nerve and true grit, and his bones deserve burial at the hands of man.

WHAT CLOCK JONES DID.

THAT winter we were in camp on Panter Creek was one never to be forgotten, even by a miner who had blasted rocks in the hills and worked knee-deep in the cold waters of the valleys. No one was making a fair living, to say nothing of adding to the store which was to some day carry the possessor back to the States and to wife and children.

It was not enough that times were hard, the weather bad and a good share of the men sick, but the blacklegs came down from Thunder Bend and up from Aunt Sally's Town and made themselves quite at home among us. They were well stocked with whisky and gambling devices, and more than one of our men who had dug and delved for months to get a few dollars ahead saw it pass into the hands of these hyenas.

When Richard Smith lost his dust and raised a kick one of the gamblers put a knife into him to settle the argument. That action stirred up the town, and in the row that followed four or five men were killed and as many more wounded. After this affair the town was pretty quiet for a fortnight, and then occurred the incident I set out to relate.

One of the best-natured men in camp was a man from Connecticut, generally known by the name of Clock Jones. Whan he left 'Frisco for the diggings he carried with him an old-fashioned family clock, and for a year or two he and the clock were " pards " and traveled in company and were never out of sight of each other. In this way he came to be known by the front name of "Clock," and if the title did not please him no one ever heard him object to it.

I repeat that he was one of the best-natured men in camp. He was never discouraged, never out of sorts, and had never been known to have a row with anyone. He had money saved up to return home to his dear ones, and was only waiting for spring to open to take his departure.

At some time in the past Clock Jones had been a drunkard. Perhaps the tears and prayers of a loving wife had wrought his rescue. He had braced against the awful vice, and none of us had ever known him to taste the stuff.

Well, it might have been curiosity that one day led the man to enter the shanty of the worst black-leg of all. If not that, then he was drawn there, as Fate has drawn her victims here and there before. He was a man who would not touch cards, and, as I said before, we had never seen him taste liquor. And yet within half an hour after he had entered that den he was whooping, drunk and being plucked of his money. Several of his friends made efforts to get him out of the clutches of the blacklegs, but their kind words were answered by threats and curses. The man had changed from a quiet, God-fearing miner to a howling, reckless, brawling demon in thirty minutes. One sip of whisky had created a craving for a drink and dram had followed dram with frightful avidity.

We couldn't let him go on that way, and finally a miner named Williams was prevailed upon to make another effort. We selected this man because at home he was a neighbor of Jones, and because he, too, had saved up a snug little sum and would go home in the spring. The two men, after a hard day's work, had sat together by the cheerful fire of evening and anticipated their return home. They had planned how they would reach home in the evening, still wearing their old clothes and long beards and rough looks, and after an absence of seven years no one would know them as they walked the streets of the village. They would quietly approach their own homes, and their knock would be answered by the wife who had waited and hoped and lived by hoping. He would speak to her as a stranger, and he would be on the point of turning away when something in voice or gesture would tell her that the long-gone husband was home at last.

So they had planned, and neither had been ashamed of the tears which welled up to his eyes at the recollections of home.

We sought out Williams and entreated him to interfere to save his friend, and he walked straight to the gambler's cabin. Jones had lost every dollar of his money and was fighting drunk.

"Come, Clock, come away," coaxed Williams.

"I won't! I want more whisky and a chance to win my money back!" shouted Jones.

"For your wife's sake, come away," entreated Williams.

" I tell you I won't, **and if you don't go away I'll kill** you !" yelled Jones as he flourished **his shooter** around.

Williams walked over and laid his hand **on his** friend's shoulder and whispered :

" Come, **old** neighbor, remember wife **and** children !"

" D——n wife **and children** and you, too !" was the fierce exclamation from **the** maddened man, and with that he fired to kill.

The bullet did not kill. **Indeed, it did not hit** Williams at all, but the flame **of the powder blinded** him in a flash and forever. He carried his hands **to** his face, stepped back a pace or two, and I **can never** forget how his voice went to every heart **as he cried out :**

" Oh ! man, you have **blinded** me, and I **shall** never see wife and children again !"

The demon fled from Clock Jones' heart as that wail reached it. In a moment he was pale as death and as sober as at any hour in his life. Slowly, as **the** darkness **of** his brain was lighted up by the return of reason, he comprehended what he had **done.** He looked from face to face and saw the horror resting on each countenance. Then he took **poor** Williams' hands down from his face, kissed him **on** his cheek, and stepped back and blew his own brains out before **a** hand could be raised to prevent.

HANGING THE WRONG MAN.

You see, William Bovers was as much to blame as any of us, and being he was the man who was hung, he ought to have entered into particulars to a further extent than he did.

I shall always blame him that he didn't.

William was placid. I knew him for three years, and only three times did I know of his countenance undergoing a change for even a second.

Once he met a grizzly face to face, and that placid expression gave way to a look of surprise and interest. He was pursued on another occasion by twenty-four Indians, and his countenance expressed homesickness. The third change is what I am going to tell you about.

There has been a good deal of robbing and killing around the camp that summer, and somehow it had been impossible to lay a hand on one of the perpetrators. The men had become roiled and desperate, and it was generally understood that the first offender who fell into our clutches would step off the head of a barrel to be brought up suddenly by a rope and a limb.

One day when some of the boys were returning from Pot-Luck Creek with flour and pork, they came upon the placid William Bovers in a bad situation. He was bending over the body of a man named Powers, who had been settled by the thrust of a bowie, and his hands were bloody.

The placid William was **nabbed.**

What did he do? Nothing at all.

What did he say? Why, **when** the **boys** laid hands on him he quietly remarked that he discovered the body only **five minutes** before, and was inspecting it in hopes to discover signs of life.

Too **thin.**

And too placid to fit that crowd.

The camp didn't waste any **valuable time over William's** case. Within the hour **a court was convened,** William was arraigned, and the dead body was placed in sight of all. Circumstances were against the **prisoner,** but there were some things we forgot. William had been a quiet, honest, civil resident of Diamond **Gulch.** He had never been known to carry a bowie-**knife.** He had been down the trail to wash some shirts, and had discovered the body on his return. He scarcely knew the murdered man by sight, and could therefore **have had** no grudge against him. The victim had little **or no** money, while the accused had the biggest pile of any man in camp.

But placid William should have kicked.

Which he didn't do worth **a** cent. He pleaded **not** guilty in a careless, indifferent manner, as if the result was of no particular consequence to him. He told about going to wash his shirts, and of the finding of the body, but there was nothing anxious about him.

"If you believe me let me go; if you don't believe me bring on the rope!"

That was **the** sum and **substance of** his defense **and it was bad** for William.

When it was too late we saw where he could have proved his record clear if he had tried to, but we had sent him to answer before the highest court of all.

Well, the court could scarcely fail to convict under the circumstances, and in less than an hour it became the painful duty of the judge to arise and remark :

" William, you have been found guilty of murder. Does it make any great difference to you whether you are hung this afternoon or to-morrow ? Weather's liable to change, you know, and we may not have such an arternoon again for a week."

The placid William replied that he would be ready in half an hour, and he was.

He went to his shanty, accompanied by Col. Smith, and when he had disposed of his property and written a letter to friends in the East, he walked coolly to the gallows-tree, mounted the barrel, and never winked an eye when the noose was slipped over his head.

Then came a painful pause.

William was about to be launched inte the great unknown.

It is a serious thing to kick a barrel from under the feet of a fellow man and let a rope catch and choke him to death. We felt it so, and when the pause came we could hear each other's hard breathing.

" William Bovers !" solemnly remarked the judge, " you are about to hang !"

" Yes," calmly replied the prisoner.

" And **now** once more **I ask you if you are guilty**
of the awful crime ?"

" No," was the equally calm **reply.**

But he had been tried, convicted **and sentenced,**
and the **sentence must be** carried **out. It was** when
the man **advanced to** pull **away** the barrel that William's **countenance lost** its placidity. **For** five seconds he seemed a stranger **to us** all. A white shadow
crossed his face, a look **of fear** crept into his eyes
and his jaw fell.

Then placid William **was himself again.** He
braced right up, shut his **teeth** hard and **he died with**
a countenance as unreadable **as a stone.**

A week afterward a **robber** who **was** fired on **and**
fatally wounded confessed that he was guilty of **the**
murder for which William Bovers had been hung.
That was **a** nice **mess** for us, and there were many
solemn faces as we gathered around the judge and
asked him **what** could be done about it.

" Wall, **I** reckon we'd better have an inquest, if
thar' be **no** objections," was the reply, and we had
one.

We viewed the **rope,** the barrel, the tree and the
grave, and the verdict was :

" Hung the wrong man and sorry for it."

But placid William was half to blame. He should
have seriously **objected to** being hung.

DEAD IN THE GULCH.

A GULCH dividing two foot-hills. It is lonely enough for a canyon, and rugged enough for a ravine, but it is a gulch. It dips here—rises there—turns to the right and left in an erratic way, and one who picks his path through the place must feel the solemn stillness chill his very soul.

Look there! Just where the gulch widens a bit, as if to expand its lungs, a great cinnamon bear is taking his afternoon nap in front of his den. Men read of the fierceness of the grizzly and forget the terrible hug, the sharp claws and the awful teeth of the cinnamon. Look at that paw covering his nose! The claws are iron hooks with points like needles; the paw is a mass of meat and muscle ten times as hard as the fist of a pugilist, and more dangerous than the kick of a horse. That leg, almost as large as the limb of a strong man in his prime, has muscles which never tire, and a bone which would stand a blow from a sledge-hammer. Better open the throttle of a locomotive and let the mighty machine rush away than to arouse this sleeping bear to anger!

Hark!

The cinnamon opens his eyes. The reports of rifles and the yells of Indians come to him from down the gulch where the immigrant trail crosses. These are no new sounds to his ears, but as he drops his jaws and lifts his head he catches something less familiar. It is the frightened cries of a child—

shouts of terror in which there is a mingling of sobs of grief. Above these cries come the shouts of the red-men, and the bear utters a low growl as he realizes that he may be disturbed.

Patter! Patter! Patter!

It is the footsteps of some one in flight—some one coming up the gulch. A still deeper growl, a snort of astonishment, and a boy eight or nine years old, bare-headed, white-faced, and eyes full of terror comes running for his life. Behind him is an Indian warrior with tomahawk ready to strike. In the brief but terrible struggle around the wagon this child crept away, and terror lent him wings to fly.

In another moment the warrior will be within striking distance. Pity? Look into his bronzed face, daubed here and there with war paint, and find trace of pity or mercy! He will not even make the child a prisoner. A scalp is a trophy, whether from the head of an adult or a babe. Curious that the boy should hold him such a race, when fright and horror are pulling at the muscles to weaken them; he strains every nerve and heads straight up the dark and rugged gulch as if the lonely shadows would wrap him in a mantle of safety.

A brown body suddenly rises up before the boy, and there is a growl and a roar in his very face. He throws up his arms with a shriek and falls upon the rocky path, and the brute leaps over him to face the pursuing warrior.

Strange tableau!

They are not ten feet apart. The cinnamon sits

up and stretches **out one** fore-leg **and** then the other, as if making **ready** to box, and his lips part to reveal teeth almost **as sharp as** the warrior's tomahawk.

The Sioux stands with one **leg** thrown forward **and his** hatched **half** raised, and he looks straight **into** the eyes of the foe barring his path.

Tomahawk *versus* **teeth** !

Hunting-knife *versus* claws !

The grasp of an athlete *versus* the **hug** of a cinnamon !

The boy rises to his knees and creeps to the side of the gulch opposite the den, and with **his** back to **the** rocks he becomes a spectator of the tableau.

One ! There is a long growl from the bear. He **is** looking into **the eyes** of the Indian, **and** he sees defiance written there.

Two ! **The** warrior's clutch tightens **over the** handle of his tomahawk. He sees the wicked claws working and he knows what is coming.

Three ! A roar—a yell—a rush, and two bodies **weave to** and fro in the gloom—wrestle from side to **side, and the** cinnamon is victor. **It** is well for the boy. **Better be in the** power of the bear than the warrior. **The** cinnamon bends over his conquered enemy with growls and sniffs, and then slowly turns and approaches the boy.

The child does **not** move. **He** lives and breathes and sees and hears, but the acme of terror has killed **all** muscular action. **The** bear comes close to him—smells of his feet—sniffs **at** his breast—breathes into his face, but he neither draws back nor cries out.

His great blue eyes ask for **pity, and the cinnamon** turns back to the body of **the dead.**

Craunch! Those terrible teeth seized an out-stretched arm and crushed the bones as if they **had** been pipe-stems.

Gurgle! The severed arteries and mangled veins **pour forth their hot** store **of** blood, **but** it is not wasted. The cinnamon is thirsty. **Here is** something better than the cold spring water of the foot-hills.

Rend and tear! The feast has begun. **The** boy closes his eyes, but he cannot prevent those horrible sounds from filling his ears.

The sun was not two hours high when **he fled** from the wagon. The **feast** is not ended when **dark** shadows begin **to** troop up and down **the** gulch—**now halting** beside the boy, now running swiftly up **and** down—by-and-by gathering in such force as to **welcome** night.

The boy shivers and his blood seems to stand still. He can no longer see the cinnamon at his banquet, and the craunching and tearing and gurgling have almost ceased.

What now!

Now comes the silver moon of a summer's night, gloriously bright and full of peaceful rest. Up—up—**and** now its bright rays fall into the gulch and pour streams of soft white light over the rugged rocks. **U**p—up—and now the rays fall upon the poor little figure braced against the wall of stone.

Here comes the cinnamon! His banquet is finished. Pat! pat! pat! echoes his footsteps as he shuffles along. **There** is no growling—no warning of anger **as** he comes. He halts before **the boy,** and **the** summer moon throws her full light down **into** the gulch to whiten a pale face until its ghostly pallor **makes it** terribly distinct. The cinnamon touches that white face with his nose. **There is** no movement **in** response.

Now the shaggy form stretches and yawns, and presently the great beast lies down at the boy's feet and closes his eyes in sleep.

Adown the gulch is a heap of bones and bloody fragments. Here sleeps the victor. Pressed close to the flinty wall is the form of the child—asleep. No! Dead!

KING AGAINST KING.

From this grove of cotton-woods sheltering the **spring** across to that peninsula of thicket running out **from the forest in a** clear space of ten miles. Call it a valley and you will not be far wrong. Write that it is almost as level as a floor, and covered with rich green grass, and you will give the **reader** a true picture.

The grove contains not over a **dozen** trees, and in the center a spring bubbles up and throws off a **stream** which steals away through grass and weeds **and** is finally soaked **up** by the parched soil. In the spring-time the stream becomes a rivulet and runs its course for fifty miles. In the hot summer **the thirsty** wolf must cool his tongue at the **spring or cross to** the forest and lap at the creek.

Skeletons? Yes. Two—three—five. Not **of** men, but **of large** animals. Three of them rest on the ground **almost** within shade of the trees; the other **two are** out in **the** sunshine, and the grass is shooting up between **the** bleaching ribs and fast concealing the hideous skulls. You look about expecting to see the rusting iron-work of an immigrant's wagon, and there is a sudden fear that the grass may be hiding the story of a terrible **butchery.**

Look out! There is a gurgle—a growl—a **warning of** danger which sends the chills creeping over **you,** and from the high grass springing up around **the skeleton** furthest away a head is lifted into view. It is **the** head of the American lion—the puma of the plains! Its glassy eyes are watching you—its yellow fangs work as if they were tearing your flesh! Is he crouching for a spring? Has he been waiting and watching for this last half hour?

Now there is a whine **of** hunger and pain, and as you watch for that horrible head to be raised again a tawny form creeps out of **its** hiding-place and pulls itself out upon the short grass and into the full glare of the sunshine. So-ho! The king is a cripple! He is dragging **a** shoulder and leg after him as he moves, and he is willing to vacate without **a** fight.

Now you have the mystery. The key is five miles up the valley, where you see that band of wild horses coming down at a round trot. The king has

12

had a fat thing of **it.** The grove was his palace. That big cotton-wood with his claw marks showing by the hundred **was** his throne. The wild horses came here to drink, and his royal highness has feasted **as** becomes a king. A fat horse on **the** grass—a spring at his heels—no one to molest him at his meals or during his slumbers—who wouldn't be a nabob?

These skeletons **are** clean-picked. That proves much. **It was weeks ago that the** last horse was borne to the ground in a terrific struggle for life. He did not save himself, but he inflicted such damage that his royal highness has been a plebeian cripple ever since. Pain and hunger have made him whine and beg, and the coyotes have dared to invade his realm and gnaw at the bones within a hundred feet of **his bed. In** his strength they feared and respected him ; in his distress they mock him and exhibit contempt.

The palace of **his** royal highness had been invaded, and he **must go.** He who has never shown **mercy can expect** none. The forest will give him a **hiding** place, **if** not food and drink, and he will drag **himself** across that weary stretch of grass to secure a cover. He moves slowly. Every foot of progress gives him pain, and at every ten feet he pauses and looks back and seems to wonder **if** it would not be **more** in keeping with his record to limp back and **have** it out with **the** invader.

Let him alone and watch the horses. The whole **band** have halted. Every head is up, **every nostril**

is sniffing the air, and every eye is watching the crippled king as he slowly increases his distance from shelter. He is growling and complaining, and has eyes only for you. Now he hobbles on three legs, uttering short barks—now he draws himself along on his belly and growls as if he had a victim within reach of his fangs.

Watch the horses! They stand stock still, every head thrust out and every eye marking off the distance between the crippled king and the grove. In a quarter of an hour there is half a mile of open ground between the first cotton-wood and the spot where the fugitive has halted for a long look backwards. He has turned his face towards the forest, when there is a sudden movement among the horses.

The band divides. A portion rush to the right to cut off retreat to the grove—the rest bear straight down upon the king. He hears the rush of feet—he raises his head for one swift glance, and then there is a roar of mingled defiance and despair.

His royal highness is cornered, his escape cut off. He makes a dozen bounds forward, forgetting for the instant his broken shoulder, and then he halts and faces the rush, whining, begging, growling—a coward in the face of danger. A coward? No! He weakened in the first moment of despair, but now his courage returns and he roars defiance. If he must die, it shall be the death of a king.

Watch the horses! They have formed a circle about him and are closing in—not with a rush, but slowly and coquettishly—pawing at the earth—snorting in alarm—tossing their heads **to distract his at-**tention. But for his hurt the king would ride away **upon** one **of their backs.** He settles down in the grass—his eyes glare—his tail moves nervously—his **claws dig into** the sod—look out for him !

The circle is not fifty feet from him when the advance suddenly **ceases,** and a stout, rangy stallion whose muscles stand out in ridges and whose eyes are brighter than stars, steps out alone. He is the king of the wild horse band. It is king against king. He looks straight into the **eyes** of the crouching beast as he advances, and every nerve and muscle is playing with excitement. Step ! step ! step ! Look out ! That growl means blood ! The eyes of the crippled king take on a greener glare—the claws dig deeper—there he springs !

Pity **him** a little. **He was** game, but he was crippled. His bound **brought a** shriek of pain to mingle with his roar for vengeance, and ere he could **recover** from the false spring there was a whirl—a **flash,** and the heels of the wild horse king sent him rolling over and over on the grass. There was a rush— **wild** neighs—howls of despair—and as the grand old king of the prairie gallops away at the head of his band the king of the grove lies trampled and bruised and dead on the grass.

BURYING THE BABY.

I REMEMBER that the far-away reports of rifles roused us from sleep in the gray of dawn, and as we stood on our feet and listened more intently, we could now and then catch the echoes of an infernal war-whoop.

There were twenty of us, miners all, and we were in the foot-hills of the Rockies, not more than half a mile from the great Overland Trail.

"Boys, them sounds means an Injun attack and a butchery," whispered our leader, as we listened ; and without another word we picked up our traps and headed for the spot at a half run.

Two immigrant families, farmers from Indiana, who had started for the land of gold, and had separated from the train from whim or accident, had encamped in a bit of green valley beside the trail. There were thirteen souls of them, and one might wonder if the bravest among them did not shudder with fear as the night crept down and the howl of the wolf came from the Rocky hills.

The men had seen their danger, and both had set out to act as sentinels through the long night. Hour after hour had passed away without an alarm, and just as dawn was breaking the merciless savages, creeping along like snakes, had found one of the sentinels asleep. A thrust from a knife finished him so quickly that he did not even throw up his arms. Perhaps he uttered a single cry, or a groan and alarmed the other, for the second one was shot while running toward the wagons.

Then, with both men dead, came the rush upon the women and children. Only fiends could do such work as was done there, and when we came to look at it the strongest men in the party grew white and faint. Every head but one was scalped, and no doubt the scalps had been taken while the victims lived. The bodies were hacked and gashed—hands and arms severed, brains beaten out—children flung into the camp-fire, and the spectacle was one to live in memory when all else had been forgotten.

The fiends had finished their work of butchery before we were near enough to open fire, and it was poor consolation to save the wagons. While all the bodies were yet warm, life had departed from each and every one. We were collecting them in a heap, to make ready for burial, when a sudden wail startled everybody.

"Ow—ow—ow—ow!" came the sound, and each man looked in the air above and on the ground below.

"That 'ere noise purceeds from a baby, or I'm not the father of thirteen children back in Ohio!" exclaimed Jackson as he made for the nearest wagon.

He was right. Down beside a chest, almost smothered under bed quilts, was a year-old boy baby, but alas! when he was handed out we found that he had been fatally wounded by a bullet. Jackson sat down on the grass and chirped to him and rocked him to and fro while the rest of us looked on in wonder and doubt, but in a quarter of an hour the baby was dead. It had **gone to sleep** the night before in his mother's arms, a battered old rattle-box clutched fast in his tiny hand, and he never let go of it. There it was in his hand as death stiffened his fingers around it.

Well, there **was a** general breaking down when we saw that the little **one was** going. He **threw** up his hands, gasped **once or** twice, and **then** settled back with such a smile on his face as babies wear **when** their dreams **are sweet.** Old Jackson **was crying** like a child, and some of **the men** hid from **each** other behind **the** wagons. **It was** a long time before the old man arose, laid the little body down among the prairie flowers, **and** huskily whispered:

" We'll bury him by hisself. **One** of them bodies out there was his mother, but as we can't tell which **from** which **we'll** make no mistake."

There was **one** large grave for the mutilated re- **mains,** and when the earth had been pressed down above them **and** rocks rolled down to prevent the work of the wolves, we went to the center of the dell and there, under a lone pine, we hollowed out a resting-place for baby. When all was ready Jackson took the body up in his arms, dropped his hat on the grass, and looked around, and said :

" Hats off, men ! We are nearer seein' angels this mornin' than any of us will ever come agin !"

Slowly—tenderly—grievingly the little form was **laid** away, and it was Jackson's coat that came off his back **to** cover it before the earth was filled in. Every single man in our band **took** the shovel by turns to fill in **and** round up the grave and protect it, and before **we** went away there was a head-board to mark the spot, and on the board a **knife had en-**graved the single **word:** " BABY "'

<hr>

THE DOCTOR **IN** CAMP.

You may wonder how the miners got along without a doctor in camp, for there indeed times enough when the services of a skillful physician were in demand. That winter we put in at Calico Flats there was somebody **on** the sick list all the time, and there were days when we had three or patients **in hospital at once.**

As to medicines, **our mainstay** was **a** hot sweat. When a man began **to dump** around **we** didn't **lose time** by feeling of his pulse or looking at his tongue. Three or four stones were put into the fire to heat, blankets borrowed for the occasion, and when we got steam on, the knots and twists and kinks in that chap's case had to unravel. He'd come out as long and flat and thin and white as you please, and if any **one** pointed a finger at him for the next week he'd **cry** like a baby.

Next to a sweat we had decoctions of herbs, **barks** and roots, and once or twice we tried **the earth** cure. On one occasion **when a** red-headed miner from Ohio was laid **up with a pain in the side, a**

stranger came along from White Dog Bend and said he could cure him by laying on of hands. For three long hours he smoothed away at the patient as steadily as clock work, and then there was a row. The "smoother" asserted that the cure was complete, while the patient denied that the pain was a whit easier, and, of course, we stood by our comrade and gave the stranger a tumble off a cliff twenty-eight feet high into an old snow drift eighteen feet deep.

But as I said at the start, sickness became so prevalent, and our plain remedies had so little effect, that it was finally decided to send up to Sacramento for a doctor. The idea was to have him come down and brace us all up and leave medicines and remedies, and the expense was to be borne by a shake purse.

A letter was sent to a dealer in the town, asking him to forward a doctor, and in about five days along he came. He was a young man of 24, just out of college in the East, and just landed on the slope without a dollar in his pocket, and all he brought to camp with him was a lancet, some prescription blanks and a stick of salve for making sticking-plasters.

There were four men in hospital that day, and after a bit the doctor entered to take a look at them. It happened that he came to Big Jim Smith first. Smith was threatened with inflammatory rheumatism, and was in no mood to take nonsense.

"Run out your tongue," said the Doctor, as he bent over the man.

Big Jim displayed it, but in such a begrudging

12*

way that it was plain to see that he thought it all bosh.

"Your pulse," said the Doctor, as he reached over for Jim's great paw.

"Pulse? I hain't got any," growled Jim.

"Oh, yes, you have. Here it is in your wrist. Keep still for a moment."

"Stranger," said Jim, after the doctor had dropped his hand, "d'ye mean to tell me that ye kin feel a man's wrist and tell what ails his insides?"

"Yes, in a measure."

"Excuse my not calling you a liar, but some of the boys will do it fur me afore you are an hour older."

"What are your symptoms?" asked the doctor.

"Never had any."

"But how do you feel?"

"Sick."

"How were you taken?"

"Stranger, what are ye driving at?" demanded Jim, as he sat up in bed.

"Have you got pains?"

"In course, I have! D'ye 'spose I'd be lying flat on my back here if anything less'n a ton was holding me down?"

"Do you ache?"

"Rayther!"

"Any fever?"

"Wall, I git away with a quart of cold water at a gulp."

The doctor sat and studied the case for a few minutes, and then he came over to the shanty where the committee had assembled, and said :

"Gentlemen, the case of Big Jim is a serious one. He needs a change of diet, scenery and air. My advice is that you brace him up as well as you can on chicken soup and beef tea, and then send him off for a trip to Cuba. I'll look at the other cases in the morning."

But he never did. When the boys found that he had come without even a dose of quinine, and they heard him talk about chicken soup and trips to Cuba for a man who hadn't five dollars to his name, they waited upon him in a sort of hilarious body, and at midnight he went up the trail at the rate of twelve miles an hour, with a crowd behind him aching for his ears as relics.

Next day we heated half a ton of rocks, took six or eight blankets, and gave Big Jim such a sweat that all his toe-nails shed off, and rather than be cured in the same way the other men got well.

"I did have some faith in the chap," exclaimed Jim—"just a leetle bit until he axed my symptoms. That floored me. The idea of sending 200 miles fur a doctor to walk in on ye and not be able to tell symptoms from the all-firedest back-ache a man ever had, topped off with chills galloping up and down the spine-wall. I'm only sorry that you moved the procession on him afore I was able to head it !"

SANDY OF ROARING FORK.

ONE of the real good men in our camp on Roaring Fork was J. M. Sanders. It was years afterwards before any one knew that he was anything but plain "Sandy," but if a man has a front name it is bound to come out sooner or later.

It was later when it turned out that "Sandy" was not only Sanders, but J. M. Sanders, and like as not some of his letters had "Esq." at the end of the name.

Well, Sandy was a good man—a real good man. He always had a remedy for every complaint, from chills and fever to being so homesick that the patient would have given his left arm for a sight of the old red farmhouse in the States. He was also a praying man, and on Sunday, when he didn't have too much patching and darning to do he read from the Bible and exhorted us that the road to Heaven led through trials and tribulations and over hills where a man shod with the strongest faith had to look out for his footing.

Which I may remark right here was also the belief of several others in camp, including your humble servant.

Sandy didn't play cards nor drink nor howl around with his hat on his ear and his teeth on edge, and for this reason he was despised by some and admired by others. If he had a weak point it was his too forgiving spirit. Once in a while,.when one of the men rubbed him **a little** too hard, **there was a** warning of danger in his big blue eyes, but he let **a** half-drunken miner spit in his face one day without betraying the least show of anger.

The same was talked **over** in camp, and we were divided as to whether it was fear of the miner's fist or pity for his befuddled condition which prevented **a** knock-down. However, there came a day when the old man settled the long-standing query **of** whether he had fight in him **or** no.

Two miles above us was the camp of the " Howling **Wild Cats.**" One day big Jim Stevens, standing six feet two in his boots and having a fist **as big** as a two-quart jug, got hold of some particularly good whisky, and after licking the best man in his own camp he came down to give us a whirl. Some of our men, probably out of mere deviltry, told Jim that Sandy was our fighting man and the hardest hitter west of the Nebraska prairies.

What did big Jim do but hunt up our parson and give him to understand that the awfulest, bloodiest, fiercest and most desperate struggle ever known on the face of this globe was about to take place.

" **James** Stevens, you go home," replied Sandy.

" Sandy, **I'm** going to lick you till you can't **beller !**" chuckled Jim.

" Go away ! I've nothing against you," warned the parson.

" Sandy, prepare to be driven head first into the sile !" yelled Jim, and with that he spit on his hands and turned on a full head of steam.

We were all there, you know, but there was a sort of understood law or custom in the mining camps that a fight must be fought out without a third party chipping in. And besides, some of us had a sneaking suspicion that Sandy would astonish the country if cornered and compelled to use his muscle.

Big Jim rushed in like a locomotive going for a spring lamb, but **he** didn't get there. When he **came** within striking distance Sandy shot out and keeled him **over in** such style that some one called for three cheers. Jim got up slowly, made another rush, and the result was the same. He wouldn't have tried it again but for the jeers and taunts of the men. The third round was a beautiful affair. **Jim** advanced slowly, hands up, prize ring fashion, and for **a minute** we weakened a bit on our man. Foot to foot they eyed each other, and sparred for an opening. Then, like a streak of greased lightning, Sandy shot out with his left and Jim went **down** like a log and had enough.

Then who washed the blood from his face? The parson.

Who brushed his clothes and brought him a drink? The parson.

Who lifted him up and walked **him** away, speaking as kindly as a woman? The parson.

Yes, it was, and it was the same parson who walked to his camp with him, and on the way up the **trail** sowed such good seed that Big Jim changed from a drunken, brawling good-for-nothing to a sober, industrious miner; and when **he** struck a " pocket "

PHOTO-I. ENG CO NY

and had the wherewithal to **return home, the parson**
was the first to congratulate him **and the last to**
shake his hand **and** bid him God-speed.

"Which I desire to explain," **observed our camp**
shoemaker, **one** day some months after the fight,
"some men can be coaxed or **reasoned** into being
good, and some others **never** begin to mend their
ways until after the third knock-down."

"LITTLE FORTY-TWO."

WELL, now, but weren't we surprised!   You see,
we had encountered such a run of hard luck up at
Point Despair that one morning we packed up bag
and baggage **to the** last man and set off down the
trail in search of a show for something better.   I
well remember **it was a** hot July day, and there was
exactly forty-one of us.

Seven miles down the trail we came to what was
then called Uncle Joe's Road, and right at the inter-
section was where the surprise hit us.   An immigrant family had strayed **from** the main party for
some reason which we never ascertained, and right
at the crossing they had **been** attacked by Indians.
The wagon broke down there, and there the pioneer
made his defense and fired his last **shot.**   That he
was game we needed no other proof than that visible
to our eyes.   Three great blood-spots showed where

three savages had fallen before they charged, and when they rushed in on him he had killed or disbled **three** more with his revolver.

The family had consisted of five persons, and there **they all** lay—hacked, cut, shot, and a horrible spectacle under that bright sun and birds singing **around** us. It was a horrible heap which we surrounded, and for a minute no one spoke. Then the astonishment and horror of the men brought forth deep and **angry exclamations, and amidst** the rumpus Uncle Ben **Turner suddenly called out :**

" Stand back !—stand back ! Here's a live young 'un !"

There was **for a** fact. Half hidden under **the torn** and blood-stained garments of it dead mother, **was a** boy about **two** years old. He had a terrible bump **on his** head, and **as** we talked it over we concluded that his mother fell from the wagon with him **in** her arms when the wheel broke down, and that **the** bump rendered **him** insensible. In the excitement **he had** been overlooked or thought dead, and **had cried himself** to sleep, to be awakened by the voices **of our** men. The attack had been made early in the morning, and it was near noon when we came upon the scene.

Well, the best we could do with the poor victims was to bury them, but didn't that boy leave us in **a** nice **fix !** There we were, forty-one gruff, growlish, rough-handed miners, and there he was, a milk face baby calling for ma and pa and shivering with terror at sight of **us.** What could we do with **him ?** We had no kisses, no pet words, no **dainties nor little** clothes. We looked from the baby to each **other** and scratched our heads, and no man knew what another man thought until finally old Uncle **Ben** called out:

"Boys, it's a token of good luck! If this 'ere what d'ye-call-it don't bring **us a** rich find then we've all forgot our homes and wives and children!"

That's all we were waiting for. Up went our hats, cheers made the rocks echo, and **the** little toddler was one of us—one of the forty-two. Graves were dug and the victims laid away, and **we made a** hunt to identify them. If the immigrant had had **any** papers with him they **had** been burnt or taken **off, and** we found nothing on the boy's clothing which gave us a clue. When we were ready **to** go he stood in the circle, screaming out as **we** coaxed **him in turn,** but when old Ben finally advanced the young cub held up his arms and nestled against his shoulder as if he had found his own true father. I believe the rest of us were a bit jealous, but we were also helpless. Ben had a kind, fatherly face, a quiet voice, and the boy had only to look into his eyes to trust him.

As to the luck, the old man was right. **Four** miles farther down the trail, the boy pointed to some flowers growing off to the right, and right there we **halted** and founded what was known for **years** as **Lost** Boy Diggings. It was the richest spot for fifty miles around, and all on account of "Little Forty-Two," as we called the youngster.

As to the boy himself, he took to old Ben in such a way that they could not be separated. He could be enticed to sit with one of us now and then, but it was plain to see that his love was elsewhere.

If Ben wanted a kiss he got a dozen, and all the gold in California wouldn't have bribed the boy off his knee. At night his arm was the child's pillow, and the slightest move of the youngster brought the old man's eyes open. You might have expected that "Little Forty-Two" would die on our hands, living as we did, but he never had a moment's sickness. Old Ben had a way of preparing nourishing dishes out of our coarse provisions, and from the clothing found with the wagon he was kept comfortably clad. Old Ben was no dress-maker, and the boy would have looked queerly dressed in the States, but as long as he was comfortable we didn't care for looks.

"Little Forty-Two" had been with us thirteen months, and was, to our figuring, a little over three years old, when some of the men who had made their stakes announced their intention of going home. Then the question arose: "Whose boy is our boy?" It was a stumper. Each man felt that he owned a share in the little chap, and each man would have been glad to take him home. We argued and discussed without avail, and old Uncle Ben sat there saying never a word, but his face as white as chalk. "Little Forty-Two" belonged to the old man in every sense, but I believe there would have been some trouble if Fate hadn't come stalking up **the rocky** trail and halted at our diggings.

This was the **way** of it. Some were packing up, some using the pick and bar, **and** down near the creek powder **was** being used to blast the ledge. **It** was about 10 o'clock **in** the morning, and a blast had been prepared and the fuse lighted, when from our retreat, full ten rods away, we suddenly saw Little Forty-Two turn the thicket and run straight for the blast. He was laughing and shouting, having been playing " tag " with Uncle Ben. We sprang up and shouted and screamed, and the boy halted within ten feet of the **blast** and waved his **cap at us.** Next instant he was hidden in the dust and smoke, and **when** we reached him some of the men sat down and covered their faces. He was dead.

Well, that wasn't the end of it. That afternoon, after old Uncle Ben had made the poor little body ready for burial, and moaned over it, and while we were digging a grave, the old man went down to the blast, placed the muzzle of **a** revolver to his heart, and was dead before the report reached us. He had lost his boy and found him again.

ABANDONED.

A BROAD prairie with blue-topped mountains fifty miles **to the** right—a column of cavalry riding by fours at **a** walk—a dozen white-topped wagons—a

rear guard—and while you are looking at the picture
you notice a slight commotion among the score of
troopers following the wagons.

What is this?

Nothing—nothing but a troop horse taken **sud-**
denly ill after days of hard riding and poor provender.
The cruel spur urges him along for a few rods further,
but **then** he stops and groans and shivers, and it is
evident that he will soon fall.   Trooper and saddle
are off in an instant, and the gallant old horse, bearing the scars of war and faithful to the **end,** falls to
the ground and seems to be struggling with death.
In five minutes the marching column has passed
almost beyond hearing, and in another five the body
of the **poor old** horse on the grass is almost hidden
from the view **of** the men in the saddle.

The wagons are not three miles away when strange
shadows begin to dance about on the grass around the
horse.   He is not dead.   The terrible pains which
racked him, caused perhaps by a poisonous weed,
have passed away, and though weak and dripping
with perspiration he feels life coming back to him.
He raises his head to look at the shadows.   How
swiftly **they flit** to **and fro!**   How curiously they cross
each other's **track!**   Shadows, and yet the **horse** sees
nothing but **grass and** flowers **and weeds** on every
side.

"Croak! Croak! Croak!

Ah! there is the clue to **the** strange shadows!
Five **hundred** feet above his head there are a score
of buzzards sailing to and fro, and the horse is on his

feet before the last hoarse note has **been uttered.** Does he realize that the buzzards saw him from afar off and called each other to the feast? If **not, why** did their direful croaks bring him to his feet, and why **does he** tremble as he gazes after the disappear-**ing column?**

"Croak! Croak! Croak!"

The tone has changed. The call betrays surprise and anger, and the birds rise a little.

The horse is moving away. His steps are **slow** and short, but his eyes are fastened on the far-away wagons. He trembles with fear as he hears the **flap** of wings above his head and sees the strange **shadows** flitting over the grass before **him, but** desperation has nerved him as it nerves the man who sees but one chance for life. His steps grow steadier and his limbs feel stronger as he moves onward, and the angry and disappointed buzzards are rising higher and higher, when the horse suddenly stops.

What is that? Off to the left and a hundred rods ahead a grey object comes creeping out of a hidden ravine and skulks through the grass. Then a second —a third—a dozen. Shadows? No! They **are** wolves!

As long as he kept moving **the** buzzards dared **not** descend, but here was a new and savage foe from which the fleetest horse could hardly escape. Now they divide to the right and left to form a circle, and the buzzards descend again and unnerve the poor **beast** with their ominous cries.

Is there a hope? Bracing himself just as a man

would to take advantage of a desperate chance, the
horse suddenly darted forward on the trail at a gallop.
To **reach** the wagon was to live on. **To** fail now was
to be dragged down **and** torn to pieces while alive.
A sharp cry from **the** buzzards—a howl from the
wolves—and the race had begun. **Brave** old troop-
horse! Every leap was a gain on the wagons—every
rod opened a new chance for life. Fear made him
forget those racking pains—terror **gave** him such
speed as he had never shown. **He was out** of the
circle. With ears laid back and head pointing straight
for the wagons, he was leaving the red-mouthed wolves
behind.   Hurrah!

No! Out from the grass—from hidden gulch or
grass-grown buffalo wallow more wolves appear, as if
stationed there and told to wait their time. They
are right ahead **of him.** With a groan of despair the
horse swerves to the right, but it is too late. The
old pains come back—great clouds of foam fly from
his mouth to stain the grass, and all of **a** sudden he
plunges forward to rise no more. Next instant there
is a struggling, fighting, yelping mass of gray covering the **spot,** and the air is rent with one long, quivering shriek **of** agony which the buzzards catch up
in wild delight.

An hour hence a trampled spot, a stain of blood
and a few bones **will** catch the red **man's eye** for an
instant as he rides **apace,** but the gorged **wolves** will
have hidden away and the buzzards be watching else-
where.

JUDGE LYNCH.

You may have seen a street riot. That is simply the outer **circles of a** whirlpool. **A shower** of brick-**bats—a** surge up and down—a dozen broken heads— **a cry** of " police !" and your crowd scatters like sheep and slinks away like curs.

A mob sets out to resist the authorities. **Nine** out of every ten men in it are cowards. They boast and brag and encourage, but they keep their **own** bodies in the background. **They** want to **see** some-one hurt, but **they know that** law will triumph, and they want to be able to prove that they **were simply** lookers-on. One brave man will walk into **a** mob **and defy** and overawe it.

*   *   *   *   *   *

A brutal outrage has been committed. It is an affair that stirs the blood of sons and brothers and brings a dangerous light to the eyes of husbands and fathers. There is no boasting or shouting. Knots of men gather here and **there,** and they speak with fierce earnestness, but in low voices. No mob surges up and down—no wild yells rend the air—no cowards furnish drink to excite young men to foolish deeds.

"Lynch him !"

It is not shouted, but spoken in whispers, or read **in** each other's eyes. Every man has obeyed the laws—every man would peril his life in aiding to en-**force** them, but there is a feeling that legal punish-ment does not always punish sufficiently.

" Lynch him !"

When men who never partake of a meal without bowing the head in prayer, whisper those words, look out ! The heart burns and thrills. For the time being law is nothing. Fathers whisper it to sons, brothers to each other, merchants to mechanics. Lips tighten and grow pale, teeth shut close, eyes flash as you never saw them before.

The knots of men swell into groups—the groups consolidate into a crowd. The leader takes his place, and instinctively the crowd realize that he is the proper person. Speeches and orations are not in order—ropes are !

See now ! Teeth shut tighter as the crowd moves. Not a man would turn back from a loaded cannon. It moves ahead, but it swirls and hisses and gurgles like a river vexed by rocks. It is the whispers—the quick answers—the pale faces—that tell you what danger lurks in the crowd. A noisy crowd can be scattered. It will fall to pieces of itself. A silent body of men will take your life if every man has to peril his own.

It is the jail. Key or no key the prisoner must come out. That crowd would have him if a score of grated doors had to be battered down. He does not plead for mercy. One look around him tells him that his life is hungered for with such intensity that prayers would be mockery. He may look up at the harvest moon and the star-studded heavens, but he sees nothing. He is dazed and awed by the grim silence of the band.

" Halt !"

No voice commands, but here is the **tree.** The whirlpool stands still for **a** moment. Faces grow **a** little whiter, but the eyes of every man show a dogged **determination** that would blaze into desperation if opposed. **The noose** is rapidly adjusted, there **is a** falling back and with a groan of terror and despair trembling on his lips the guilty wretch swings in the air. **The creak** of the limb— the calls of **a** night-bird—the deep breathing of men—are plainly heard as the body swings **to** and fro **or turns round** and round as the death-struggle goes on.

*   *   *   *   *   *

It is morning. Merchants are behind their counters, mechanics at the bench, sons **at** school. There is no sign that last night was not one of tranquillity and peace. Men speak again, women and children **laugh** as they walk abroad—the cyclone has passed. The jail doors **are** being repaired—the tree no longer holds a corpse, and **a** stranger would look upon this face and that and whisper to himself : " What good-nature I see in every line of their countenances ! They are obedient to law and enforce the best of order."

Riots are the work of demagogues and boasters. **Mobs** are created by cowards. When men turn out with shut teeth and whispered voices to take the law into their own hands, Judge Lynch has opened court **and** sentenced a man to die.

DOMESTIC SKETCHES.

THE BROKEN PANE.

T was **spring time.** The buds were **bursting** into blossom—the birds sang joyfully **as they built their** nests—the green grass **was** hiding **the ugly** scars of winter. A child's pale face peered through a broken **pane out** upon the glorious sunshine, and the **soft wind kissed** her cheeks and whispered :

"Bye and bye !"

Outside the house was life and health **and happi-ness. Inside** was sickness, sorrow **and poverty. Child though she was,** the shadows **had** settled down about **her as the** fog gathers round the **ship** which the rocks **thirst to destroy. There were children there,** but no childish **laughter. The** sunshine streamed **into** the bare rooms, **but it warmed no** hearts. It was **a poor** widow's **struggle against** that gaunt, grim shadow whose **other name is poverty.** Hunger and **cold and rags dwarf the** body, and give the face the **look of one hunted for** years by an implacable enemy, **Despair will watte** whoever dares enter the struggle,

[290]

and anxiety leaves its **mark so plainly that no one can** mistake it.

This child **of 12** had known nothing but shadows, grim, **silent,** stealthy shadows, stealing upon her young life **to rob it** of every happiness. Even as she looked **out upon the** glorious world she felt that she was **no part of** it. It **was** around her, but beyond **her reach.**

————

It was mid-summer. Every tree was a thing **of** beauty—every flower a silent tribute of praise **to the** Creator. The grass had become **a** velvet **carpet**— the blossoms were young fruit—the sun **was** sending **his** warm rays to cheer the darkest corners. **The** world was joyous under the blue skies of summer as **the** pale face again looked from the broken pane. Out in the world around her the children shouted in their glee. In the dark old house children hungered **for** bread. **The same** grim shadows were there—the same struggle for bread—the same burdens and anxieties and bitterness of heart. The child had **grown** paler, and the hunted look had chased every other expression away. Her eyes saw the trees, the flowers, the streets, the busy world and its happiness, and her ears heard the summer breeze as it softly whispered :

" Bye and bye."

What would it bring? What is the bye and bye to those hunted by hunger and striving against poverty ?

The other day when the north wind shrieked and moaned and the **snow-flakes** whirled and flew, another face appeared **at** the broken pane. It was that of a boy who could not resist the temptation to look in. On **a poorer bed** than he had ever seen—in a room **so cold and** bare and cheerless that he shivered as he **looked—lay** the corpse of the child who had looked **out upon** the spring **and the summer.** The snow-flakes which strayed **in** at **the broken pane were no** whiter than her face. There was no **smile to cloak** its coldness, but around the mouth were lines to melt the heart. It was as if the dead were whispering: "Snow and poverty and despair have beclouded and cut short a young life. Have pity!"

The soft winds had whispered: " Bye and bye!" It had come. **In** life the tears in that boy's eyes would have lighted her sorrows **and** made her heart braver. They had come too late.

A STRANGE BATTLE.

Nothing but the wail of a child—a child two years old—asleep on **the** bed, and yet it broke out so suddenly, and **it** had such **a** long-drawn quaver in it that the mother started up with a scream.

A stove, table, bed, two or three chairs—a home **in which** a weak **woman** was battling with sickness and poverty, only asking for **the** bare necessaries of life, and yet finding the battle going **against her** more and more as the days passed on. On this night there was not a mouthful in that house to eat. **A** hungry mouse could not have picked up crust or crumb. **The** last bit of bread had been given to the child **at** dusk, and now as it wailed out the mother **clasped her** hands and gasped:

"If he awakes and cries for bread—what then?"

Well! What then? It was only a square to the river with its cold, dark current. She could say to the angels in Heaven: "It was either that or starvation," and they would not judge her too harshly.

As she sat there with beating heart and anxious fears, the dim light making queer shadows dance about the room, a low, fierce growl made her heart stand still. The door had not swung open, and yet a gaunt wolf had found its way into the room. It stood there with its blood-shot eyes looking into hers —its red tongue lolling from its mouth and flecks of foam falling to the floor. Its shaggy fur was stained and discolored—its yellow fangs clashing and grinding—a spectacle to have made a hunter's heart beat like a caged bird.

It was the Wolf of Starvation—the fierce brute which never tires—which is ever on the hunt for the helpless and weak—which growls with delight as the wails of hunger and despair reach its ears. It had scented its prey from afar, and its fangs were sharpened to rend, and tear and devour.

For a moment the mother's heart stood still and

she gasped **for breath. Then, as she** realized **the** horror **of the** situation, she rose **up and** cried **out :**

" **You have** come to drink the blood of **my child : I'll fight you to** the death !"

She had no weapon but **the thin hands which had toiled and** ached for long years—no hopes but those **born of a** mother's love and affection for her offspring, **but she** sprung at the gaunt, strong beast and the battle began. **Despair gave her** strength—love steeled her heart. **The** beast **retreated** with fierce growls as she sprang forward to clutch him, and as she stood in the center of the room she **became a** magnet round which he circled.

Now he slowly circles to the right, his red eyes watching her bony fingers, as they nervously work, **and every hair** on his **back** standing up in anger. She **turns** slowly, always looking **straight** into **his** eyes—ready to clutch at his throat **when** he springs. Now he halts and glares **at** her, growling, sniffing— flinging the flecks of foam to the right and left and grinding those horrible fangs. Now he circles to the left—cringing, skulking, crawling like **a serpent** —**watching to** find her off her guard.

The **child is** aroused **by** the patter of the beast's feet and the labored breathing of the mother, and he sits up a silent witness **of the scene. His** face is whiter than snow—his eyes are **big** with terror—his heart chokes him.

Now the beast springs. With a cry of rage and triumph he springs full at his prey, and the woman's hands clutch his throat. They weave **to and** fro.

They stagger this way and that. His yellow fangs graze her flesh and draw blood, and the foam-flecks are stained crimson. The child looks on with a fascination born of horror. He hears the clash of teeth as the jaws meet—he notes the fury of the vengeful eyes—his young heart seems to be stabbed at the sight of the mother's grim despair.

Such a battle! Such a prize if the gaunt, hungry beast succeeds—such a victory if the strength of a fainting, despairing woman holds out to save the life of her child. With a cry to heaven for aid she calls up all her strength for one great effort and hurls the beast across the room. He is back again in a moment, and now he circles to the right—now to the left—now——!"

A step on the stairs! The beast halts in his circling, his ears work nervously, and as the steps come nearer his growl changes to a whine and he slinks into the darkness—away into space. The door is thrown open and Charity steps within, food in her basket and kind words upon her lips.

The battle is ended.

ADOPTING GRANDPA.

An old man—not ragged, but clad in old and faded and time-worn garments, and moving with feeble steps and weary air—sat down under a tree on John R. street the other day to rest a bit. Three or four children were playing in the yard at his back, and directly a mite of a girl looked through the fence and asked:

"Would you hurt a little girl?"

"Bless me, no!" he replied. "Why, I'd even step aside to pass a bug or a worm! No, child, I wouldn't hurt a hair of your head for all the money in the world."

"Are you anybody's grandpa?" she inquired as the other children crowded up.

"No—not now, child. There was a time—dear me! but it hurts my old heart to remember it—when children called me grandpa. It was years ago—years and years, but I can almost hear their voices yet."

" Be you crying?"

"N-no. The tears will spring up as I recall the past, but I'm not crying. There are days when I can't keep 'em back—nights when I am a child, but I'm trying to be strong just now."

"I guess I'll come out and see you. My doll's broke her neck and is most dead."

"Come right along, child! I used to mend legs

and arms and necks when the children brought their dolls to me."

The little one passed through the gate and sat down beside the poor old man, and while he sought to save the life of the "most dead" doll by means of a stick and a string the child observed:

"You must be quite old, grandpa; you are all skin and bone."

"Old? Bless you, yes! I was 81 only a week or two ago. Yes, I'm poor in flesh as well as in purse."

"So your grand-children had dolls, eh?"

"Yes, dear—dolls and toys and fine clothes and books and everything they wanted. I was rich then."

"And did they comb your hair?"

"Oh, yes."

"And sing to you?"

"Yes."

"Well, I guess I'll sing you a song, for I'm going to ask ma if I can't adopt you as my grandpa. You must excuse my voice, for I swallowed a pin the other day and ma expects it to work out of my shoulder this fall. I guess I'll sing about the three little graves. Don't look at me or I shall forget."

And in a voice full of childish quavers, and frequently stopping as if to swallow some of the words she sung:

> "Under an elm three little graves—
>   Under the sod my children three;
> The years may pass, but my heart will grieve
>   And sorrow will ever rest with me.
> Under the elm I walked to-day,
>   I looked————"

13*

" Why, grandpa, **the** tears are **just running** down your cheeks !"

" **Y-yes**, child--I can't help **it ! My** poor old life is **full of grav**es and griefs !"

" **Is your** wife dead ?"

" **Long** ago, child ?"

" **And all the** children ?"

" **Dead or scattered. I am all alone.**"

" Well, that's funny. You **can wipe your** eyes on my apron, if **you want to.**"

" Here's your doll—good as **new.**"

" That's nice. **If** I should adopt **you I'd keep** you mending dolls all the time. Have **you** got **over** crying ?"

" Yes, **child.**"

" **Well,** then, you **must be hungry. I'm always** hungry **after a** good **cry.** Wait a minute."

She ran into the house to return with a generous slice of bread and butter **and** a piece of meat, and as **she** handed the food to the old man she said :

" **I've** got to go in now, but we'll remember that **I've** adopted you as **my** grandpa. Don't cry any more, and come back to-morrow. Good-bye, grandpa !"

" Good-bye !"

And men who passed by saw an old man with his face in his hands to hide his tears, and when they asked the matter, **a** child who stood by explained :

" Why, sir, he's crying **because he's all alone in** the world, **and a** little girl has **adopted him !**"

THE MAN WITH A BEAR.

AMONG the baggage coming down on a Flint &
Pere Marquette train the other day was a full-grown
black bear. Bruin had been in captivity for two or
three years, and was on his way East for a zoological
garden. His owner was allowed to ride with him in
the baggage-car, and he seemed to think his bear
was the greatest animal on earth. He was ready to
bet that Bruin could out-hug and out-bite anything
human, and was rather disappointed when the railroad men refused to dispute this point with him. He
was indulging in his brag when an old man came into
the car to see about his trunk. He saw the bear, of
course, but the glance of contempt he bestowed on
the animal instantly kindled the indignation of the
owner, who called out:

"Mebbe you think I'm toting an old hyena
around the country!"

"I guess it's a bear," slowly replied the other,
"but I see nothing remarkable about him."

"You didn't, eh? Well, I do! Mebbe you'd
like to see him hug that trunk of yours? What he
can't sliver when he gets his paws around it has got
to have roots forty feet under ground."

"I've got a son back in the car——," reflectively
observed the old man and then he stopped and looked
at the bear.

"Your son? Egad! Will you match your son

agin my bear!" chuckled the owner as he danced with delight.

"I guess so."

"You do! Bring him in! Trot him out! I'll give him all the show he wants and bet five to one on the bear!"

The old man slowly took in a chew of tobacco, left the car, and when he returned he had his son Martin with him. Martin seemed to be about 27 years of age, and a little taller than a hitching-post. He was built on the ground, with a back like a writing-desk and arms which seemed to have been sawed from railroad ties.

"Martin, this 'ere man wants to bet five to one that his bear can out-hug you," quietly explained the father as the son sat down on a trunk.

"Yes, that's it—that's just it!" cackled the owner, "I'll muzzle him so he can't bite, and I'll bet five to one he'll make you holler in two minutes!"

"Muzzle your b'ar!" was all that Martin said as he pulled out a five-dollar bill and handed it to the baggage-man. The bear-man put $25 with it, grinning like a boy in a cherry tree, and in a minute he had the bear ready. Martin removed his coat and paper collar and carelessly inquired:

"Is this to be a squar' hug, with no gouging?"

"Jess so—jess so!" replied the bear man. "You hug the bear and he will hug you, and the one who squeals first loses his cash. Now, then, all ready."

As Martin approached, the bear rose up with a sinful glare in his eye, and the two embraced. It

was a sort of back-hold, with no sell out on the crowd.

"Go for him, Hunyado!" yelled the bear man as they closed, and the bear responded. One could see by the set of his eyes that he meant to make jelly of that young man in a York minute, but he failed to do it. Some little trifles stood in his way. For instance it wasn't ten seconds before he realized that two could play at hugging. Martin's hand sank down in the bear's coat, the shoulder muscles were called on for duty, and at the first hug the bear rolled his eyes in astonishment.

"Go in Hunyado—go in—go in!" screamed the bear-man, and Bruin laid himself out as if he meant to pull a railroad water-tank down.

"You might squeeze a little bit harder, my son," carelessly suggested the father, as he spit from the open door, and Martin called out his reserve muscle.

Each had his best grip. There was no tumbling around to waste breath, but it was a stand-up, stand-still hugging match. Little by little the bear's eyes began to bulge and his mouth to open, and Martin's face slowly grew to the color of red paint.

"Hang to him, Hunyado—I've got my last dollar on your head!" shrieked the bear man, as he saw a further bulge to his pet's eyes.

But it was no use. All of a sudden the bear began to yell and cough and strangle. He was a goner. Martin knew it, but he wanted no dispute and so he gave Hunyado a lift from the floor, a hug which rolled his eyes around like a pin-wheel, and then dropped him in a heap on the floor.

"Well, may I be shot!" gasped the bear-man, as he stood over the half-lifeless heap of hair and claws.

"Martin," said the father, as he handed him the thirty dollars, "you'd better go back thar and watch our satchels!"

"Yes, I guess so," replied the son, as he shoved the bills in his vest pocket, and he retired without another word or a look at the bear.

That was the bear they were feeding gruel in a saloon on Randolph street two evenings ago—one man was feeding him gruel and another feeling along his spine to find the fracture.

"BABY CRIED AND JACK CRIED."

It has been going on for a year past. Jack is a carrier for one of the dailies, and, one day last spring a baby crowed at him from an open door, and Jack tossed an apple into the hall. The next day the baby was watching for him, and after three or four days the boy made bold to slip up the steps and pat the little chap on the head and leave the stick of candy he had purchased two miles away. As time went on Jack came to know that the baby was fatherless, and that its mother was pale-faced and hardly able to drag about. It was weeks before she spoke to him, but the baby took to Jack right away and was always ready for his coming. After the first week it was always clean-faced, but it was a good while before Jack roused up the courage to give him a kiss and to ask for one in return. After that it was plain sailing, and the neighbors became interested. It was queer enough that a boy like Jack, having his own way to make and roughing it until he had become suspicious and hard-hearted, should catch on to a little whitehead, and be more than a big brother to him, but that was what happened.

And something more. One day he brought up a quarter of a pound of tea and left it where the mother would find it, and this was followed by other parcels and articles. One day he missed the baby and crept into the hall to find that he had cried himself to sleep and that the mother was ill and helpless. Jack roused up the neighbors, and whatever was eaten in that house for the next two weeks was purchased with Jack's money. The mother could only thank him and weep. She could not speak ten words of English.

A fortnight ago Jack missed baby again, and again he found the mother ill. Friends were with her this time and she did not suffer for care. A week ago there was crape on the door as the carrier went his round, and baby had been carried off by a neighbor. When Jack came around next day, the mother had been buried and people were watching to tell him, that the house was **to be** vacated and baby was to go to a distant **city.** He had **been** brought back to bid the carrier good-bye, **and** the poor and lowly people drew off with tears in their eyes, and **J**ack sat on the door-steps and took baby **in** his lap and smoothed his white head and kissed **his** red cheeks. Baby clunk around his neck and **seemed to** realize that he was to lose a friend, and, as **one** who stood by expressed it:

"Then baby **cried** and Jack **cried,** and the women put their aprons up and sobbed like children. When they finally took the child away Jack's heart was big enough to break, and throwing **his arms** around the little chap for the last time he turned and **ran** away and never looked back!"

WHAT THE PASSENGER WITH ONE EYE DID.

There **was an** army officer, **a** sutler, **a** surveyor and two men who might have been mine inspectors in the stage when it drew up at Burt Hill to take on another passenger.

"Howdy," said the new passenger, as he crowded **in.**

As he stood for a moment in the light of the station lamp, all saw that his left eye was gone. He wore no shade or patch to conceal the **loss, and those** who gave him a second look felt that the **fire in his** remaining eye was bright enough to answer for two. Dark **as** it was in the stage he seemed to have "sized up" every man inside of a minute, and, seeming **to** be satisfied regarding the crowd, he set-tled himself back in his seat, and had no remarks to make.

By and by the army officer mentioned something about road agents, and directly the conversation be-came interesting. Coaches had been stopped at vari ous points on the line within **a** week, and **it was** pretty generally believed that a bad gang **had de-**scended on the route and were still ripe for business. The man with one eye had nothing to say. Once or twice he raised his head and that single eye blazed in the darkness like a lone star, but **not** a word es-caped his mouth. The captain had said what he would do in case the coach was halted, and this brought out the others. It was firmly decided to fight. The passengers had money to fight for and weapons to fight with.

The man with one eye said nothing. At such a time, and under such circumstances there could be but one interpretation of such conduct.

" A coward has no business traveling this route," said the captain, in a voice which every man could hear.

The stranger started up, and that **eye** of his seemed to shower sparks of fire, but after a moment he fell back again without having replied.

If he wasn't chicken-hearted, why didn't he show colors? If he intended to fight where were his weapons? He had no Winchester, and so far as any one had seen as he entered the coach he was without revolvers. Everybody felt a contempt for a man who calculated to hold up his hands at the order, and permit himself to be quietly despoiled.

"Pop! pop! halt!"

The passengers were dozing as the salute of the road agents reached their ears. The coach was halted in a way to tumble everybody together, and legs and bodies were still tangled up when a voice at the door of the voice called out:

"No nonsense, now! You gentlemen climb right down here and up with your hands! The first man who kicks on me will get a bullet through his head!"

We had agreed to fight. The captain had agreed to lead us. We were listening for his yell of defiance and the click of his revolver when he stepped down and out as humbly as you please. The sutler had been aching to chew up a dozen road agents and now he was the second man out. The surveyor had intimated that he never passed over the route without killing at least three highwaymen, but this occasion was to be an exception. In three minutes the five of us were down and in line and hands up, and the road agent had said:

"Straight matter of business! First one who drops his hands won't ever know what hurt him!"

Where was the man with one eye? The robber

appeared to believe that we were all out, and he was just approaching the head of the line to begin his work when a dark form dropped out of the coach, there was a yell as if from a wounded tiger, and a revolver began to crack. The robber went down at the first pop. His partner was just coming around the rear of the coach. He was a game man. He knew what had happened, but he was coming to the rescue. Pop! pop! pop! went the revolvers, their flashes lighting up the night until we could see the driver in his seat.

It didn't take twenty seconds. One of the robbers lay dead in front of us—the other under the coach, while the man with one eye had a lock cut from his head and the graze of a bullet across his cheek. Not one of us had moved a finger. We were five fools in a row. There was a painful lull after the last shot, and it lasted a full minute before the stranger turned to us and remarked in a quiet, cutting manner:

" Gentlemen, ye kin drop yer hands!"

We dropped. We undertook to thank him, and we wanted to shake hands, and somebody suggested a shake purse for his benefit, but he motioned us into the coach, banged the door after us, and climbed up to a seat beside the driver. His contempt for such a crowd could not be measured.

QUEER SHADOWS.

IT was twilight. The red flashes thrown on the window-panes by the setting sun had slowly faded out and given place to the first soft shadows of night, which bring the cricket from its hiding-place and send the bee and the butterfly to sleep. There was a feeling of rest in the room—a feeling of quiet contentment and perfect satisfaction. The hum of voices from other rooms lulled instead of annoyed; the voices of children on the street seemed far away and had a touch of pathos.

The old man lay at perfect ease. His eyes rested on the wall at the foot of the bed—his thin, wrinkled hands were folded one over the other—there was no pain to deepen the lines on his kindly face. He had seen the sun go down, and he had listened for the voice of the cricket and the call of the whip-poor-will.

What was that?

A shadow suddenly flitted across the wall in front of his eyes. Now another and another. Now the first shadows flit back to head a procession. Passing from right to the left the procession moves—a procession of queer shadows. They take on faces as they move along, and the old man's heart beats faster as each face comes before him. Here are the friends of his youth—faces which grew white in death so long ago that he had forgotten them. This one was a child—that a youth—that a fair young girl when he

stood by and saw the earth **cover them.** They smile at him, and his heart grows younger.

One procession ends and another begins. These are **the** faces of men and women stricken down in the noonday of life. Some of them had shared his hopes and sympathized with his sorrows—all had been his friends. The sea, the lake **and** the forest gave up their dead to the procession of shadows, and each face was recognized and remembered. The procession moves on and on. He is shocked to realize that so many of his friends fell in the **battle of life while** he was spared to grow old and rest **in peace.**

Now comes the third procession. **There is a father, old** and bent **and feeble;** a mother with wrinkled, patient face; brothers in youth and middle **age;** sisters who wept with him over some of the graves. Every face looks as it did in life; every eye meets his with **a** glad look of recognition. The shadows wave their hands and move on, and the old man's **heart grows** childish and big.

There is another procession. The first shadow is that of a loved wife, who died while the snow-white locks had scarcely turned gray. Then came the children—sons and daughters—five in all. **One by** one they had grown weary and rested by the wayside, leaving husband and father to pursue the journey alone. The procession halts, and every shadow holds out its hands to the poor old man as if in supplication. His heart swells—tears fill his eyes, and he cries out **to** them :

" I see you all—I am coming !"

Back with your light! But it is too late. The glare of the lamp flings the twilight out of the room with hasty hand, and the shadows which crept along the wall are gone forever. No one saw them but the old man, and yet there is proof of there presence. His poor old hands are outstretched—on his white cheeks are tears—on his wrinkled face a smile of joy and gladness.

His spirit had joined the shadows!

WHO KISSED AWAY THE TEAR?

Is anything stranger than the human heart? Nature sends a frail, green vine creeping across the earth to reach a grim wall and cover its ugliness—to reach a dead branch and cover it with life. We bless nature as we see these things, and yet we do not realize that human hearts are ever doing the same. One day, months ago, a rosy-faced child looking from a window saw a queer old man go limping past. It tapped on the pane and the old man looked up. The sight of that sweet face opened his old heart, and he went on his way feeling richer than for many a month past. He was the grim wall— the child was the green vine. He passed again, and again the child was at the window, and for days and weeks they never missed seeing each other. At each meeting the vine crept nearer to the wall—the wall appeared less grim and forbidding. One day the "wall" laid aside his old hat for a better one. Another day he had a new coat. Again he was clean-shaved, and the "vine" scarcely recognized him. No one knew the old man, but all knew that he was feeling the influence of the vine.

A week ago as the old man passed he missed the face at the window. Was he too early or too late? He lingered and looked and seemed lost. It was the same next day, but a kind heart pitied him and sent out word that the child was sick. The green vine had reached the wall only to be blighted. Two days more and there was crape on the door. The child was dead. It had fallen asleep in death without a struggle, knowing nothing of the grand hereafter, but having no fear. On its pale check was a tear—a single tear which glistened like a diamond. No hand dared wipe that tear away. It seemed a tie between the present and the past—the living and the dead.

"Please can I see the—the child?" It was the old man—the grim wall—who knocked timidly at the door and spoke thus. They knew him by sight, and they led him into the room where the vine lay dead. He stood over the coffin for a moment, lips quivering and eyes full of tears, and then he bent over and kissed the face which would watch for him no more. When he had gone they looked for the tear. He had kissed it away! Old and poor and unknown, he had reaped a treasure such as all the millions of the world could not buy.

ONE CHRISTMAS MORN.

I**T** was twenty years ago, and yet when the thought springs to my mind **I feel for a moment as if** some one **had** stabbed me.

I was guilty, without crime. **Doing** only as millions of others have done, I laid up a burden of guilt which has humbled me a thousand times in the presence of men.

It was Christmas eve, and the city **was in excite**ment. It seemed as if every human being in **the** big city who had money to buy with and a friend to buy for was to contribute to the joy of the morrow. I had money and a wife and children. **I** was warmly clad and in the **best of health. The** bitter cold was nothing to **me,** and those at home had every comfort.

I halted with the crowd before a grand show-window, and there, so near that I could have pulled her rags, was one of my victims. She was **a woman of 50,** gaunt, pinched, ragged, and great black eyes which had the look of some hunted animal. I saw all this at a glance and turned **away.** What was it to me whether she wore silk or rags? Why should I care whether she was penniless or had plenty? Was it my business to ask whether she had food and fire —whether she was wife or widow—whether children waited for her **in** some wretched room, **or whether** she lived alone and had money hoarded up?

You wouldn't have asked. No **one man in** ten

thousand would have cared. **What is one poor old woman** more or less to the crowds **who surged up and** down the busy streets **of** a busy city ?

I **was** going home with **presents** for all—with bright anticipations—with gratitude in my heart that I had **some one to love,** when that woman met me face **to face. Snowflakes were** falling **on** the old shawl covering **her head, and** the face which hunger had pinched was pinched again with the cold. Her great, fear-haunted eyes looked squarely into mine as she held out her hand. She did not speak. **That** bare arm—the skeleton fingers—the **rags were** enough.

Then I committed **a foul crime. I** did not strike **her, nor** brush her aside, nor curse her. I read her **poverty** and her suffering in a single glance, and I turned away and passed on. **She** was a beggar. Perhaps she was **a** drunkard as **well.** How did I know that **she** had not been released from the work-house that very afternoon ? If she was old and poor and friendless **her place** was in the poorhouse.

I looked back over my shoulder and there she stood, hand outstretched towards me as if she were praying **to** God to soften my heart and bring me back, and had faith that He would answer her prayer.

But I did not halt. **I** felt a stab, but I conquered **it and** said to my accusing conscience : " Be still ! **you** might give every dollar **you** possess **to** the poor **and you** would receive no thanks !"

That night, when all the little stockings had been filled, and **wife** and I had expressed our gratitude for the blessings of life and the good health which had been ours for years, I slept to dream. I dreamed of the gaunt woman who had asked for alms. I dreamed of a hovel in which there was neither food nor fire nor lamp. I dreamed that I followed her home and heard moans and sobs and prayers as I listened at the door. I tried to open it, but it would not yield. I tried to cry out that I had come to help her, but the words would not come. I wanted to give her money, and tell her that I had misjudged her and would help to make it a happy Christmas by sending food and fuel, but while I struggled to speak a form stole past me into the wretched abode and whispered :

"It is too late !"

When the morning dawned I could not rest. I hurried out and walked the streets, scanning every face and figure, and hoping against hope that I would meet my victim. I could not find her. Then I left the streets and journeyed through alleys where I had seen the pale faces of the poor peering through shattered panes. By and by I came to a time-beaten, desolate-looking hovel half buried under the snow. Frost covered the panes and snow had drifted over the doorstep. I looked for smoke from the chimney but none came forth. I listened for sounds of human voice, but I listened in vain.

Then I felt myself a criminal, and trembled as if the law had laid its hand upon me. I would have run away, but some strange power prevented and urged me nearer. I knocked at the door. No answer. I tapped on the window. All was silent. Then I opened the door and stepped in. I had committed murder, and like other murderers, had been drawn back to the scene by some strange fascination. In a chair—the only one in the hovel—sat the woman who had held out her hand to me. Her face was held in her hands, and she seemed to have shriveled up. On the bed—on the rags and straw—covered with rags and locked in each other's arms, were the children—a girl of 9 and a boy of 12. On the wall near by were two stockings—faded and ragged and worn, but hung there for Santa Claus.

The stockings were empty. I touched the woman and called: " Good morning!" but she did not move.

" I bent over the children and shouted : " Merry Christmas!" but they did not awake.

They were dead! In my dream I had seen a spectre pass me and enter. It was the spectre of Death. Hunger and cold and sickness and despair had invited him in.

And I—where is my defense? I could have given and I did not. One single coin would have given them bread that night. The hundredth part of the contents of my purse would have lighted and warmed and fed them and placed tokens of a mother's love in the ragged stockings.

That was my crime. It accuses me by day and comes to me in my dreams by night. I give and give, but that voice is ever whispering : " It is too late !"

A BOOT-BLACK'S EULOGY.

"Brandy is dead !"

So the men said, so the **women** said, and so the children called to each other as a piece of news.

A drunken, good-for-nothing. **A** so-called man whose **brain** had **become dissolved in** liquor, whose mind **was enfeebled, and who had** disappointed everybody by **not** dying in the **gutter,** instead **of** having the roof **of a** tenement house over his head.

Why should anyone grieve when such a vagabond **passes** away? The world may owe him room for his **bones to rest, but nothing further.** So in "Brandy's" **case men said that he was well out** of the way, the **women clattered** their dishes in the rooms **below, and cared not** for the presence of the **dead.**

When the undertaker came to bear the **body** away a dozen **people** crowded into the **room,** and **among them was a** boot-black. Some said that **"Brandy"** looked well in a coffin; others spoke **lightly about** his face having at **last lost its ruby** color, and the dead pauper was **no more than a dog** in their minds, and why should he **have been?** One can be a **man or he can be a** vagabond. If he becomes a vagabond let him lose the respect of men. **All had a heartless remark except the boot-black. He stood at the head of** the coffin and looked **from face to face and** said :

"Brandy was low-down, and he died like a beast,

and you are all sneering at him! Did any one among you ever give him a chance? Did he have a home when he was a boy? Did men try to encourage him and guide him aright? Is there a man in this room who ever took him by the hand and spoke one kind word? Didn't everybody abuse and ill-treat him? Didn't everybody look upon him as a dog?"

There was no answer.

"Aye! Brandy was low down!" whispered the boy as he laid his hand on the coffin. "He was ragged and hungry, and poor and homeless, and without one single friend. What man among you could have stood out against it any better? Poor old man! They know all about it in Heaven! Let me help to carry him down."

And when the dead had been driven away, and the boy had disappeared, more than one man said:

"After all, we might have made it easier for the poor old man. I wonder that some of us never sought to make a man of him, instead of helping him down."

TEAR AND TEAR.

WHEN they found her dead in her old chair the men noticed nothing but the poverty surrounding her. The women saw a tear in her eye before they noticed anything else. Some had called her a hag, and spoken of her home as a hovel. Some had heard her curse and seen her reeling along, and they looked closer to see if it really was a tear. It *was* a tear—a great, round tear, and it rested on her wrinkled cheek as if human hand had placed it there.

"Isn't it strange that she shed a tear, even in death!" they whispered.

So it was, and yet it was not. When death comes slowly the crust melts from the wickedest heart, and human nature comes back with all the love and charity and sorrow and pity which heart ever had. Death came slowly to her. As she sat in the old chair and watched the sun go down and the shadows come, she knew that she would not live to again hear the notes of the morning birds. Men and women passed her door, but she did not cry out. Over the heads of the gleeful children playing at the curb-stone she saw a darker shadow than the rest. It was the shadow of death. It floated over the heads of the children as fog drifts along the river's surface, and as it stopped at her open door, she knew that the shadow was chilling her sunshine of life.

There was not a living thing in or around the house for her to love—for her to part with. No birds built their nests under the lonely eaves—no cat or dog basked in the sunshine creeping in through the dusty windows—even the rats and mice seemed to avoid the place. The husband had been dead so long that she scarce ever gave his memory a thought. Her boy—! Ah! that was it. As the shadow entered the door and cast its chill over her, she whispered :

" John was wicked. He ran away—he stole from me, he beat me !"

He had gone to the war. She had not heard from him even once. Yet, when the heart's crust melted, the love of a mother crept in, and she whispered :

" Poverty vexed me. Despair made me drink. Desperation made me curse louder than my boy could. He was a good boy once—I made him bad ! I, his own mother, drove him into the streets—beat him —abused him, and when I could have won him back by a kind, motherly word I would not speak it ! If he were here to-night I would sing those old child-songs to him—I would tell him those old stories—I would look upon him as my own precious child ! Here, in the shadow of death, I ask his forgiveness —I ask God to forgive me !"

Later, when the dusk was deeper and the black shadow had crept yet nearer, a boy searched about her door for a lost ball and heard her murmur :

" John, won't you forgive your mother ! I am dying, John, but all the old love has come back to me ! I am your mother—I want to hold you in my arms and kiss you as I used to—I want **to hear your** voice and know that you forgive !"

Her arms were outstretched. Her fingers felt of the darkness—nothing **more.**

" I want you to call me ' mother ' again !" she entreated. " I want **to** smooth back your hair as I **used** to—I want to look into your eyes and see if you still hate me !"

And those who **found her knew not** the feelings that had brought the tear, nor that it was the last of many which had burned her cheeks as the gloom grew deeper and the chilling breath of the shadow made her **heart** beat slower.

It had been a **fierce** fight. Shoulder to shoulder the line swept **out** from **the** cover of the woods, dashed across **the** long field **and** found death beyond it—death **in such** terrible forms that the line fell back in wild disorder. Again and again the pale-faced but courageous men dashed at the position, almost gained it, and melted **away** under the fire of **shot** and shell **and** bullet. By and by the slaughter **ceased.** The living left the field in possession of the **dead** and wounded, and the deafening roar of battle drifted right **and** left.

On that **meadow there was no** patch of grass without its **stain of** blood—dead men with eyes **open shared the** ground with those who shrieked for **water or** screamed out with the agony of their wounds. **John** was there. **A shot** had mangled arm and shoulder, and he **knew that** the blue cloud of powder smoke could **not shut him in from the shadow of** death. He had **been wicked.** He was loudest in his curses—the first to sneer at good—the last to speak **of home.** Comrades feared and **hated** him, and officers wondered why he was there instead of in a convict's **cell. Yet,** when he saw the shadow coming, **his face** lost its bronze, his tongue forgot its familiar oaths, and he dragged himself to the side of a wounded comrade and said :

"Have you got a mother, comrade ?"

"Yes—God bless her !" gasped the **other.**

"So have I," said **John.** "I was thinking **of** her for the first time **in a** year just before I was hit. She used to beat me. Our home was **a** hovel, and I **knew** the alleys better **by** night than I did the streets by **day.** I have been the wickedest man in the regiment, but she is **to** blame !"

The dusk **of** evening helped the **blue** cloud to shut out some **of** the horrible sights, but it could not disguise that dark shadow which moved from man to man and stilled the awful cries. It was coming nearer as John whispered :

"I have been thinking. I alone am **to blame.** In an **hour I** shall be dead ! You will live, and you will some day **go** back to our old home. **Will you** seek out my mother and tell her that in **my last hour** I asked her forgiveness—I wanted to hear **her voice** —prayed for the motherly touch **of** her hand on **my** hot cheeks ?"

"I will !"

"And say **to her that** good thoughts crept into

my heart—that I prayed—that I remembered her as the dear old mother who prayed at my bedside and taught me Heaven.   Say that—— !"

When the living stealthily advanced under cover of midnight, feeling of this and that dark mass to **see if** the heart was still, or flashing their lanterns **into** pale faces to see what comrade it **was,** a voice called out:

" **Come this** way—here **under** the bushes !"

They were lifting **him** upon **a** stretcher, but **he** said :

" Here is our John.   Turn your light **upon his** face !"

They bent over the figure, and one said :

" He is dead !"

" **And he** must have wept," **said** another—" see this tear on his **cheek !"**.

No stone marks the mother's grave—no flag or wreath, or tribute has ever pressed the turf above the dust of the soldier **son.**   It is well.   Could there be a greater tribute than the tears of **the dying—of** the forgiving **and** the **forgiven ?**

"A LITTLE BIT OF A CHAP."

"I USED to think it was my duty to cut 'em with the whip, and I **took** satisfaction in striking hard, but I wouldn't strike a boy now for the best thousand dollars ever coined."

He was a car-driver, and his attention had been called to three or four boys stealing a ride on the rear platform.

"Yes, I **was** a sort o' **terror on** this route **to** the boys," he continued **after a time.** "Not one of the crowd could put his foot **on** the step and get away without a cut from the whip. Big or little, rough or gentle, I served all alike, and if the passengers scowled at me for lashing a little kid of seven or eight, I solaced myself with the reflection that it was my duty."

A passenger was dropped at the corner, and as the car started up again the driver went on:

"Well, one day when the boys had bothered me more than usual, I dodged through the car and found a little bit of a chap, not over seven years old, seated on the lower step. He was all humped **over and** softly crying about something or other. **At** another time I might have felt pity, but **the boys had got my** mad up and what did I do but **give** the little chap a cut **with the lash** and call out **with such** a voice that off he **tumbled** into the dust. I saw him rise up and limp away, and there was something **in the** look he gave me that I shan't forget in a hurry. Whoa! now!"

The car stopped to take on two ladies, and presently the driver resumed :

"Do you know that I felt so conscience stricken that I kept looking for that boy on every trip, calculating to make up with him and secure his forgiveness for my brutality. I did not see him again until the afternoon of the second day."

" And what did he say ?" was asked as the driver hesitated.

" He was in his coffin !" was the reply. " It was his funeral procession which stopped my car for two or three minutes. That child was ill when he tried to steal his way home with me, and death was not twenty-four hours away when I lashed him and chuckled over the way he rolled into the street ! I tell you, sir, when I saw his coffin in the hearse, and caught a look from the mother, which seemed to charge me with being his murderer, I got a stab at my heart that pains me yet, and I wouldn't strike another boy if the reward was to be the whole line and its outfit."

THE END.

www.ingramcontent.com/pod-product-compliance
Lightning Source LLC
Chambersburg PA
CBHW031136120726
47905CB00006B/1712